T0008668

Through the Rain

The Hidalgo Brothers series

Through My Window

Through You

Through the Rain

Ariana Godoy

Through the RAIN

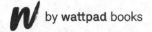
by **wattpad** books

w by **wattpad** books

An imprint of Wattpad WEBTOON Book Group

Copyright © 2023 Ariana Godoy

English translation by Susy Alvarez

All rights reserved.

No portion of this publication may be reproduced or transmitted,
in any form or by any means, without the express written
permission of the copyright holders.

Published in Canada by Wattpad WEBTOON Book Group, a
division of Wattpad WEBTOON Studi-os, Inc.

36 Wellington Street E., Suite 200, Toronto, ON M5E 1C7 Canada

www.wattpad.com

First W by Wattpad Books edition: December 2023

ISBN 978-1-99077-846-9 (Trade Paper original)
ISBN 978-1-99077-847-6 (eBook edition)

Names, characters, places, and incidents featured in this publication
are either the product of the author's imagination or are used
fictitiously. Any resemblance to actual persons (living or dead),
events, institutions, or locales, without satiric intent, is coincidental.

Wattpad Books, W by Wattpad Books, Wattpad WEBTOON Book
Group, and associated logos are trademarks and/or registered
trademarks of Wattpad WEBTOON Studios, Inc. and/or its
affiliates. Wattpad and associated logos are trademarks and/or
registered trademarks of Wattpad Corp.

Library and Archives Canada Cataloguing in Publication
information is available upon request.

Printed and bound in Canada

3 5 7 9 10 8 6 4 2

Cover design by Lesley Worrell and Niko Dalcin

Author photo by Kat & Jay Photography

Images © Stefano Cavoretto via Alamy;
© mgitg, © ifoung via Shutterstock

Typesetting by Delaney Anderson

This book is dedicated to all my Wattpad readers.

Thanks to you, the Hidalgo Brothers trilogy has made it this far, reaching a wider audience. I'm thankful today and always for the love and support you have given to Ares and Raquel, Claudia and Artemis, and now Apolo.

I love you dearly, with all my heart.

Prologue

It's raining. I'm drenched in a matter of seconds. My clothes cling to my body, but at this moment that's the least of my worries.

Everything hurts.

My whole body aches. My face, in particular, throbs with pain. Blood runs down my nose to my mouth. It mingles with the rain that pours over my face and slides to my chin. One of my eyes is half shut, and I groan every time I try to open it.

I've never been someone prone to violence, nor one to instigate a fight, so I find my current predicament ironic to say the least. I'm a crumpled mess lying in an alley with my back against the wall; I can barely manage to sit up. Heavy blows have left my face punctured with small cuts that sting when hit by the freezing raindrops. The same goes for my bruised knuckles, which were ripped open as I attempted to defend myself.

I wince in pain.

Do I just have the worst luck? It's my first night in college. I was out on the town, hoping to get acquainted with Raleigh nightlife. I came out of a pub and got jumped—beaten until I lost consciousness. I didn't put up much of a fight, and willingly gave up everything I had on me, so I don't understand the reason for such a brutal attack.

C'mon, Apolo. Don't pass out, I tell myself, struggling to stay conscious.

I have been kicked in the head repeatedly, and I need to stay alert until a doctor checks me. Or at least that's what I remember being told by my brother, the one who has been studying medicine for a few years. Yet I am having a hard time managing in my present state.

My vision is blurry. I swallow saliva. Even an action so simple has become very painful. I realize I should get up on my feet. Except every time I try, my body gives out and collapses against the wall. Shouting for help is not an option, as my cries will likely be drowned out by the sound of the rain pelting against the pavement and the trash cans around me. The autumn chill makes me shiver, and numbs my limbs. I decide to doze off for a brief moment, until the rain stops.

Just for one second . . .

My eyes close and my head falls to the side.

Citrus.

I'm half awake and scrunch up my nose when I pick up the scent of a citrusy perfume. I realize I no longer feel the rain on my skin. I open my eyes slightly and catch sight of a blurry silhouette standing in front of me, holding an umbrella and sheltering us from the downpour.

"Hey, hey," a woman's voice whispers as she leans closer to me. "Can you hear me?"

I lack the strength to reply so I simply nod.

"I've already called 9-1-1. They said they'll be here in five minutes. They told me to keep you awake." Her voice is very soft and calming. It's making me want to doze off.

"Hey!" Her hand cups my bruised face and pain shoots through my body, making me wince. "I'm sorry, but I can't let you fall asleep."

The icy air turns my breath visible as I exhale through parted and trembling lips.

"Coooo-cold," I stammer, shivering.

"Of course you're cold. Agh." I pick up a hint of hesitation in her voice. "What should I do? Can you hang in there a little longer? Okay?"

I weakly extend my hand and grab the hem of her shirt, pulling her toward me. She lets out a squeal when she falls forward on her knees and lands between my legs, which are currently outstretched on the pavement.

So very cold.

I lift my other hand and manage to wrap my arms around her waist. I hug her and bury my face between her breasts.

"Oh! Hey!"

"Warm . . ." I whisper, shivering against her body and getting her clothes wet.

She stops trying to push me away and lets out a sigh. "Fine. I'll allow it because you look awful and you're freezing," she mumbles. I take comfort in her warmth and her scent, a combination of citrusy perfume and the fragrance of her skin. "And just so you know, I never let guys hug me on the first date. So consider yourself lucky."

I'm not sure if she's kidding. I just want to stay still, right here. Her heart is racing. I wonder why. Is she afraid?

"Hey. Don't fall asleep on me, okay? I can hear the ambulance siren getting closer. You're going to be fine."

I can hear it too. Footsteps follow shortly after. She pulls away and clears her throat. I want to protest, but once again I succumb to the cold. Suddenly, several individuals stand before me, shining flashlights. And from this moment on, everything becomes muddled and fuzzy.

From the stretcher I reach out my hand and she takes it.

"You'll be okay," she whispers, giving it a tight squeeze before letting go.

I can only make out the shape of her silhouette, standing in the alley holding an umbrella. She saved me, and I am certain I will never forget her.

I will never forget the girl I met through the rain.

PART ONE

RAIN

One

APOLO

I missed jogging.

It took me four weeks to fully recover, and for the doctor to give me the go-ahead to get back to exercising. Physically speaking, I've healed. Mentally, on the other hand, it's a different story. I still have nightmares about the guys who attacked me. What's more, every time it rains, it puts me in a shitty mood.

It's half past six in the morning when I enter the apartment. The hall is partially cloaked in predawn darkness. I shut the door and make my way down the hall, switching the light on when I reach the spacious kitchen. A disheveled Gregory pokes his head in from the doorway that leads to our bedrooms.

"Why are you up at this hour?"

"I went jogging."

"At . . ." He squints in an attempt to read the time displayed on the microwave oven. "At six o'clock in the morning?"

"Six thirty."

"Not even my grandfather would get up at this hour to go for a run."

"Your grandfather didn't jog," I remind him, placing the keys on the counter of the kitchen island.

"Exactly."

"What are you doing up?" I ask as I open the fridge to grab a bottle of water.

"Uh . . ."

"Good morning!" A perky brown-skinned girl with an all-too-familiar face squeals excitedly as she makes her way past Gregory.

What's her name, again? Kelly. She's Gregory's I've-no-clue-what-I-should-call-her someone, who frequently spends the night. Sometimes they act like a normal couple, and then other times they don't even acknowledge each other when they cross paths. To be completely honest, I don't get what their deal is, but I also don't care to figure it out.

My priority is to get along with Gregory. I met him through my brother Ares, and he's become a good friend. Living together has been great during these first weeks in college. I haven't felt as lonely. Gregory is always coming up with things to do, and doesn't leave me with too much free time to feel depressed or homesick. I miss my grandpa, my brother Artemis, his wife, Claudia, and my dogs. But most of all—and to my surprise—I miss Hera. I never thought I would miss my little niece this much.

"Apolo?" Kelly stands next to me and waves her hand in front of my face. "Are you still asleep?"

"Good morning," I reply, with a friendly smile.

Gregory yawns. "Well, since we're all awake, should we have breakfast?"

I raise my fist to bump his. Gregory is a great cook, an under-rated quality that is greatly appreciated now that I live away from home. I'm not good at it—at all. The only things I can manage to make are desserts. But you can't live on sweet bread rolls and cupcakes alone.

"What do you fancy today? A continental breakfast? A full American?" Gregory suggests as he bends down to get the pans out of the drawer.

Kelly seizes the opportunity and gets behind him. She grabs him by the hips and gyrates against his backside.

"Stop," Gregory whispers, turning around to kiss her passionately while pressing her against the island.

I grimace, and shift from side to side while staring at a rather interesting painting of a pear that hangs on the kitchen wall.

I should be used to this by now.

After breakfast, I take a shower, spending more time than necessary with my eyes closed under the spraying water. I lower my head, stretch my arms forward, and rest my hands against the wall. The water washes over me, and I feel as if I'm not exactly here. My body may be standing there, but my mind has discon-nected. I'm falling deep into a void.

The irony is that I came here to study psychology, and during my first week in college I became the victim of a traumatic expe-rience in the form of a violent beating. Numbly, I turn off the faucet. I stand still for a brief moment, and then shake my head in an effort to get rid of the excess water left in my hair and snap my head back to this reality.

Each bedroom in the apartment has its own bathroom. And my bedroom is quite spacious. I quickly dry off, but realize that all my underwear is in the dryer, so, wearing one towel wrapped around my waist and another placed on my neck, I leave my room to retrieve it. Kelly is lying on the couch in the living room, fiddling with her cell phone.

When she notices me, she puts down her phone and arches an eyebrow. "So you've been hiding *all that* behind your nice-boy exterior?"

I frown when I hear *boy*.

"And what makes you think I'm a nice boy?"

"Oh please. You give yourself away too easily." She props herself up on her elbows. "I bet you're also a virgin."

Her remark makes me laugh. I give her my back and move to retrieve my clothes from the dryer, putting an end to our exchange. It could be my imagination, but it sounds like she's flirting with me. Maybe it's the way she's looking intently at my abs and biceps. The last thing I need right now is to create problems between me and Gregory.

When I turn back, she's sitting on the armrest of the couch, staring at me with amusement.

"Did I scare you?"

I flash back to Ares explaining the various flirting techniques used by different people. *I call that particular approach the Challenger, because the questions made are meant to pose a challenge with the sole purpose of proving an assumption is wrong. The overall goal is to get you to confirm something that's already established.* It's hard to believe how often that idiot's sweeping generalizations happen to be spot-on. I suspect his former life as a serial heartbreaker has granted him considerable experience in that department. And one thing is certain—I have yet to meet someone who has broken as many hearts as my idiot brother. However, I am not the type of person who makes assumptions about others, so I smile at Kelly and decide to give her the benefit of the doubt.

"Not at all," I answer, shrugging.

She smiles back, then moves to stand right in front of me. She presses a fist against my naked abdomen and cocks her head to one side. "Nice boy, you have a lot to learn."

There's that word again. I clench my jaw and wrap my hand around her wrist in an attempt to remove it from my stomach.

"I'm not a boy," I reply, keeping my cool. "But you're entitled to your opinion about me. I have no intention of proving you wrong."

I let go of her wrist and walk back to my room.

My morning class is guidance, so it's easy. It consists of mostly tips and pointers to guide us through our first year in college. The classroom is packed with students, and the professor is going over some information about the syllabus for the next couple weeks. My notebook lies open before me, and my restless hand begins scribbles something in pencil on the blank pages. When I'm done, I read what I've written down: *Rain*.

That's her name.

Rain Adams is the name of the girl who came to my rescue that rainy night. She's a student here, and that's all I know about her.

That's all the information the doctors who cared for me were able to provide when I woke up the next morning. From what I understand, she cooperated with the police and gave a statement. My case is still open, and the investigation is ongoing because the attack didn't fit the profile of a typical mugging. The police said it was too violent considering that I gave up everything without any resistance.

But I have not seen Rain again. All I have is a faint memory of her and that icy-cold night: her voice, her silhouette, the scent of citrusy perfume. Nothing more. I'd like to find her and thank her. I want to see what she looks like and get to know her. I've tried searching on social media. But when I type *Rain*, all the results I get are about rainy days. Maybe I'm spending too much time thinking about her, while she has already forgotten about me.

I break into a smile. *C'mon. I just started college and here I am, obsessing over a girl.*

"Rain?" A feminine voice pulls me out of my reverie and back to the present. I look around and find a girl with glasses and wavy hair sitting next to me. She is attractive. Her coffee-colored eyes have a slight sparkle when she talks. "Do you like the rain?"

I understand what she means. She's taking the word literally. Ironic given the circumstances in which I met Rain.

I take my time to answer, simply because I'm taken aback; this is the first time someone has ever spoken to me in this class.

"Actually, I'm no longer fond of the rain."

She nods. "And here I was expecting a speech about how much you love the sound of the rain, how it relaxes you and makes you feel nostalgic."

I'm speechless. She smiles and offers me her hand.

"I'm Erica. I'm retaking this course."

I shake her hand, and am about to introduce myself when she cuts in.

"It's nice to meet you, Apolo."

"How do you know my name?"

She arches an eyebrow. "Apolo Hidalgo, everyone on campus knows your name."

"What are you talking about?"

"You've been in the campus bulletin for several weeks," she informs me. "I'm sorry about what happened to you. Are you all right?"

I detect pity in the look she's giving me, and it bothers me.

"I'm fine," I tell her, and get up. I excuse myself to go to the washroom, and leave in a hurry.

Outside the classroom, I head over to check the faculty bulletin board, and find a bunch of articles posted that have been written about me. They have my name and show my face. I realize that my story has been heavily covered in the college news.

Surely Rain has heard or read about me somewhere. She knows my name, my major, and where to find me. Yet she hasn't made the effort to look for me.

I frown when I consider the possibility that Rain has no intention of finding me. And why would she? She saved me, and doesn't owe me anything. I rub my face with one hand and turn away.

I feel my cell phone vibrating inside my pocket so I pull it out and read Gregory's texts.

> **Cockroach:** Housewarming party at our place! See you tonight, looooooser. And save my contact under a different name or I'll kick your ass.

I snort and text back a reply.

> **Me:** Dream on, cockroach. Who did you invite?

Cockroach: A few friends from my department. I'm throwing you a "debutante" bash so wear your best suit.

Gregory has been enrolled for a year, so he has a wide social circle and many friends. Meanwhile, I'm new, and he is my one and only friend. I missed the first two weeks of class due to my recovery, so I skipped the crucial phase in college life when most students have the chance to socialize and meet new friends. And I feel left out yet again. I've never been good at meeting people on my own. In high school, I met people through my brothers. I ended up being friends with their friends simply because I happened to be around. I'm not complaining; it's how I met some of my very best friends. Still, I've never managed to make friends without external help. I guess the moment to change that has finally arrived.

Me: How many people did you invite?
Cockroach: Numbers are abstract concepts entrapped in space.

Sometimes I wonder if everything is all right inside Gregory's head. I have yet to figure out exactly how his brain works.

I sigh and give him a call. I hear a racket in the background. Did he made it to class? Or did he skip to hang out with friends instead?

"How many people?"

"Twelve and a half." He laughs, and I narrow my eyes.

"And a half?"

"One of the girls is bringing her dog."

I love dogs, so this actually makes the whole situation more tolerable.

"What's her dog's name?"

"Cookie."

"Okay. Fine."

He hangs up before I can point out that he exploited my weakness to distract me. I have a feeling he's going to squeeze a crowd into our apartment.

The hallway leading back to class is packed with people. Some look at me with curiosity, others with pity. Even though the bruises are gone, I still have stitches on the left side of my jaw and above my right eye.

So I pretend to check my phone.

Citrus . . .

I look up when I catch the scent of citrus. It immediately takes me back to that night—the cold, the pain, and the words softly whispered in the midst of it all.

You will be okay.

When I turn around, I focus on a group of boys and girls walking away from me, about to blend in with the rest of the crowd. I stand still in the middle of the throng of moving bodies, and stare. I barely manage a glimpse as they keep moving farther away from me.

Stop it.

I start walking but my mind is stuck again, thinking about her.

Will I ever find you, Rain?

Two

APOLO

Addition is certainly not Gregory's strength.

There is no way in hell that there are only twelve people in this room. So far I've counted over thirty. If it wasn't for the fact that we have ample space in our apartment, we wouldn't be able to accommodate everyone he invited. Most people seem to be hanging out in the living room, playing god knows what kind of game while I'm keeping busy playing with Cookie, the dog that belongs to a girl named Tania.

"Gregory talks a lot about you," she mentions as I bend down to pet Cookie. "Psychology, huh?"

"That's right," I reply politely.

Tania smiles and proceeds to gather Cookie in her arms, then walks away.

Since the move here, I've noticed my behavior has become detached. Maybe it's just me adjusting to this new environment. It could also be connected to the trauma I experienced and what it triggered. One thing is for certain—I'm unable to hold a conversation, and I find it difficult to read the mood in the room. The few who have tried talking with me tired quickly and walked away shortly after. I can't blame them; socializing is not my forte.

"Apolo!" Gregory's voice carries all the way from the other side of the living room, and I scowl. "Apolo! Come here!"

I put on a fake smile and make my way to him.

Tania is sitting next to a guy I don't recognize. He has his arm snaked around her side. I remember they were introduced to me as boyfriend and girlfriend. Kelly is hanging out with two girls and four guys whose names I can't recall. Clearly, this is what happens when I meet over thirty people in under half an hour.

"Everyone to the living room!" Gregory calls. I sigh and stand next to him, facing the large crowd. Everyone is well dressed. A few behave very much like my roommate, boisterous and carefree.

"I've already introduced this guy to you." Gregory puts his arm around my shoulders and holds me to his side. "He's got my seal of approval." Then he winks at the girls in the room. "And he's single."

I break free from his arm. I can feel myself blushing. "Stop it."

"What? Why did you think I was throwing this party?"

I scan the crowd and my eyes land briefly on Kelly, who looks back at me, smiles, and whispers something in the ear of another girl. I return my gaze to the rest of the people gathered in the room, and land on a pair of beautiful obsidian eyes almost hidden under a red hood. A few strands of black hair peek out. She's the only girl here who is not dressed up, who has opted for a casual, sporty look in a red hoodie with the official logo of our college. It's a bit too large on her, and mostly covers the shorts she has on underneath.

Her expression is calm as she looks directly into my eyes, and I find myself having a hard time swallowing because she's too beautiful.

I gawk at her like an idiot, and she furrows her eyebrows.

"Apolo?" Gregory breaks the spell.

"Huh?"

"Maybe you should say something so she can get to know you better?"

"Ah . . ." Everyone stares at me.

I swallow hard again, at a loss for words. I don't know what to say, and I really don't want to humiliate myself in front of all these people.

Kelly stands up. "Apolo is a psychology major. He loves dogs, and tends to look away during the gory parts of horror movies," she announces. Everyone chuckles. "C'mon, let's keep the party going."

"Boo! You always ruin my special moments," Gregory complains, giving her a thumbs-down before walking over to where she stands.

Kelly looks at me with a friendly smile, and I feel the urge to thank her for sparing me the embarrassment. I think she's the only one who picked up on my discomfort when everyone's attention was on me.

I'm surprised she's noticed my aversion to the gory parts in horror movies. We watch movies together every Thursday—it's a tradition that Gregory is committed to keeping going. I get the feeling she's been watching me more closely than I noticed. But why? I look at her again, and watch as Gregory kisses her affectionately on the cheek. She shoots me a quick glance, then fixes her eyes on Gregory. I shake my head. She's trying to be nice to me—nothing more, nothing less.

I need fresh air so I step out onto the balcony. From our apartment on the seventh floor the bright city lights make for a spectacular view.

I can make out the college campus in the distance, otherwise known as my new home away from home. Also, the place where I will spend a great deal of my time studying. I miss my real home. Though it's not that far from here, in order to get used to this new life I won't be visiting every weekend.

Those closest to me have always said I'm a sensitive person. I consider myself lucky to have brothers who never made me feel bad about being that way. I know it's a skewed notion of masculinity that showing emotion can be perceived as weakness, hence a man who cries during a sad scene in a movie or in the midst of an emotionally charged situation could certainly become the target of ridicule.

It's one of the reasons I'm studying psychology. The human mind is a complex organ with so many attributes yet to be discovered. And I would like to play a part in helping others.

Initially, I'd wanted to study veterinary medicine, but I changed my mind after visiting an animal hospital and observing firsthand what that job would entail. I left with my heart broken. Sure, there were animals that were saved and had happy outcomes. However, there were many others that didn't enjoy the same fate. I realized that day I wasn't cut out for that type of work. I couldn't bring myself to put small, defenseless animals out of their misery forever. I wouldn't be able to bear the death of someone's pet if anything were to go wrong during a procedure. I know myself very well and I know that over time each loss would have shattered me little by little. And so here I am.

"Are you okay?"

I'd been so lost in my thoughts that I failed to notice that the pretty girl with the obsidian eyes who caught my attention a few minutes ago has joined me on the balcony.

"Yes, I'm fine."

"You don't look like you're enjoying yourself." She walks over and stands next to me at the railing.

"I don't do well at parties," I admit.

"Well, you'll have to get used to it. After all, on this campus…" She makes an overly dramatic expression. "Gregory is known as the party monster."

"I'm not shocked, to be honest."

She extends her hand to me. "My name is Charlotte, but my friends call me Char."

I reach out and give her hand a shake. "Nice to meet you, Char. I gather you already know my name, given that Gregory has mentioned it to everyone at this party every other second."

She lets go of my hand. "Yes, Apolo."

My gaze drops to her lips, intently watching them as they breathe my name. Once again, I struggle to swallow.

"So tell me, Char, how did you end up becoming friends with the walking, talking lunacy that goes by the name of Gregory?"

"Who could ever resist Gregory's friendship?" She snorts. "Sure, he's a pain in the ass. He's loud and can't shut up, even underwater. But you can always count on having a good time in his company. And he can make you laugh nonstop. You know what I mean? He's the life of the party."

I understand her perfectly. Gregory has been like that since high school.

She turns and stares at the view of the city. And I do the same before I speak again.

"I'm the opposite of Gregory."

"And that's a good thing," she replies. "If we were all the same, this world would be a boring piece of shit."

I let out a sigh. "I'm not sure. Sometimes I wish I could be just a little more . . . outgoing."

"Nah." She returns my gaze. "You're fine the way you are."

"You don't really know me."

"That's true, but my first impression of you is a good one."

I turn toward her, resting my forearm on the railing. "And what is that impression, may I ask?"

She also turns to stand face-to-face with me. "You're a quiet and kindhearted guy who doesn't like to be the center of attention," she states. "I've also noticed that when you become preoccupied, you tend to disconnect from the reality around you. It's why you have a hard time making friends. You seem to enjoy your own company over that of others, and would rather be left alone with your thoughts."

"Wow. That's a very in-depth analysis, don't you think?"

"I'm a third-year psychology major. If I wasn't capable of making a thorough evaluation at this point in my studies, I would consider myself a complete failure."

"You're enrolled in psychology?"

"Why are you surprised?"

"I assumed Gregory was only going to invite his engineering buddies."

"Gregory's colorful personality has a massive reach that extends far beyond the confines of his department."

"I see."

"So please don't think twice about asking for my help when and if you need it. I know it can be daunting at first. So I'm happy to be of assistance."

I stare at her, appreciating the maturity of her attitude and her words.

"Is that why you came out on the balcony?" I ask, curious. "To psychoanalyze me?"

"That's a misconception. Just because we happen to study psychology, and happen to become psychologists, it doesn't mean that we're going to spend all our time analyzing everyone we meet. It just means we have acquired a more enhanced understanding of the human mind and behavior."

Her statement renders me speechless. I find myself once again staring at her like an idiot. She's beautiful, smart, and she's pursuing the same discipline as me. Would it be too bold to ask her out? What's the worst that could happen? A rejection? On the other hand, I could scare her away. And so far, she's the only person I've managed to have a conversation with.

Apolo, don't ruin this by thinking with your dick.

"What?" she asks, noting my reaction. "Is there something on my face?"

"You're very attractive."

Nice going, Apolo. Way to not fuck it up, huh?!

But she doesn't seem fazed by my slip, and gives me a big smile.

"Thank you very much, Apolo."

"You're welcome," I reply quickly.

A pause follows. She takes a step toward me, and then another, until there's only a small gap between us. She leans closer and kisses me on the cheek.

"I'll see you around, Apolo."

She gives me a parting smile, and goes back inside.

I bring a hand to my chest, and feel my heart racing a little.

Well, how else is my cardiovascular system supposed to react in response to that move? Unbelievable. I'm starting to think more like Ares. A full summer spent in his company and his endless medicine study sessions have clearly made a mark.

Back in the living room, the party appears to have taken a raucous turn. Everyone is dancing and singing at the top of their lungs to a song I don't recognize. I stand in the corner, watching everyone. I search for Char, but she's no longer around. Unintentionally, my gaze lands on Kelly, who is dancing with two friends. She grabs the hem of her dress and drags it up her thighs in a seductive way while swaying her hips. I press my lips together, and try to look away. But my eyes keep coming back to her. The way she's dancing, so confident and sexy—I find it difficult to look away.

She lets go of the hem and moves her hands up to her hair. She lifts it up, then lets it slowly fall down; all this is done in sync with the easy sway of her body. Then she turns to face me, and her eyes lock with mine. A mischievous smile creeps across her lips. And now it's like she's dancing for me alone. She runs her hands over her hips, to her waist, then up to her breasts in such a sensual way that, for a moment, I forget that we're surrounded by a crowd of people.

She starts moving toward me and I shake my head, but she ignores me. At no point does she stop dancing. She bites her lip, turns around, and wriggles her hips, brushing against that one particular place on me.

Her ass lightly rubs against the crotch of my pants, making me clench my fists. I'm enjoying this way more than I should be. God, when was the last time I got laid?

She presses her backside firmly on me, and my breath hitches a little.

After months of no action in this department, it doesn't take much for me to get an erection. I need to put a stop to this immediately. I firmly grab her by the hips and bring her movements to a halt. But she leans back, and her hands begin to stroke my hair. From this angle, I can see the outline of her face.

"We're just dancing, Apolo."

Liar. She knows exactly what she's doing.

I dig my fingers deep into her hips and whisper in her ear.

"Stop provoking me."

I press my erection against her and she pants.

"Or else what? Are you going to punish me?"

Her words bring up images in my head, and I picture her assuming several intimate positions.

I shake my head in an effort to drag my thoughts out of the lust-filled gutter they've fallen into. I summon the strength to gently push her away, and head to my room. I hear her call my name but I keep walking through the crowd as my breath comes in short gasps.

In my room, I close the door and rest my back against it. I close my eyes and try to calm my breathing. The feel of her body and the way her ass was pressed to me are still vivid in my mind. I run my hand over my face before I throw myself on the bed. Maybe sleep will help.

At first, I have a hard time dozing off, but eventually I manage to succumb.

A knock on my door wakes me up. I sit up and switch on the lamp that's on the bedside table. I don't hear any more music or commotion outside. The party must be over by now. I check the time on my cell: it's 4:20 in the morning. I rub my eyes gently and go to the door, expecting to see Gregory, but it's not him I find.

"Kelly." I use a serious tone.

She gives me a smile and walks into my room, which is partially cloaked in darkness. She proceeds to close the door behind her and lock it.

"What are you doing here?" My voice comes out raspy and deep. Though her makeup doesn't look as flawless as it did earlier, she still looks very pretty.

She purses her lips before breaking into a naughty smile. And just like that, she reignites the feelings that she stirred a few hours ago.

"What are you so afraid of, Apolo?" Her soft and seductive voice fills up the room. I slowly inhale, hoping yet failing to calm myself down. She has physically provoked me, and has wreaked havoc with my emotions. She moves her hand down to the crotch of my pants, but I grab her wrist. Her eyes search mine, and she cocks her head playfully.

What in the fuck am I doing?

One thing is certain; Kelly has become my wanton tormentor. And I frankly have no clue how to handle the situation, or what to do about her.

Three

APOLO

An open invitation . . .

A beautiful girl has slipped in my room . . .

Her motive is crystal clear when I look into her eyes . . .

And here I am, mulling over what to do next . . .

If she wasn't seeing Gregory, this would be a no-brainer. Even though their involvement may be considered casual, I don't think it's wise to let my urges influence my decision. I don't want to make things awkward or uncomfortable for my friend and me. Truth be told, the times I've let myself get carried away and given in to my impulses have not ended well. There was the time I ended up with a broken heart. And another when I almost ruined my relationship with my brother Artemis.

So I fight these urges triggered by what I'm feeling from the waist down, and keep a firm grip on Kelly's wrist as I gently pull her to the door, which I manage to open with my other hand.

"You've had too much to drink," I tell her softly. "I think you should go to sleep."

She breaks free from my grip, surprised. "Seriously?"

I give her a nod. "This is not what I want."

She tries to keep her cool, acting as if nothing has happened, and clears her throat. "Okay. I'm truly sorry. I misread the signals and got it all wrong."

"It's fine, we're good."

She purses her lips, and I can tell she is holding back tears. I didn't mean to hurt her feelings. She turns and disappears down the hallway.

I slam my fist against the doorframe. This has been quite the night.

Kelly's face, flushed with embarrassment, haunts me as I try to go back to asleep. I didn't want to hurt her but she's responsible for her own actions. Still, I don't want her to think that she's not attractive. Or that I rejected her based on her looks. She must know it was because of Gregory. Right?

I hope that what happened won't have an effect on her.

Ugh. Shit.

The more I think about it, the worse I feel. Or maybe I'm blowing what happened out of proportion and being arrogant, thinking I have the power to crush the self-esteem of a girl who always seems so confident and self-assured.

Go to sleep, Apolo.

"And then I said, 'That's exactly why you're going to fail Intro to Psychology, you idiot.' And I know all about it, because that's exactly what happened to me."

Erica is going over an argument she had with a guy in one of her classes. Apparently, the one conversation we had the other day was enough to turn us into instant friends. We've chatted a few times during a couple of classes we share. We even had lunch together at the cafeteria on campus.

When I entered our last class of the day, she waved at me, motioning to the seat she saved next to hers. I don't have any complaints. I'm grateful that people like her exist in this world.

She adjusts her glasses and looks intently at me as I use my hand to wipe my face, as if she is studying me in great detail.

"Someone had a rough night," she states, interrupting her own story.

Although we've only known each other a very short period of time, I realized immediately she's the type of person I can trust. It feels like we were friends in another lifetime, meant to come back to this one and rekindle our friendship.

"Party monster," I mutter, and take a sip from the water bottle in front of me.

"Is party monster your friend?"

"Yeah. Do you know him?"

Erica has been talking without a break from the moment I sat down and I haven't managed to get her to stop. Yet all of sudden she's silent when I mention Gregory. She's sitting very straight, but her head is bowed. Her wavy hair hangs loosely, covering her face, and her fidgeting hands are restless in her lap. I furrow my eyebrows and take notice of the cute outfit she has on. A baggy blue sweater paired with dark jeans.

"What's wrong?" I ask her.

She turns away and shrugs while staring at the opposite side of the classroom.

"Nothing."

It really bothers me when she talks to me without making eye contact. "Erica."

She abruptly jumps out of her seat, and I lean back so I can look up at her.

"I have to get some candy. Do you want anything?" she asks.

"The class is about to start."

"I'll be right back."

"Erica."

She leaves the classroom, as if she has to get out of here in a hurry. I keep glancing at the door, hoping she will come back and apologize to the professor for being late. But she never returns. I look down at her seat and notice that she left with all her things.

After class, I walk down the main corridor of the department and search for Erica without any success. I notice someone is waving at me in the distance, so I stop and wait. As Charlotte approaches, I think she looks more attractive in broad daylight than she did the night before. Her black hair falls loosely, framing her cheerful face. Her dress hugs her figure, accentuating every curve and contour perfectly. I didn't expect to see her so soon, so I raise my hand and wave at her like a fool.

Relax, Apolo.

"My midnight chatterbox," she says softly, standing in front of me.

"My not-quite-there-yet psychologist?"

She laughs, and I'm relieved she finds my response amusing.

"Done with class already?" she asks, and I reply with a nod. "How about we get a coffee, huh?"

I draw a blank for a few seconds, and she looks at me, amused. I wonder. Is she . . . ?

No, Apolo. She's just being nice.

"Sure."

Charlotte leads the way to a coffee shop that's close to campus. We find a table next to a large window, and sit across from each other. She then informs me that she's about to hand in a paper on a very important topic, and proceeds to go over it in detail. I try hard not to stare too much at her lips when she's talking. Damn. She has beautiful lips.

"Apolo?"

"Yes?"

"Are you okay? I'm sorry—once I start talking, I find it hard to stop. I think I may have made your head spin."

"Don't worry. I'm a good listener, and enjoy it."

She takes a sip from her coffee, and I do the same.

"Do you want to go to my apartment?" she asks.

I choke on my coffee and cough a little. "Pardon?"

She smiles. "Would you like to come see my apartment?"

C'mon, Apolo. Don't let you mind go there. Maybe she just wants to show you her place.

"Sure." I wipe my sweaty palms on my pants.

"Great. Let's go." She gets up and slings her purse over one shoulder.

Charlotte is tall and striking. She has a knockout figure and a gorgeous face. She walks with the confidence of someone who knows she's attractive and doesn't need validation from others. In addition to being gorgeous, she's incredibly smart. I can't deny I'm feeling a little intimidated.

I follow in her footsteps until we catch an Uber that takes us to her building. We sit in the back, and she smiles at me then looks out the window. My hand rests in the space between us.

Then she places her hand on mine, and I am having a hard time swallowing. Her gaze remains fixed on the window.

Okay. I think that's a signal. I really don't want to rush to a conclusion or get ahead of myself. Wait. Do I have condoms on me? I feel a sense of relief when I remember I'm in the habit of carrying a few at Gregory's insistent advice—which was punctuated with one of his signature silly made-up proverbs: *You never know where along the way you may step in a puddle and slip.*

The building looks nice and it's in a busy corner of the city. Charlotte talks about her experience of moving far away from her family. I tell her how difficult the experience has been for me.

Her apartment is small but decorated in a way that's welcoming and cozy.

All right, Apolo. Stay calm.

Charlotte tells me to take a seat on the couch while she prepares a couple of drinks. I notice the sun is setting when I look out her window. No. She couldn't possibly have invited me to . . . ? In broad daylight? But maybe she did.

"So, what's your story, Apolo?" She sits next to me, handing me a drink in a clear glass.

"What do you mean?"

"Your romantic history."

I give her an unhappy smile. "It hasn't been great. Nothing exciting."

"Ouch. Did you already have your heart broken?"

"Everyone has to go through that. Right?"

"So, is that why you're so closed off? Are you afraid of getting hurt again?"

"I am not closed off."

"You hardly ever say a word."

"According to your analysis from last night, I'm an introvert. Didn't you conclude that? And introverted people don't talk much."

She places her glass on the small table across from the sofa, then moves toward me. My breath quickens when I see her face inching closer to mine. Her hand cups my cheek, and I lick my lips. She smiles again and asks. "Do you want to kiss me?"

"Very much."

"Then, what are—"

I don't let her finish, and kiss her madly. My urges rule my actions, and I intensify the kiss. She tastes like wine, or whatever it was she was drinking. Her lips feel soft, just as I imagined. I'm kissing her recklessly, like a madman. In my defense, it's been a while since the last time I had any physical contact with someone.

I shift my body and move forward, pouncing on her. She has no choice but to lie on her back with me on top. We're both breathing heavily. I'm surprised when I notice she's slipped a hand under my shirt to caress my abs. But it doesn't stop there. She reaches down to unbutton my pants. How did she manage to do that with just one hand?

It seems that Charlotte is very skillful. My assumption is soon validated when the very same hand makes its way inside my boxers. I let out a moan against her lips. She knows exactly what to do. I keep kissing her all over: her neck, her lips, and every spot that's within my reach.

My too-long dry spell combined with Charlotte's ministrations make for a disastrous combo. It only takes a few hand strokes to push me close to the edge.

"Wait. Wait. Wait," I repeat against her lips in an attempt to stop her.

She just smiles, bites my lip, and increases the speed and intensity of her strokes. I close my eyes and rest my forehead against hers, whimpering and moaning as I enjoy this incredible feeling. The heat in me rises, and I can feel myself coming. And it is in this moment that for some inexplicable fucking reason my brain brings up Kelly's face and the feeling of her body pressed against mine when we danced in the living room.

No. No.

When I open my eyes, I see Charlotte. She's the one here with me. She's the one I want at this very moment. I kiss her again, feeling needy and desperate.

Or else what? Are you going to punish me?

Enough.

But my mind is clouded with lust and my body is so close to orgasm that I lose all control of the situation. I keep fantasizing that it's Kelly lying under me. Her legs are wrapped around my waist while I prove to her that I'm not the innocent and naive boy she thinks I am. Charlotte keeps stroking me until I reach my release, spilling myself on her hand as well as on her clothes.

"That was fast," she says in a playful tone.

And I don't know what's worse: coming too fast and embarrassing myself with a beautiful girl like Charlotte or fantasizing about my friend's girlfriend during my climax.

What a memorable way to start college, Apolo.

Four

APOLO

Sex.

Is it simple? Or is it complicated?

I guess it depends on the type of guy you happen to be. Or at least, that's what I've heard. For some guys, those whose attitudes are clearly straight out of the Stone Age, it boils down to a number, or it's more of a competition. Their attitude is informed by a "the more girls you fuck, the bigger a man you are" mantra. These guys are Neanderthals, period. Then there are the guys who view sex a conduit to self-exploration, and a way to find someone worthy of their attention. These guys go by the "if she's a good lay, I will date her" mentality. Then we have the ones who see sex as a simple act in the pursuit of pleasure, no explanations given and no strings or commitments required. This is the "I fuck because I enjoy it, and that's all" camp. And lastly, we have the guys who consider sex a sacred act—something they will only do with someone they really care about.

And then there's me. Where do I place myself among these categories? To be honest, I don't understand myself well enough to have figured out what sex truly means to me. I lost my virginity to a girl I had fallen head over heels in love with. So there were feelings involved, which made the experience so much better. After she walked out of my life I tried casual sex with other people. No feelings involved, no names given, and no attachments. And I abysmally failed at it when I tried hooking up with several people—it went very badly. I realized casual sex wasn't for me, so I stopped.

So what am I doing here with Charlotte? I just met her and have no plans of sleeping with her. I did let her finish what she started, and proceed to return the favor in kind. I let my fingers get to work. My hands are quite skillful, and I have received many compliments in the past. Charlotte certainly seems surprised at how quickly they get her to orgasm. She tries to touch me again as she reaches her climax, but I shake my head. I don't want us to go any further.

Right after we're done, Charlotte heads to the bathroom and stays there for a few minutes while I button up my pants. I sit on the couch and hold my head, leaning forward. It seems I haven't completely fucked everything up today, and she enjoyed herself. What now? Should I take her out to eat, or something like that? Would that be too much? Perhaps we can get to know each other better and see where that leads.

I sit up straight and rub my face, then stare at the huge television set on a stand in front on me. I frown when I notice a bunch of frames stacked on the various shelves. Every one displays a picture of Charlotte with a tall, blond-bearded man. In one, they're kissing in front of the Statue of Liberty in New York.

I immediately realize he's not a relative. In a handful of photos she looks younger, which confirms to me they've been together for a few years.

Shit, shit. Did I just hook up with a married woman? That's a line I would have never crossed if I had known—after everything my family went through because of my mother's infidelity, all that it destroyed and the effort it took for us to heal. I would never put myself in a position where I would mess with someone else's family.

What the fuck am I doing here, anyway? I've only met Charlotte twice, and I've already given her an orgasm in the middle of the apartment she shares with her husband? Or is it a boyfriend? I completely lost control, and I don't feel like myself.

Charlotte comes out of the bathroom. She's changed into a knee-length dress. A bright smile lights up her face, but I have so many questions. The words stick in my throat. The look on my face must give me away, and makes her smile fade. Her eyes follow the direction of my gaze to the photos.

"Oh." She sighs. "Don't worry about him."

I'm not sure what to say. She smiles again before taking a seat next to me on the couch. She tosses her black hair over her shoulder.

"We have an open relationship."

"An open relationship?"

Just when I think I've seen and heard it all.

"That's right. Loosen up, Apolo." She hits me playfully on my arm. "He knows what I do, just like I know what he does. We're not monogamous."

Does such a thing exist?

"And you're both okay with this arrangement?"

Now my curiosity is piqued.

She nods.

"Honesty is key between the two of us," she tells me. "And to avoid any complications, we never hook up with the same person twice."

"You mean we'll never do this again?"

"Exactly."

And here I was thinking this was the start of something, planning to invite her on a date. Meanwhile, to Charlotte, this was just a fling.

So I stand. "I need to go."

"Apolo."

"I should get back to my place before it gets dark." I'm telling the truth. Since the beating I don't like being out at night. "Thank you for everything." I look at the framed photos. They both look very happy. "See you around. Or maybe not, I guess. I'm off."

I head toward the door. Charlotte follows me, grabs my arm, and makes me turn to face her.

"Hey. Don't leave like that." She smiles. "How about we talk, okay?"

What is there to talk about? Should we have to go over the fact that I tend to misunderstand cues and suck at reading the signs?

"It's all good." I free my arm from her hold and leave.

Whiskey tastes like dirt.

I've always said this. I've had many fun discussions with my brothers about it. Yet here I am, sitting on the big L-shaped couch in our apartment's living room, holding a glass of whiskey.

Maybe I'm punishing myself for messing around with someone else's girl. Though technically, the other guy is fine with it. Still, it doesn't make me feel any less uneasy. Why do I always manage to get myself right smack in the middle of situations like this without intending to?

I've drunk more than half of a bottle of eighteen-year-old whiskey that Gregory had stashed in one of the bar cabinets. That's right—our apartment includes a small bar area where Gregory gets to play the role of bartender whenever he hosts a party. It's well stocked with all the necessary ingredients. Naturally, given the fact that I'm an idiot, I decided to consume my least favorite spirit. Also, whiskey is the drink that gives me the mildest hangover.

I don't drink often, and my tolerance is low, so I'm already feeling sick after just a few sips. I sink deeper in the sofa, turn my face to the side, and stare out the windows facing the balcony. Orange stripes appear in the sky as the sun sets. As the sunlight fades away, my mind takes a trip down memory lane to the day I spent hanging out at the beach with my brothers and friends before most of them were set to head off to college. It's one of my fondest memories. At the time, it was just another crazy get-together—just another bonfire and day spent at the beach. Now, in retrospect, I realize how magical that moment was. And now here I am, living in this town and adjusting to this new life. I don't think I'm coping as well as I should. But at least I have Gregory by my side.

I hear the main door open and I immediately assume it's Gregory, so I keep on drinking. However, it's Kelly who makes an entrance. She looks surprised. I guess she's reacting to the glass in my hand as well as my entire demeanor.

"Drinking on a Thursday?" she asks as she places two boxes of pizza and a bag containing two bottles of Pepsi on the counter of the island. "Having a rough week?"

Shoot. It's Thursday. Movie night Thursday. I completely forgot about it.

"Life is not easy," I whisper.

"Pardon? I didn't hear you."

She pulls her black hair up and gathers it in a bun. She takes the Pepsi bottles out of the bag and places them in the fridge. I stare at her like a drunken fool. She's wearing tight jeans and a tube top that shows off two thin lines on each side of her collarbone where her skin tone is slightly lighter. Tan marks from sunbathing in her swimsuit.

After she's completed her task, she walks over and drops onto the other end of the couch. "Are you okay?"

"Why shouldn't I be?"

She grimaces. "I don't know. You're not a drinker. Much less one to indulge on a weekday."

"You don't know me very well."

Her face falls. She wasn't expecting that answer. And honestly, I'm having a hard time pinpointing where this feeling of annoyance and this anger are coming from.

"Okay, Apolo. You're in a bad mood, but drinking isn't going to solve your problems."

I stare at her briefly. And I ask myself, *Why her?*

Kelly is attractive, but so is Charlotte. So why did I keep picturing Kelly while I was with Charlotte? Do I want Kelly because I can't have her? Is that it? Suddenly, I recall the laughs we've had over stupid things while we were cooking or watching movies with Gregory. I think of the effort she puts into telling a joke even

39

when no one laughs. Or her weird obsession with tuna spread on saltine crackers. I come to a too-obvious realization: I like Kelly. And that's the difference between Charlotte and her. I find Charlotte very attractive, but I don't know her well. Not in the same way I know Kelly. And I happen to like what I know about Kelly.

Well done, Apolo. You're crushing on your best friend's girlfriend. This is going from bad to worse. First you hooked up with a pseudomarried woman. And now you're setting your sights on your friend's girl.

I down the glass of whiskey in one gulp. There's a burning sensation as the alcohol makes its way down my throat. Briefly, I try to focus on the sensation and nothing else. I open the bottle to pour myself another glass but a hand grabs mine.

"Apolo." Her voice has become softer, gentler. "That's enough."

I look up to find her leaning over me. Her hand covers the one I'm using to grip the bottle by its neck. A few unruly locks have freed themselves from her messy bun. The look in her eyes is warm and understanding. Her lips are parted, and I look away.

"This is not the way to deal with problems," she tells me, and tries to take the bottle. But I pull it back and pour myself another drink.

"And how should I deal with them?" I ask.

I don't know what's wrong with me. I realize this isn't just about Charlotte or Kelly. It goes deeper than that. There is a part of me that is wounded and hasn't managed to heal or can't figure out how to address the root cause of the problem. And whatever is afflicting me goes deep—very deep. What happened to me in that alley seeped all the way down to my core, and it rears its ugly head anytime I experience something intense. Or whenever I happen to drink. But why is that? I thought I was doing fine. Or that by now I would be fine—that all I needed was time. My family wanted me to go to therapy but I swore to them that I was doing okay. Maybe I should have gone. Should I still go?

This anger I feel, and this annoyance—I don't understand where they're coming from. I've never been an angry person, nor do I ever resort to violence. So why the short fuse lately? Where are these feelings coming from?

"Did you guys start the party without me?" Gregory enters the room and drops his books on the island right next to the pizzas. Kelly takes a step back and sits back down on the opposite end of the couch. "Wow. Whiskey? Very fancy, Apolo." He walks over to the fridge and gets a beer. "I'm in the mood for a beer. Mr. Hidalgo, please accept my apologies for joining you with such an inferior beverage choice."

"Gregory." Kelly draws his attention and reprimands him with a gesture. "This is not the time."

"Babe, when did you become such a bore, huh?"

Gregory takes a swig from his bottle, and sits next to me.

"So what's the occasion?"

"Life is full of shit."

Gregory nods. "Cheers to that." He raises his beer and makes a toast with my glass. The alcohol has clearly impaired my motor skills so the impact causes me to almost drop the glass. Gregory grabs it and lets me get a firmer grip. "Everything okay, bro?"

"Just perfect."

"I haven't seen you this drunk since my graduation."

He watches me closely. I smile and shake my head.

"Do you really want to know the reason?" I raise my glass of whiskey in Kelly's direction. Gregory furrows his eyebrows and casts his gaze on her. "How about it, 'reason'? Why don't you get up?"

Kelly looks tense and says nothing. I drink without taking my eyes off her. Right after I put the glass down, I address her one more time.

"What's the matter? Not feeling so brave anymore?"

Gregory looks at me again. "Is there something going on that I should know?"

Kelly purses her lips. "Greg, he's just drunk."

"Kels, drunks tend to tell the truth," my roommate replies. Of course they have nicknames for each other.

"Anything you would like to share?" he asks me, point-blank.

I stare at Kelly. She looks very pale, and seems to be holding her breath. Unfortunately, my inebriated brain is not thinking clearly and flashes back to a conversation with Ares when he explained to me why he always tells the truth.

It's never easy being honest, Apolo. But it's important to tell the truth, even when it's uncomfortable or even painful. The truth always comes out. In the end, when the time comes to repair friendships, relationships, or circumstances, it makes a huge difference whether it comes from you, or from another source.

I have chosen the worst time to follow my brother's advice. "I'm attracted to Kelly."

Dead silence.

For a few seconds, all I can hear is the sound of the ice cubes hitting the glass as I lift my hand to take another swig. Kelly places her hand over her mouth, and Gregory looks down at his beer bottle. I would be way more worried about how awkward this situation has become if I wasn't feeling so groggy.

I put the glass down on the table and stand up, swaying from one side to the other.

"I think . . . I have to go . . . the bathroom."

Gregory stands up and offers me his support by slipping my arm over his shoulder. "Come on. I'll take you."

I puke my guts out. Everything is blurry. Gregory takes me to my room, where I fall into bed, landing on my back. He helps me take off my shoes. Before he gets up to leave, I grab him by his shirt to stop him.

"I would never do anything to hurt you." My words come out a rambling mess, though Gregory appears to understand. He lets out a sigh and sits down next to me. "It's just that . . . I had to be honest with you."

"Bro, you're cute," he tells me this with a smile. "What Kelly and I have, it's not serious. But I appreciate your honesty. Though I would have preferred it if you'd shared this information when it was just the two of us around."

"I'm sorry," I mumble. "I'm an idiot. Things never work out the way I expect them to."

Gregory lets out a chuckle. "Apolo, you have to stop taking life so seriously." He shakes his head. "You're eighteen, in college, and girls are coming at you in droves. Just enjoy yourself."

"But that's not me," I admit, staring at the ceiling. "I overthink and worry about everything. I want to date someone. I want to give all my attention and affection to one person at a time. I'm not looking to just have fun and split my affection into multiple meaningless hookups." I snort. "I'm not well, am I? I'm not normal."

Gregory laughs again. He takes my face in his hands and gives it a squeeze.

"Apolo Hidalgo, you're too fucking cute." He lets go. "Bro, you are who you are. Don't ever feel like you have to be like everyone else. If you want to date Kelly, that's fine with me. I always respect her choices."

I think back to Charlotte.

"We three should have an open relationship." I giggle like a silly fool.

Gregory laughs with me. "My sweet Apolo, where have you learned about these things?" He keeps laughing. "Who is filling my innocent Apolo's head with these ideas, huh? They have defiled the sweetest boy in this household!" he declares in an overly dramatic tone.

"Shut up."

"Try to sleep it off, you boozehound." He stands up and heads to the door.

"Gregory?" He turns around. "I won't try anything with her. I need you to know that."

"Whatever she wants, I will respect and accept," he tells me, shrugging. "Honestly, you need to relax. I'm fine."

And with that parting comment, he leaves. I close my eyes and am about to fall asleep when the sound of the rain hitting the window puts my senses on alert. It reminds me of that night, and I refuse to relive all over again the fear and the pain I felt then. So I use a pillow to cover my face. Unfortunately, the memories keep coming back.

For some reason, it was the first blow that hurt the most. It was the one that disoriented me and disconnected my perception of the world from reality. Evil can exist without justification. There are people who hurt others without a justifiable reason or provocation. I gave up all my belongings without a fight yet the blows and kicks kept coming at me, packed with red-hot fury. Why, though? The lack of answer to this question is partly the reason why I feel this way.

I don't want to listen to the rain anymore. I clumsily reach for my EarPods, and get my phone from my pocket. I sync them and put them in my ears. I choose music that's soothing, and close my eyes again. Sure enough, her image comes to mind.

Rain.

My memory of her is blurry: she leans over me, her hair shifting to one side, her umbrella keeping her dry. I can almost smell the citrusy scent she wore that night. It's amazing how the rest of your senses are heightened when your sight is impaired. Her presence gave me a sense of peace and hope that I desperately needed, since I was ready to give up and die right then and there. I never imagined I could end up in such a state, and at that moment I was terrified. No one had ever hurt me like that before. I never thought I was someone who deserved to be treated that way. I'd always been good to others, tried to give my very best to the world. So why was I lying in the middle of an alley bleeding to death? Why?

You'll be fine.

My obsession with Rain doesn't come from a romantic place. It's rooted in appreciation and gratitude. I want to be able to look her in the eyes and thank her from the bottom of my heart. She came to me in my darkest moment, when I had lost all hope. She stepped forward and gathered the pieces right when the idea of the just and good world that I had fabricated inside my head came crumbling down. And through her actions, she delivered a message. *Don't stop believing; goodness still exists out there in the world.*

Perhaps it was the logical thing to help someone in my condition. But her actions meant everything to me. Enveloping me in her warmth as we waited for the ambulance in the cold made all the difference. There are no words that can explain the fear you feel when you think you are going to die alone with no one by your side. A hug may be the one thing you need to keep you fighting and awake just a little longer.

I log in to my Instagram and create a post for no reason. Maybe Rain doesn't even have an account, and the chances of her seeing this are close to zero. Still, I feel the urge to do something. The post is the word *rain* in all caps, set right in the middle, and nothing else. I put my phone down and watch the raindrops slowly roll down the window. I have managed to calm myself a bit, and my eyelids feel heavy with sleep. It's difficult to believe in something again.

And just so you know, I never let guys hug me on the first date. So consider yourself lucky.

The universe conspired as I slept and recovered from my drunken night. Rain noticed my post. Maybe she sensed my desperation. Or realized how much I need to hear from her. For one reason or another, she has finally come out of the woodwork and revealed herself. Not only did she like my post, but she also left a reply. So shortly after I wake up this morning, I'm greeted with a surprise in the comments.

My mouth curves into a smile when I read her comment, which feels like a heaven-sent reminder telling me that it's okay to have faith again. That even when we go through terrible

experiences, there's always a chance for unexpected, silly outcomes that bring a smile to your face. And that hopefully this
could be the foundation of my journey back to new normal.

Five

RAIN

I did what I had to do. Period.

"Rain."

I can't hide forever.

"Rain."

I've never been a coward.

"Rain!"

A thumping sound startles me and brings me back to reality. My mother is standing next to the table. Her brown hair is gathered in a messy bun and she's watching me intently, eyebrows raised.

Over her shoulder, I notice the glow from the sunset reflecting off the window. And for a fleeting moment, I'm distracted all over again.

"Did you read it?"

I look down at the manuscript in front of me. It's titled *Burning for You*. I scrunch my face. It's one thing to read erotica.

But it's another thing entirely when the erotica was written by your mother. And as tends to happen in my case, I couldn't help but picture my mother as the protagonist in this story. In order to get through it, I forced myself to pretend it was a random book I had picked up somewhere out there in the world.

"I read half of it."

"And what do you think?"

There's a look of anticipation on her face. I must admit that the story is quite good, despite my personal inner conflict as a reader.

"I like it. Although I would lengthen the buildup of the sexual tension between the main characters." My mother takes notes. "I don't know—maybe two or three more chapters before they finally sleep together."

She nods.

We've always been open when talking about sex. At first it was awkward but with time we got used to it. Besides, my dear mother, Cassey Adams, has been establishing herself for over ten years as an author in the erotica genre. She is very talented and her books sell like hotcakes. She started out by self-publishing, and then a small publishing house took a look at her work and gave her its full backing.

She has more than thirty published books under her belt. I suspect that's why she has such an open mind on the subject. As an expert on erotica, she's not one to censor herself when it's time to discuss the topic with her children.

She agrees with my feedback about adding to the buildup.

"I felt the exact same way. Anything else?"

"The part in the story when the ex enters the narrative, and she's characterized as evil—don't you think it's a bit trite?"

"You think so?"

"One hundred percent."

"All right."

I provide her with a few additional pointers, mostly about grammar and filler scenes, and she writes them all down. My mother takes my advice very seriously. I think it's helped create a special bond between us. I really appreciate her work and I never tire of telling her how good she is. Who could disagree?

"And what filth have you written this time?" Vance, my older brother, walks into the living room and reaches out to grab the manuscript. My mother sighs.

My dad isn't particularly interested in my mother's career, but at least he's not against it. Vance on the other hand spends all day belittling her and letting her know how much she embarrasses him. I'm not sure in which century this jerk lives. He's twenty-three for crying out loud. I can attest with all certainty that as a twenty-year-old, I'm way more mature than he is. In spite of Vance becoming independent and moving out of the house, he keeps getting in trouble. And I'm the one who has to step in and clean up when he messes up.

I stand and snatch the manuscript back. Then, with my free hand, I pretend to wipe something off the front of his shirt.

He pushes my hand away.

"What are you doing?"

"Oh, I was cleaning a smudge of misogyny and stunted intellectual growth off your shirt."

"Ha-ha, Rain, as always, the comedian."

Jim appears from behind Vance. He's holding his high-school notebook, and is wearing headphones under his straight blond hair. My younger brother lives in his own world and isn't influenced by Vance, thank god. Jim takes off his headphones, walks over, and kisses my mother's head.

"How was your day?" my mother asks him with a smile.

"Good. I got an A in chemistry again." He shares the news then proceeds to remove his backpack and hang it on a wall hook in the corner. "Mr. James thinks I'll make it to the top ten percent of the class."

"Wow." I walk past Vance, discreetly flipping him off as I move closer to Jim. "And who did you get your smarts from?"

Jim smiles at me. "From my amazing sister."

We share a few laughs before dinner. When we're done, I walk Vance to the door as he gets ready to leave.

"Tell Dad that I dropped by," Vance says, then turns to face me. He inherited our mother's dark eyes and tall stature. "Are you okay?"

"I'll be better when you stop bugging Mom," I tell him sincerely.

Vance runs his tongue over his front teeth, leans closer to me, and whispers: "Same goes for me when you stop meddling in my business, Rain." He runs a finger along the contour of my face, and I grab his hand to stop him.

"I don't know what you're talking about."

He snorts and removes his hand.

"Yes, you do," he says with certainty, and I'm having a hard time swallowing. "I hope you're smart enough, and keep yourself together." He kisses my forehead. "I would never hurt you," he informs me as he pulls away. He moves his hand to caress my cheek. "However, I wouldn't be too sure about those close to you."

And after delivering this parting statement, he leaves, and I feel the air returning to my lungs. Vance is more dangerous than

I'd like to admit. Ever since he moved out, he's been acting recklessly. Back when he was living with us, our parents could restrain him to a certain degree.

It's astonishing he managed to become financially independent. Thanks to social media, my older brother has become an influencer. Yet no one truly knows who he really is. His pretty face and chiseled muscles have earned him a large group of dedicated followers who are oblivious to the type of person he is behind closed doors.

I head up to my room. That's when it hits me. I remember what I've done and let out a long sigh. I'm not the kind of person who runs away and hides. And that's exactly what I've done since the night I came to the rescue of the Hidalgo boy: run away.

But not anymore. I thought that if I carried on without drawing attention to myself eventually he would forget and stop looking for me. That post on his Instagram account tells me the opposite. He doesn't seem to be the type of guy who lets things go easily. I didn't intend to play the role of woman of mystery, but I have my reasons for keeping my identity anonymous. I grab my phone, throw myself onto the bed, and stare again at his post.

"Apolo." I recite his name as a whisper in the darkness.

Isn't Apolo the name of a Greek god?

I don't know what prompted me to reply to his post. It was like I could feel his despair. And though I posted my comment last night, he waited until this morning to send me a direct message.

> Hi, Rain. I know that technically we don't know each other, but if I could, I'd like to thank you in person for coming to my rescue that night. I'll send you my number. Apolo H. (I completely understand if you'd rather not meet.)

I have left him on Read, and he has not written again. I appreciate that he's giving me some space and hasn't bombarded me with messages. Okay, he just wants to thank me. I get it. If I was in his position, I would want to do the same. Besides, I'm fed up with Gregory.

Rain, I don't like keeping secrets. You know that, he told me yesterday at school. *I don't like lying to him.*

You're not lying.

I'm withholding information, he contended. *Do you have any idea how many times I've heard him talk about you? He wants to thank you, that's all. You should let him do it.*

Gregory, it's complicated.

Argh, there you go with the mystery. You should change your name to Rain "Mystery" Adams.

And you should change yours to Gregory "Overzealous" Edwards.

He gave an ironic chuckle.

Rain, it's your decision and I'll respect whatever you choose to do, you know that. But he's a good guy, so please give it some thought.

Okay, Gregory. You win, I tell myself now.

This is me accepting his thanks and nothing more. I pick up my phone and copy the number he shared in his Instagram message, but I don't save it to my contacts. I'm only using it once. I consider sending him a text message, but change my mind. A call will be more to the point. This way he can tell me exactly what he needs to share. Still, I can't help but stare at his number for a moment before pressing the Call button.

The memory of the cold rain falling that night is vividly imprinted in my brain. The echo of the chunky raindrops hitting my umbrella. The splashing sound of my shoes stepping in the puddles of water. And then there was him. My heart stopped because I thought I was too late and he was already dead. And then he let out a soft, barely audible whimper. So I began to talk to him as I fumbled with my hands, trying to dial 9-1-1 for assistance.

He caught me by surprise when he reached out and grabbed the hem of my shirt to pull me toward him. I gave out a squeal when my knees brushed the cold wet pavement as I landed between his legs. He encircled me with his arms and rested his face on my chest. Though this position could be perceived as too intimate, it didn't bother me. Still, I couldn't help myself from cracking a joke simply because it's what I do when I'm nervous.

Fine. I'll allow it because you look awful and are freezing, I'd muttered, admitting defeat. *And just so you know, I never let guys hug me on the first date. So consider yourself lucky.*

My finger remains frozen on the phone screen. *What's the big deal, Rain? It's just a phone call.* He'll thank me and that'll be the end of it.

I shake my head when I recall how his arms felt around me. With the bumps and bruises it was hard to get a good look at him that night. I confess I have since checked his social media feed, and he's very handsome. I shake my head again, and press the Call button.

It rings once, twice, then three times, and I bite my lip. Maybe he doesn't answer calls from numbers he doesn't recognize. I should I have texted him first. Right? I don't like situations with too many uncontrollable variables that might alter the outcome.

"Hello?"

His voice reminds me of that night when he whispered the word *warm* as he lay against my chest.

"Hi," I reply matter-of-factly. "This is—"

"Rain."

Hearing him say my name makes me feel strange somehow.

"Yes. I saw your post on Instagram."

There's a brief silence. Then I hear a sigh. "I found you, at last."

I let you find me. At last.

"Yes. I'm happy to hear you're doing well."

"I wanted to thank you for coming to my rescue that night. I don't know what would have happened to me without your help." I wasn't expecting his voice to sound so sweet. "Truly, I'm very thankful."

"Don't worry about it." I don't know what else to say, and hope this is enough for him. Although, to be honest, deep down I would like to get to know him better.

"I'd like to invite you out to lunch as a thank-you. Or maybe you'd prefer to do something else instead." He sounds hesitant, maybe a little nervous. "Of course, it's not a date or anything like that. It's just, you know, me wanting to thank you in person." He is definitely nervous, and it makes me smile. I think it's adorable.

"Fine. We can meet at Café Nora. Do you know the place? It's always full of people, and a safe spot for a quick meeting."

"Yes, I know the place. Although I'd rather take you somewhere more upscale. You saved my life, Rain. I don't want to repay you with coffee and day-old pastries."

"Apolo, please. Don't insult my Café Nora." I said his name. I'm surprised at how it rolled out with ease, and how relaxed I sound while speaking with him. "Besides, their baked goods are freshly made and their doughnuts are delicious."

"Okay, then. It's your decision. Wherever you want to go is fine with me."

I arch an eyebrow. "Are you always so accommodating?"

There's a pause.

"I believe I am."

I let out a sigh. "Fine. You can choose when."

"How about tomorrow?"

This guy doesn't know how to hide his emotions when he speaks. I'm not used to dealing with someone who is so open and up-front.

"Sure. We can meet after I'm done with my classes. I'll let you know when I get out." I'm not sure why I say this with a smile. I guess his excitement is contagious.

"Great. Thanks for reaching out, Rain. I've been looking forward to talking with you."

"No worries. I'll see you tomorrow, Apolo."

"Great." He's quiet for a brief moment. "Fingers crossed it doesn't rain." He lets out a short, deep laugh, and there's a flutter in my stomach, so it takes me a few seconds to respond.

"True. Let's hope it doesn't."

"Although then I won't have an excuse to hug you again."

He delivers this line with ease and subtlety. I know he's kidding. But he could also be flirting with me. Is he?

No, Rain. Stop it, he's joking.

"Good night, Apolo."

"Good night, Rain."

I hang up. I know I should have declined his invitation and only used the call to provide him with some closure. But I couldn't resist. Besides, we're only going out to eat once, and I'll only see him this one time. It shouldn't be a problem. He needs to do this, and it's no big effort on my part to accept his thanks in person.

I fall back on my bed and stare at the ceiling. So why do I feel this way? True, he's very good looking. There's also the part about meeting under unpleasant circumstances that will be difficult to forget, for both of us. Yet that shouldn't mean I will be instantly attracted to him. Right? That could stir up trouble, for everyone.

Although then I won't have an excuse to hug you again.

I sit up and mentally give myself a slap. I'm not going to over-dramatize this in my head. It's quite simple. There's no reason for me to make life complicated. So I won't. I'm only going out once with Apolo to eat, and I'm not going to feel anything toward him, period.

Six

APOLO

It's not a date.

I repeat this to myself while I look for something to wear. I don't usually make a fuss over these things, so a pair of jeans and a T-shirt should do. But for some reason, I'm obsessing over this outing. I think about the impression Rain must have of me. The only time she's met me I was soaking wet, beaten, and bleeding.

That first impression of me sucked. Still, I don't want to dress too formal because this isn't a date.

Ugh. Stop worrying too much, Apolo.

"Yeah, yeah. He's around here somewhere."

I hear Gregory's voice coming from the hallway just before he pokes his head through the half-closed door to my room.

"Are you decent?" He stares at me, and notices that I'm still in my underwear. "Were you heading out? Well, it doesn't matter."

Gregory walks in and turns his phone around. On the screen,

the person on the other end of the call is prepping something in his kitchen. His black hair is a mess. He's not wearing a shirt and I'm able to see the tattoo he got on the side of his chest a few months ago.

"Bro!" Ares greets me with a smile that shows off the line of perfect, straight teeth that all Hidalgos have been blessed with.

"Hey!" I reply, as I wasn't expecting to see him. I quickly try to find a pair of jeans. I don't want him to notice my indecision over what to wear; he knows me too well.

"Gregory told me you have a date," he adds.

I shoot a murderous glare at Gregory, who plays dumb. "What?"

"It's not a date," I tell Ares.

"Then how come you aren't dressed yet?" Ares replies, leaning over the island where he has set his phone.

"Because you interrupted me."

I hear a voice in the background.

"Who's that?" That sweet voice never changes. Ares calls my name, and then I see her appear on the screen. "LOLLO!"

I smile at her. "Hi, Raquel."

Raquel pushes Ares to the side. "Lollo, look at how much you've grown."

We video call from time to time, since we all miss each other a lot. It's one of the reasons I don't feel awkward standing in my underwear in front of everyone.

"Hey!" Ares tries his hardest to push her off camera, but she won't let him. "It's my brother."

"Wow. No greeting for me?" Gregory puts one hand on his chest, feigning wounded. "Really, Raquel. I never expected this from you."

"Ooh, cockroach! You know you're my favorite." Raquel blows an overly dramatic kiss to the camera and moves away. Then she asks curiously, "What are we getting ready for?"

"Apolo has a date." Ares lets it slip, and I roll my eyes.

"I've told you, it's not a date," I repeat.

Gregory whispers, "It's with the girl who came to his rescue! Doesn't that sound sooo romantic?"

"Really? Is it Rain? I can't believe it—" Raquel makes herself comfortable. Of course she's up to speed on everything that happened, and knows all the details.

"I'm just going to meet her, and thank her," I explain.

"Yeah . . ." Ares turns his back to us and checks on whatever he's cooking.

"Ares, are those scratches on your back?" Gregory asks, because he never misses a thing. Also, they're hard to miss on my brother's pale skin.

Raquel blushes and changes the subject. "We were talking about Apolo."

"Raquel, you're a wildcat. I'm shocked," Gregory says, shaking his head.

I grimace. "Can you leave me alone?" I ask them. At this rate, I'll never be able to figure out what to wear.

Ares turns to face the camera. "If it's not a date, why aren't you dressed? You're trying to figure out what to put on. You wouldn't be this indecisive if it didn't mean anything." I hate that my brother is so perceptive.

"I just want to dress casual." My clarification falls on deaf ears.

"It's a date! That's exciting!" Raquel exclaims, sounding delighted. It'd be a waste of time to keep denying it, so I give in.

"Can you all please stop acting like this is my first date ever?" I scold them, feeling a little embarrassed.

"It isn't?" Ares jokes. "How's that possible? I haven't been out of the loop for that long."

"Now, now, Ares. Stop making fun of him," Raquel defends me with that giant smile of hers.

"Thanks, Raquel. To be completely honest, he's still as annoying as ever."

"I'm everyone's most favorite annoying person." Ares winks, and I grimace.

"My vote is for the jeans and the black sweater with the red letters." Raquel gives me her feedback. "Black really suits you, Lollo. You look both adorable and sexy."

"Hey, I'm still here." Ares gives her a kiss on the cheek.

She laughs, and I can't help but smile along with them. Whatever love might be, these two certainly have it between them.

"Hey! Stop feasting in front of the hungry," Gregory complains with a grimace.

"You? Hungry? Don't you have a girlfriend?" Raquel asks. "Her name is Kelly, right?"

"Nah. We're not really boyfriend and girlfriend."

I lick my lips. Following the night of my drunken confession to Kelly and Gregory, things have been awkward and tense. She hasn't been coming over to the apartment as frequently. I suspect she's giving the situation some time to mellow out.

I decide to take Raquel's suggestion and get dressed. The jeans and black sweater will do.

"By the way, stop making those lovey-dovey cutesy TikToks. I've had enough of them," Gregory protests.

Raquel laughs. "Yet you watch them all, and are the first to like them." Raquel sticks out her tongue.

"It's because I like to support my friends. But enough is enough."

I spray some cologne on my sweater, and ignore the cheers coming from Raquel, Ares, and Gregory. I say good-bye to all three and head out. If I stick around, they'll tease me relentlessly the entire afternoon.

My palms are sweaty by the time I arrive on campus. Rain texted, letting me know that her class is over and we should meet at the coffee shop shortly. I don't know why I'm so nervous. I'm finally going to meet the girl who saved me. Rain was the warmth I needed in the freezing cold. The memory of her has frequented my thoughts almost every day since that rainy night.

I walk under Café Nora's oversized sign and head inside. The smell of coffee hits me instantly. Lo-fi beats flow out of the speakers as I check out the long line of tables, which are placed one behind the other and to the side next to a tall wall of windows, offering a great view of the university's ample green spaces.

I spot two groups of people taking up a couple of tables. But the rest are empty. She must not have arrived yet.

A guy with hair dyed a dark shade of blue and pierced ears stands on the other side of the bar. He greets me with a smile. "Welcome to Café Nora. Today's specials are the iced macchiato and freshly baked cookies."

His sunny disposition is infectious, so I return the smile. He has warm brown eyes, and his cheeks are slightly flushed. I hear him clear his throat and suddenly realize that I have been staring at him.

"Ahh. I'm not ready to order. I'm waiting for my—"

Your what, exactly, Apolo? You don't even know her.

The guy stands there waiting for me to finish my answer. But my brain is not cooperating, so he takes pity on me.

"It's complicated, huh?" He sighs. "We've all been there. Take a seat. When your 'someone' arrives, I'll be right here to take your order."

"Thanks."

I turn my back to him, chagrined. After I find a table, I sit, wiping my sweaty palms on my jeans. I need to calm down. I keep my eyes locked on the main door. I try to distract myself, hoping to bring to a stop my obsessing with every passing minute. But I fail. I swallow hard, and then it happens.

The small bell attached to the front door announces her arrival. I freeze. It's hard to explain how I know it's her. Maybe a part of me remembers the shape of her silhouette, or something about her face, because it's immediately clear to me that this is Rain.

The first thing I notice is how her tousled blond hair falls all around her face. It's styled with a slight wave from the middle down to the tips. She's wearing jeans and a pale-pink sweater. She's clutching the strap of her purse as she scans the coffee shop, looking for me. I should wave. But I don't. Rain finds me anyway, and smiles.

I feel like my heart is going to burst out of my mouth. There's something about Rain that makes me feel an instant sense of peace. Her aura radiates with warmth. I know I shouldn't be saying something like this about someone I just met, but it's exactly how I feel. She walks over to my table and slides into the seat across from me.

She's still smiling. I'm having a hard time speaking. I'm in awe of how beautiful she is. I'm not saying she's perfect in looks only. It's the whole package: her energy, the sparkle in her eyes, her smile.

"Apolo Hidalgo," she says, placing her clasped hands on the table.

"Rain."

"We meet at last." Then she points to the windows. "It's not raining, though."

"You're gorgeous," I blurt. My mouth opens wide, into an O. I feel the heat rush from my neck to my face and I apologize. "Sorry, that was—"

"Thank you," she replies with a giggle. "You're not so bad yourself."

I raise an eyebrow. "Not bad?"

"Come on, you're hot. You know it. The whole faculty knows it. I think your ego will survive without my compliments."

She leans back in her chair. Her nonchalant attitude puts me at ease, and I feel less tense. I start to unclench my fists.

"Thanks for agreeing to see me. I really needed to see you. I mean, I wanted to meet you and thank you," I clarify. And Rain laughs.

"Are you always like this?"

"Like what?"

"This adorable."

That adjective makes me think of a pair of black eyes, and the full lips that whispered that phrase in my ear a handful of times.

"I'm not adorable." My voice comes out sounding colder than I want it to, and she takes notice.

"Understood."

I change the subject. "What would you like to drink?"

"Let's place our orders together." She gets up and I follow her.

At the counter, Rain keeps rubbing her chin with her index finger as she studies the menu on the wall. Then she shares her selections with the blue-haired guy. I think they must know each other because they have a quick chat after she's done placing her order. I just ask for a coffee. I doubt I can eat anything right now.

When we return to the table, I'm surprised by the number of things Rain ordered. There's a sandwich, a biscuit, a chocolate croissant, a slice of cake, and a caramel macchiato. She wasn't joking when she told me she had a weak spot for this place. Rain takes a sip of her coffee and looks at me.

"Say what you need to unload, Apolo," she encourages me. "I know it's the reason why you were so intent on seeing me. So spill."

"Honestly, I really don't know how to begin, or put it into words." I let out a long sigh. My eyes remain fixed on the table because I can't look her in the eyes. "That night—it was the worst night of my entire life. It's an experience I'm still coping with. I wouldn't be here today if you hadn't been there. If you hadn't come to my rescue. I'm unable to find the words to fully express how grateful I am. There is nothing I can give you that's worth as much as what you did for me that night." I raise my eyes and look straight at her. "I guess I'll just have to settle for this, and tell you from the bottom of my heart: thank you, Rain."

Her blinking eyes turn slightly red. And though she's smiling, I can't help but notice she's also looking rather emotional.

"Ah, really, it was nothing. I don't deserve such heartfelt gratitude." I open my mouth to protest but she carries on. "I'm just glad to see that you're okay."

We keep talking while she eats. She recounts her day at

school, and goes over an argument she had with a teacher. Rain can talk nonstop. There are no silent gaps in our conversation. And I enjoy it because I've never been a guy of many words. I listen and watch her, committing to memory every small detail. Rain has three piercings in each earlobe, in which she wears dainty studs.

Her eyes are warm and make you want to tell her everything. Her cheeks sport a few acne scars that didn't heal properly; her lips are thin, and she frequently wets them with her tongue while she's talking. She's not wearing much makeup, just lipstick in a blush shade that matches her sweater. The more I look, the more I notice that there's nothing about her that I don't like.

Apolo, wait. Wait . . . don't.

There's nothing about her that you don't like. Really?

You just met her. You can't already feel attracted to her, Apolo.

Later, outside the café, we walk next to the lawn as I work up my courage.

"Rain, feel free to say no. But can I give you a hug?" I always imagined that when I thanked her, I would also give her a big hug.

Rain smiles. "Of course."

We're the same height, so when I wrap my arms around her, we fit perfectly. However, I wasn't prepared for the feeling that takes me over when I inhale the smell of her citrusy perfume. Rain's warmth and her scent transport me back to that night, back to that moment, and how warm she felt in the midst of so much cold and pain. My eyes are burning and filled with unexpected tears. I can't pinpoint where exactly these troubled and overwhelming emotions are coming from. I cling to her tightly, and bury my face in her neck.

"Rain . . ." I'm not sure what else to say, and my voice breaks. I'm unable to explain how her scent and the warmth of her embrace have opened the door to the place where I had locked up all the emotions I've repressed since that night, to all the fear and the pain I felt then.

Rain simply hugs me back.

"It's okay, Apolo." She pats me on the back. "You're okay. You're safe. And you're out of the cold."

I pull away from her and look into her eyes. She takes my face in her hands and uses her thumbs to wipe away the tears that have fallen on my cheeks.

"It's not raining anymore," she reassures me calmly. And I manage to smile through the tears as I reply.

"It's not raining anymore."

Seven

APOLO

I can't stop thinking about her.

And it makes me feel like a complete fool because I've only met her once. I can admit I'm a romantic at heart. Still, I don't believe in love at first sight. I've always thought it takes a little more substance to fall in love with someone. One look is not enough. Not to mention, the first time we met wasn't the best encounter either. I bet it's not in the top ten list of her favorite memories of first impressions.

Rain says good-bye right after I release her from our hug. It's an embrace that has given me a much-needed boost and a sense of renewal, so I'm left with the urge to ask her out again. But I don't want to come on too strong or scare her off.

Now that a few days have passed, I'm not sure how I should reach out. What excuse could I make up? I don't want to be too forward and ask her on a date since I don't even know if she's interested in me that way.

It's likely that she just wanted to be thanked and that's all. I sigh. I take a sip of my coffee, and use my thumb to brush the rim of the cup. I'm back at Café Nora, sitting at the same table where we sat the other day. I started dropping by before class. I feel like someone is watching me, so I take a quick look in the direction of the coffee bar. There's another guy who works here, besides the one with the blue hair. This boy has jet-black hair, is quite tall, and looks very serious. I've rarely heard him talk. He's mostly occupied preparing drinks while the blue-haired guy takes down the orders. Although the dark-haired boy doesn't interact with anyone, I've caught him looking at me several times. I don't know if it's my imagination, but he seems annoyed. Maybe he's tired of seeing me here every day, and I don't blame him.

I've also caught a significant number of customers staring at him when they come into the shop. The guy definitely plays a sport or something like it, because his arms are ripped and the sleeves of his black uniform shirt fit quite snug around his biceps. And I've noticed a tattoo peeking out from under the hem of his right sleeve. I turn my attention back to my cup of coffee, savoring its contents for a long time.

"I'd like to know what's so special about this table," the blue-haired guy whispers.

Since I've been spending all my mornings here, he and I have had a few brief conversations. He stands next to me, holding a rag in his hands. When I look up, I meet his dark-brown eyes and smile.

"I have no idea." I point to the empty chair in front of me. "Perhaps it's the view."

He raises an eyebrow, and I notice there's a tiny piercing in it.

"The view of an empty chair?"

That makes me chuckle and, for some reason, I feel comfortable.

He chuckles, too, as he points to the chair. "Do you mind if I sit down?"

"Of course not."

He sits across from me, and I can better appreciate the striking blue of his messy hair, tousled with spiky tips pointing in all directions. It reminds me of an anime character's. His cheeks always appear flushed, even when he's standing behind the bar. Maybe it's from the steam coming from the coffee machines.

"Let me guess," he begins, pausing to lick his lips. "Rain broke up with you at this table and you can't get over it."

"Do you know her?"

He nods. "Who on campus doesn't know Rain? She's brilliant and supernice to everyone. My opinion, if you care to hear it, is that her name should be Sun instead."

Her gentle smile and the twinkle in Rain's eyes come to my mind. I suppose he's right.

"I wish I had the privilege of having her dump me. But I just met her."

"Ahh. You have a crush on her." He shakes his head. "Take a number, buddy."

"What? You too?" I ask, surprised.

He lets out a boisterous laugh. "No. Rain is gorgeous, but I'm into guys."

"Oh."

He raises an eyebrow. "*Oh?* Does that make you uncomfortable?"

"Not at all."

He leans back in the chair and crosses his arms, looking amused. "Calm down. You're definitely not my type."

"I wasn't making any assumptions about—"

"Apolo," he says, and I'm surprised he knows my name. "I was joking."

"How do you know my name?"

"Do you have any idea how many times I've written down your name on orders in the past few days?"

Ah, of course. I'm such an idiot.

He gets up and stretches a bit before reaching into his apron pocket, offering me a piece of paper.

"There's a party on campus tonight. Here's the address." He smiles. "Rain will be there," he adds, hoping to fill in the blanks. "I'm tired of you lingering here, looking like an anguished lost soul. Take a shot. Do something about it."

I take the paper and notice his hand remains extended toward me. I'm greeted with a smile when I look at him again.

"And my name is—" he starts.

"Xan," I say, smiling as I shake his hand. "Do you have any idea how many times I've seen your name tag on your apron as you take my order?" I point to the left side of his apron.

He lets out another chuckle, and lets go of my hand. "Okay. I deserved that."

"Xan!" We're interrupted by the dark-haired guy. He definitely seems annoyed when I turn and look at him.

"I'm sorry. He's just a sour patch," Xan whispers as he turns to leave. "I'll see you around, Apolo."

I watch him take his place behind the bar and get back to work. The other guy keeps staring at me in a very intimidating way, so I lower my gaze to the piece of paper. I realize that today is Friday. Of course there would a party happening somewhere. I copy the address into Maps then stick the scrap of paper in my pocket as I stand, ready to leave.

After I shower, I spend a couple of hours lying on the couch. I notice that lately the apartment feels empty. Gregory never seems to be around, and Kelly still hasn't been around much since the night I got hammered and made that stupid "confession." So I haven't had a chance to apologize to her in person. And I don't want to do it by text. Although, why not just send her a message that includes an apology? No, it's better to do it in person. There's a big difference between saying something to someone's face and sending an explanation in a message. The words in text are open to interpretation, and could be easily influenced by the tone the reader chooses, which could be different from what the sender intended.

I open Instagram to kill time by browsing through other people's stories. I look up Rain's, and come across a blurry picture of her standing in front of the mirror. She's putting on lipstick that's a pale-pink shade very similar to the one she wore the day we met. The story is tagged #readyfortheparty. So I guess that's a yes, she's going to the party that Xan mentioned. My finger remains pressed against the screen; I'm holding on to her story so that I can stare at the image longer. She looks happy and excited. It makes me consider that perhaps she really has no intention of reaching out or meeting with me again.

Ugh, Apolo. Stop making up stories inside your head.

I peel my finger off, and the next story that pops up brings a smile to my face. It's from someone who follows me.

Daniela.

My first love, and my first time. She's the girl who broke my heart and mended it before she left for college.

I remember that afternoon a year ago very clearly, as if it was yesterday.

The wind at the beach was gusty and kept blowing her long black hair to one side. The sunset had painted the entire sky orange. We were sitting on the sand, facing the sea. The waves would sometimes reach our feet. We'd spent the weekend alone together at a beach house belonging to one of Dani's friends. I was unsure of our status. We weren't in a relationship but we weren't seeing other people either. Dani was leaving for college the following week.

"Don't you just love how the sea appears to have no limits?" she asked me. I fixed my gaze on her side profile. "So vast. So open. And so free."

I looked back at the ocean. "I guess."

"I identify with it." She reached out for my hand, and held it against the sand. "I want to go away for college. I want to explore, meet new people, and I wish the same for you."

Ouch.

I managed to recover enough confidence to say, "Ares and Raquel are trying a long-distance relationship. Why can't we do the same?" The imploring tone in my voice was close to embarrassing.

She gave my hand a squeeze, and brought her face close to mine.

"Look into my eyes, Apolo," she instructed me. So I did, nearly losing myself in her deep, dark gaze. "Be honest with me. Is that what you really want?"

I opened my mouth, but closed it immediately as she caressed my cheek.

"We both know we have so much more left to explore about ourselves." I knew exactly what she was referring to. "I want us to end this on a good note, here in this moment that's sweet, free, and filled with the love between us."

I couldn't help myself from getting emotional. "I love you, Daniela." I kissed her because it felt as if what we had was being swept away by the sea breeze. "I love you," I repeated against her lips.

"And I love you, too, Apolo Crazy Fingers."

That made us both laugh. And I kissed her again, because I wanted to savor every last second of our time together.

My mind traveled back further, to the night at Artemis's club when I first saw her—when she appeared next to me, smiling and dancing, hoping to distract me. I thought to myself, *Holy shit! She's gorgeous.* Her whole face lit up when she smiled.

But Dani has always been so much more than a pretty smile. She listened to what I had to say and got to know me in a way that no one else ever had before. She pushed me to explore sides of myself buried deep without worrying about taboos. And she never put her interests ahead of mine.

She was right. We owed each other a beautiful ending. Romantic and at the beach, done in love. A love that she and I still had plenty of between us. True love doesn't bind, or suffocate, or constrain.

So when I come across her story on my phone, I smile wide because she was right. For me, Dani is not a bitter or painful memory. She represents freedom and never-ending affection. The second story is a clip of her at a party with lots of lights in the background. She's holding a red glass in one hand and is jumping around while shaking her hair and screaming like a madwoman. Her happiness is contagious. In the story that follows, she's kissing a girl with red hair. My lips curve into a smile. She's been dating this girl for months and she looks happy. Dani has never bothered with labels. She sees herself as fluid and prefers to fall in love with the person, regardless of their gender. In her opinion, labels are old-fashioned.

I tap on the heart icon, giving her story a like. And I immediately get a video call.

"LOLLOOOO!" Daniela screams at the top of her lungs. It's dark and there's a lot of noise and music in the background. But I still manage to catch a few glimpses of her face. "Don't tell me that you're stuck at home on a Friday night!"

I chuckle because with that racket around her, I'm pretty sure she won't be able to hear me.

"Get out there, Apolo Hidalgo!" she squeals and there's a click, bringing the video call to an abrupt end.

On that note, I grab my stuff and head out to the party.

The nightlife in downtown Raleigh is noisy and exuberant. Walking, I follow the directions in my Maps app. I cross one street and reach a cul-de-sac with lovely houses. I keep going to a two-story house. The booming sounds coming from inside confirm that I've arrived at the right place. I wipe my sweaty palms on my jeans and give myself a pep talk.

Come on, Apolo. You've come this far. Get inside.

The door is open and no one seems to care who's coming or going. There's way too many people to keep attendance under control. The music is blaring in my ears. I slip past a group of people and I can't really tell whether they're dancing or just standing there. Actually, it might be a bit of both. I make it to a sort of lounge area. There's a huge bookshelf on one side of the room. There are several groups of people chatting, and I spot her in one.

Rain.

She's laughing. My heart starts to race, the stupid fool that I am.

I take a step in her direction, feeling hesitant and nervous. That's when I catch a flash of something blue out of the corner of my right eye. When I turn around, I notice that Xan is standing a few feet away from me, and he's not alone. The black-haired guy from the coffee shop is standing right behind him. Xan has his back to him while the guy is hugging him from behind. He gives Xan a kiss on the cheek and rests his jaw on Xan's shoulder, his eyes locked on me.

And for a second I feel a lump in my throat, making it difficult to swallow. Dani's words from that afternoon on the beach replay in my head.

Don't you just love how the sea appears to have no limits?

Yes, Dani. It certainly has no limits.

Eight

APOLO

I stand very still in the sea of people.

Rain is a few feet away but she hasn't noticed me because she's busy laughing at something that was said by the girl in front of her. I notice how her cheeks become fuller anytime she laughs.

She's so cute.

With her warm attitude and her bright smile, it's a no-brainer why she's so popular around campus. Clearly, anyone and everyone would love to spend time in her company. She reminds me of Gregory. I think they're very similar. They both have lively and magnetic personalities.

I've always been curious about what makes each of us different. I think that's part of my motivation to pursue the study of psychology. I would like to deepen my understanding of human behavior, personality development, and everything else in that spectrum. How is it possible that my brothers and I have such different personalities despite growing up in the same household?

I've never been able to refrain from comparing myself to them or their friends. Although Ares and Artemis may act cold and distant to some degree, that has never kept them from making friends or socializing with others. So I wonder why it's so hard for me to do the same.

You're an old soul inhabiting the body of a young man.

The words of my grandfather pop into my head, providing me with the answer. I think he's always been right.

"Apolo?" I'm startled by the sound of Erica's voice. I turn. She looks surprised, and I must have the same look on my face. She's the only friend I've made in school, and so far she hasn't given me the impression of being the party-going type. I guess I shouldn't make any assumptions. Her wavy hair is up in a high ponytail and she's wearing a red sweater paired with baggy jeans.

"This is unexpected," I admit.

She adjusts her glasses and smiles at me. "I agree. I didn't expect to find you here either."

"Trust me. I thought long and hard about coming."

"Want something to drink?" She raises a red cup and I shake my head. Then I look back at Rain. Erica notices. "Rain, huh? Oh wait. The day we met you were writing *Rain* in your notebook, but it wasn't because you liked *the* rain. It was all about her." She carries on as everything clicks in her head. "I thought it was weird that you didn't like the rain, yet there you were, writing that word over and over again. Wow, come to think of it, that's pretty obsessive of you to write her name out like that. It's always the quiet ones, isn't it?" she jokes.

That gets me laughing, just a little. "I'm the most open and transparent guy you'll ever meet in your life."

"I already knew that." She gently taps my arm. "So what's keeping you from talking to her?"

"I'm not good at small talk."

"I'm also aware of that, Apolo."

We move to the side to avoid people passing by. Erica leans against the wall and crosses her arms.

"We need to work on your social skills."

"Look who's talking."

She pretends to be offended. "For your information, I have many friends."

"Of course you do."

"Apolo!" I hear someone shout. I watch as a mop of blue hair moves through the crowd until it reaches our side. Xan smiles at us, and as usual his cheeks have a rosy blush. That's when I realize that this blush is not due to the heat in the shop, and it's not caused by his emotions. Xan's face is always slightly flushed.

"Apolo! Miss Erica." Xan bows his head.

"Have you met?" Erica points to both of us.

Xan nods. "Apolo is a regular at Café Nora."

"Really?" Erica looks at me. "I've never seen you in there before."

"He always comes in the mornings. And you're in the afternoons," Xan explains. Then he places his hands on his hips and looks at me. "I'm so glad you came. Have you talked to Rain yet?"

Erica lets out an over-the-top sigh. "What do you think, Xan? Can you spot the look of a lamb being led to the slaughter?"

Xan shakes his head. "Do you need help? I'm very good at these things," he offers.

"I'm fine," I say, feeling a little embarrassed.

Xan turns to Erica and starts suggesting ideas for how I should best approach Rain. Seemingly unaware he's doing it, Xan keeps scratching his upper arm. He pulls his shirt sleeve up, bringing it to his shoulder. And that's when I notice. There are bruises on his skin. I furrow my brows. They look like marks made by fingers that have squeezed way too hard. Xan stops scratching and rolls down his sleeve. When his eyes meet mine, I feel the need to ask: *Are you okay? Do you need help?*

But I know it's not something I should ask in front of Erica. Actually, I don't think it's my place to ask him about it. Still, I'm going to when I get the chance. My gaze turns to the corner of the room where I noticed Xan earlier, only to spot the black-haired boy. He draws on a cigarette, looking very serious while talking with another guy.

Something is not right with him.

Xan and Erica laugh as they recall the day she spilled coffee all over herself and they had to mop the floor together. I look back at the boy with the dark looks. They seem like polar opposites. Xan is so cheerful and vibrant. Meanwhile, this guy has a negative aura around him—a darkness that seems follow him everywhere.

"Apolo, you're doing it again," Erica complains.

"What?"

"You stop talking and get all wrapped up inside your head. It's been like ten minutes since you last said a word."

"I'm sorry."

"Well, do you have a plan?" Erica indicates Rain. In the crowd, I find the blond with the smile that never fades.

Once again, I go back to that rainy night. I recall the sound of her voice, and the shape of her silhouette, holding an umbrella in the dark. I wonder if that's what makes my heart race when I look at her. Our first meeting was definitely intense, and hard to forget.

I need to bring this intensity down a few notches because I don't want to scare her away.

"I need fresh air," I tell them before turning toward the hallway.

The night air greets me as soon as I step outside, and I sit on the front steps. There are no stars in the sky tonight. For a downtown location, this neighborhood appears to be very quiet. I hear footsteps behind me and look over my shoulder. Xan walks out and sits next to me. I look straight ahead again, and he's silent for a few seconds.

Finally he says, "This is the first time I've met someone named Apolo."

I sigh. "I know. The Greek gods and all that."

"Makes sense."

I turn and look at him, sitting next to me with the tips of his spiky blue hair pointing in all directions. "And why is that?"

Xan throws his head back, and gazes at the sky. "Do I really need to explain?"

"Yes."

He shrugs and looks at me. "I mean, to be completely honest, you do look like a Greek god."

I laugh, but he doesn't. "And of course, you've seen a bunch. Haven't you?"

He just stares at me. "No. Only you."

Silence.

My heart skips a beat. Or at least, it feels like it does. I look away and smile, shaking my head.

"You shouldn't talk like that to a customer."

"I'm simply telling the truth."

I stay quiet for a while, and Xan doesn't say anything either.

"How do you do it?" I ask point-blank.

"How do I do what?"

"How do you talk to everyone with such ease?"

"Hmm." Xan pretends to think hard. "What can I say? I was born nosy and wonderfully pleasant. It's both a gift and a curse."

I raise an eyebrow. "A curse?"

He nods and gets up. He walks down the wooden steps until he reaches the sidewalk, then looks up in my direction. "Sometimes when you get along with everyone and draw a lot of attention to yourself, you end up attracting the wrong kind of people."

His words make me think of the bruises I noticed earlier on his arm.

"Has that happened to you?"

He gives me a nod. "Many times. But I've made it through."

I stare at him there, in his worn jeans and lightly wrinkled white shirt, and I realize that I don't really know who Xan truly is. He's a very nice guy, of course. But that's all I know about him. And I'd like to get to know him better. The ease of how I get along with Erica and Xan makes me feel less lonely. They both make me feel capable of making friends, and less inadequate in that department.

"Xan . . ." I'm struggling to find the right words to ask him. I pause and lick my lips while he waits. He flashes his signature smile but his eyes are open wide with anticipation. So I just get to the point. "Are you doing okay?"

He furrows his eyebrows. "Why do you ask?"

"I couldn't help but notice the bruises on your arm."

His smile instantly fades. His hands are clasped and resting on his lower abdomen, indicating some trepidation.

"I'm fine. I bumped against the edge of a door. You've seen how small the space is behind the counter where we prepare the drinks. One moment, you're pouring coffee. The next, you're careless, and then you—"

"Xan."

"I swear. I just wasn't paying attention and hit a sharp corner. What a klutz, right? I mean, the edge of a coffee machine is pretty hard to miss."

"Wait. Didn't you just say it was a door?"

Xan turns pale. He closes his mouth for a brief moment, then opens it again to speak. "I think I've had too much to drink. I don't even know what I'm saying anymore."

I didn't smell alcohol on him when we were inside and he was standing next to me. He's lying, and I don't blame him. We barely know each other, and I've stuck my nose into a very sensitive and personal matter. However, keeping quiet is never an option when someone's well-being is at stake. If someone needs help, I have to step up.

I stand, and make my way slowly down the steps. Xan looks at me warily.

"I don't know what's going on, but I'm here for you." I look him squarely in the eyes. "I can help, if you need anything."

Xan looks away. "You shouldn't make such heartfelt declarations to complete strangers. You hardly know me."

"Acquaintance or not, if you're not safe, I'd like to help you."

"I'm doing okay."

"Xan."

"I'm going to get Rain. Since you don't have the guts to talk to her."

Xan takes a step forward in an attempt to walk past me. But I gently grab hold of his arm and bring him to a halt.

"Wait."

Xan loosens his arm from my grip. "I'm fine. You're reading too much into a situation when nothing is wrong."

I stand in his way. "Xan, listen . . ."

At first, he appears willing to hear me out. Then he looks over my shoulder, and his face goes blank. There's a flicker of emotion in his eyes. Is it fear, perhaps?

"What's going on out here?" a deep, masculine voice booms from the doorway. When I turn around, I spot the dark-haired boy who was hanging out with Xan.

"Nothing," Xan answers immediately.

"Xan," I whisper. "Was it him? If you don't feel—"

"Hey, new guy. Why are you whispering?" The boy's addressing me, and I turn to face him.

Standing there at the top of the stairs, he looks more intimidating than ever.

"Why do I need to explain myself to you?" I ask.

He cocks his head to one side. "You don't. But he does." He points to Xan.

"We were just talking," Xan says.

"And who said you could leave the party?"

Xan lowers his head. "I needed fresh air."

"Sure."

I can't believe what I'm witnessing. What kind of controlling jerk is this guy? My suspicions that he's the cause of Xan's bruises grow stronger by the second.

"We were having a conversation. Can you please give us a minute?" I ask him, because I don't want Xan to go with him.

The guy stares at me, then slowly walks down each step until he is standing face-to-face with me.

"You're Apolo Hidalgo, right?" He says my name with disgust.

"Perhaps it's because you come from a wealthy family that you think you're entitled to meddle in other people's business. But that's not how things work here—although your attitude explains why your name made headlines on the college newspapers as the boy who got beat up."

"Are you threatening me?"

Xan comes to stand between us. "Come on. Let's go inside now, please," Xan pleads with him.

"We aren't the ones who have leave," the guy replies. "He's the one who needs to go."

Xan turns to look at me. The concerned expression on his face fills me with sadness. "Apolo, please go back inside the party. Let me take care of this."

"Let you take care of this?" He pushes Xan aside, and gets up in my face. "What are you to Xan?"

"And what gives you the right to control every second of his life?"

"I'm his boyfriend, asshole."

"So?"

He scoffs. "Since we're a couple, I have every right in the world."

"You're screwed up if that's your idea of what it means to be in a relationship."

"Whatever happens between me and Xan is none of your damn business." He tries to intimidate me by using his full height and icy glare. "Go back inside to the goddamn party."

"I don't feel like it."

He tenses, and his hands ball up by his sides. "Now I understand why they beat your ass to a pulp," he mutters between his teeth.

Xan lays his hand on the guy's chest. "Let's go home, please."

The guy peels Xan's hand off and refuses to move. I watch as Xan nervously reaches for his phone.

The guy is still staring at me. "I'm just waiting for you to say one more thing to give me a reason to punch you in the face. It's too bad that you're all healed, since you're about to get your ass kicked, again."

"You don't scare me."

The front door opens. The loud music spills from inside momentarily but it quickly fades when the door is shut by someone who is stepping outside. Hurried footsteps make their way down the stairs. In seconds, there she is, standing between us with her back to me. That blond hair captures my gaze and the smell of citrusy perfume helps calm me down.

Rain.

"What the hell are you doing?" The iciness and gravity in her voice takes me by surprise. Does Rain know this jerk too?

The boy makes a clicking sound with his tongue, takes two steps back, and raises both hands. "Oh, Xan. You shouldn't have called the party pooper."

"One more fight, and you know where you'll end up," Rain threatens him.

I look at Xan, who quietly observes the exchange.

"Xan, I'll be waiting for you inside," the boy says, then turns and leaves.

I'm left confused.

When Rain looks at me, she lets out a long sigh, which is followed by a warm smile that lights up her face. "I'm sorry, Apolo."

"What just happened? How come that jerk listens to you?"

Her smile slightly fades and she looks away.

"That's Vance. He's my brother."

Nine

RAIN

"I'll take care of it."

I'm surprised by the confidence in my voice. I look everywhere, except at him, though I feel his gaze on me. I'm too embarrassed to look directly at him.

Truth be told, I prayed that this would never happen: Apolo and Vance coming face-to-face. When I asked Apolo to meet me at Nora's, it completely slipped my mind that Xan owns the place. I suppose the universe has a twisted way of conspiring to bring certain people together.

Xan takes me by the hand and faces Apolo.

"I'm going to take off with Rain. You've got nothing to worry about anymore, Apolo. Everything is fine."

I want to protest. Nothing feels right, but I understand. Xan doesn't want to get Apolo involved in this fucked-up situation. And to be honest, neither do I.

I don't want my brother anywhere near him, at all. Vance is dangerous. And Apolo is . . .

I give him a quick once-over. The worry lines on his forehead appear to be deepening. Those pretty brown eyes jump from Xan to me, and my heart skips a beat. I've underestimated how incredible he is, both inside and out. He's gentle and kind, blushes at everything, and has an angelic smile that lights up his whole face.

Enough, Rain.

"Yeah, Xan is right," I reply. "We'll be fine."

Apolo hesitates for a second and I know he's going to challenge us, but Xan beats him to the punch.

"This is a personal matter that does not concern you, Apolo."

My face turns into a grimace, reacting to the rudeness of both his tone and his words. Xan never talks like that. He's not that kind of person. Him choosing to act this way with Apolo makes me narrow my eyes. Xan squeezes my hand and I look at him. I notice him swallowing. He looks nervous. Does this mean what I think it means?

"Okay." The coldness in Apolo's tone also leaves me confused. "You've already said that. There's no need to repeat it. I understand."

Apolo gives us a parting look, then walks past Xan and makes his way down the street. I stay quiet for a brief moment then let go of Xan's hand and stand in front of him. "What was that?"

"He wouldn't have left if I hadn't treated him that way."

"It's not that. Why did you get all defensive with Apolo? And what the hell has Vance done this time?"

"It's nothing. Vance got angry because I was out here talking to Apolo." Xan stares at the now empty sidewalk, his face falling.

I take a deep breath and grab his hand again.

"How about we get a coffee? I know a great place."

When we arrive at Café Nora we turn on only the lights above the bar area, leaving the rest of the shop shrouded in darkness. This infuses the place with slightly melancholy vibe. Xan makes us both drinks: a latte for him and a hot chocolate for me. We briefly enjoy our drinks in silence.

"I know exactly what you're going to say, Rain." He sighs as I observe him. The light bulb's yellow glow reflects off his skin. His face has a look of pure sadness. The blue of his hair looks dull under the lights. "How many times are we going to have this conversation?"

"As many times as it takes," I state frankly.

"I love him."

"I'm aware."

"And he loves me."

"No." My reply is firm. "Xan, look at me." When he does, I take the hand that's resting on the bar. "Vance is my brother, he's my blood. I have every reason in the world to defend him, to advocate for him, yet I never have and never will. Because I know him and he's not a good person. He has no idea what love is. The only thing he's capable of is hurting others."

"You don't understand, Rain. Nobody understands what's between us. Vance keeps telling me that other people will try to come between us, and that he's the only person who loves me for who I am; the only one who will accept me with all my faults."

"Xan, Vance is manipulating you. He's alienated you from everyone. That includes me, your old friends, and even your family. Do you know why he did that? He wants to be the center of your world. He doesn't want you to entertain the idea of leaving him for one second. He has made sure that you have no one left to help you if one day you decide to leave him once and for all. He's turned himself into the only person you can count on by isolating you from everyone else."

"Rain, you really don't know him. He's helped me get through hard times."

"He's been the only one there by your side during those difficult moments because he's driven everyone else away. Xan, every move he makes is calculated."

Xan takes a sip from his coffee and savors it, looking pensive. His eyes wander and appear to be studying the coffee equipment as he lets out a sigh.

"When I told him that one of my dreams was to open my own coffee shop, he gave me a portion of the amount I needed to get this place." Now it's my turn to take a sip from my cup as I let him go on. "He was okay with me naming the place after my mother, may she rest in peace. Do you have any idea how happy I am every day when I'm working here? I feel her spirit with me, guiding me and teaching me how to be a great barista and brew the best coffee, just like she did when I was a kid. And, yes, Rain, I know Vance isn't perfect. But it's gestures like that one that make me stay with him. There's a side of him that is sweet and caring, and that knows how to make me happy."

"Xan, you can't possibly stay in this relationship because of that one part, while the rest of him is hurtful, jealous, and controlling."

"And why not? There are times when I'm over the moon happy when I'm with him. So when things turn ugly, I figure it's the payment I have to make to hold on to that happiness. In a way the bad and the good balance each other out."

That breaks my heart.

"Xan." I adopt a firmer tone. "You deserve to be happy all the time. You don't need to pay for anything. Love is not a debt."

Xan doesn't respond and remains quiet.

"I don't think Apolo will ever speak to me again after my little speech." I detect he's trying to change the subject, and I let him because I don't want to overwhelm him either.

"Nah. He'll be okay. Apolo is very understanding."

"He likes you," he states matter-of-factly, watching me out of the corner of his eye.

"You think so?"

"You know it, Rain. Apolo couldn't be any more obvious."

"All right."

Xan waves his hand, gesturing as if he's waiting for more.

"What?" I give him a smile.

"I dunno. What about you? Do you like him?"

I watch him with amusement. "Why do you need to know?"

He gives me a shrug. "I'm just curious."

"This is the first time you've shown any interest in my love life."

"I've already told you, it's pure curiosity."

"Out of all the guys who have come through the doors of this shop and have been interested in me, Apolo is the first one you're curious about," I tease him.

Xan snorts. "I don't know what you're thinking, but whatever it is, you're wrong. Besides, I'm pretty sure he's straight. So no thanks. My life is complicated enough as it is."

"Xan, I have faith that soon your life will stop being so complicated." I give his hand a squeeze. "I can't force you to break up with Vance. It's your life, so it's your decision. Whatever happens, I'm here for you. Same goes for your other friends. The day you decide to end this relationship, we'll be here for you. Yes, it will be heartbreaking and will hurt at first, but it will pass."

Xan gets up and leans over to give me a hug. "You, Rain Adams, are too good for this world."

I break into a smile, pressed against his chest. "At this rate, I'll fill up your shop with guys pining over me," I joke.

"I won't mind if they're all like Apolo."

I pull away. "What was that?"

"Oh, nothing. Nothing at all."

He laughs and carries our empty cups to the other side of the counter while I keep teasing him. I have a feeling that Apolo coming into our lives is a positive sign, indicating good things are on the horizon. However, this optimism is clouded by a sense of foreboding when I think of my brother and the possibility that Vance may hurt Apolo.

Ten

APOLO

I can't sleep.

I toss and turn, restless. I replay every moment, every look, and of course, the way Rain and Xan said good-bye to me after tonight's incident. No explanations, just a "this is a personal matter," and "it doesn't concern you." I wanted to ask so many questions; I wanted to pry, but I knew it wasn't my place. I've never been one to interfere in other people's problems. I value and respect privacy. However, I am very concerned about what's going on between Xan and that guy.

Vance.

Who happens to be Rain's brother. To be honest, I wasn't expecting that at all.

Rain's awkward smile haunts me. The way she clenched her fists and avoided looking me in the eye. She looked embarrassed but had no reason feel that way. She's not to blame for the kind of person her brother is. It's the first time I've seen her act like that.

She looked as if she wanted to run away. Not even on that rainy night was she that tense.

I give up trying to fall asleep, and step out of my room. The long hallway envelops me in its darkness until I reach the living room, where I'm surprised to find the lamp next to the balcony doors turned on. I'm startled when I notice a silhouette sitting on one end of the long couch.

"Kelly?" She's in her pajamas, holding her knees to her chest, looking out onto the balcony. Her hair is loose, falling around her face. "Kelly?"

She lowers her head, using her hair as a curtain to hide her face. She wipes her cheeks discreetly. Is she crying? Did she have a fight with Gregory?

I take a step closer.

"I'm okay," she assures me, and lifts her face to look at me. Her swollen eyes tell a different story.

"Kelly—"

"Can't sleep? That makes two of us," she says with a fake smile. It saddens me to see her this way.

I sit down, keeping a distance from her. I don't want to make her feel uncomfortable.

"Yeah, it's been an interesting night."

She nods.

"Apolo, the one who picks everything apart." She shakes her head. "When I met you, I assumed you weren't interested in making friends. I thought you didn't want to waste your time with us mere mortals. I took you for a snob, or something like that." I raise an eyebrow. "Ah, come on. Give me a break. With your last name and—"

"And?"

"Your good looks." She shrugs. I pretend that her confession doesn't have an effect on me. I'm not good with compliments. "Anyway, after spending time with you, I finally figured it out."

"And what's your conclusion?" I fold my arms and try to appear interested, hoping to distract her from what's really bothering her.

"You spend all day overanalyzing everything. I think you need to take it easy."

"Join the club. It's what everyone tells me."

Kelly gives me the finger.

"Honestly." I carry on because I've missed this. I've always felt comfortable around her, though this could be due to the fact that she used to spend a lot of time at our place. "You're not the first one to say it: my brothers, their girlfriends, Greg . . ." I think of Charlotte and her open relationship. "And other friends I've made here. Pretty much everyone says so."

"Then why don't you turn that around?" She turns and looks me in the eye.

"Why don't I relax? Let loose? I don't know, it's not in my nature."

"Don't you get tired of living like this? It must be exhausting to overthink everything. It's like walking through a minefield, analyzing every move."

She hugs a cushion and my gaze instinctively slips down to the V of her top, where I notice a flash of skin. I look up immediately, slightly blushing.

"What was I saying?" I lose my train of thought for a moment. Then without meaning to, I blurt, "Why were you crying?"

Nice going, Apolo. Very subtle.

Kelly looks away and sighs. "Straight to the point, huh?"

"Sorry. You don't have to—"

"It's okay. It's no big secret. I'm a basic girl."

"Don't call yourself that."

She laughs.

"It's the truth. I'm crying over a boy." I let her finish. "Over a boy who doesn't love me."

I'm at a loss for words.

"You mean Gregory?"

"Who else?" She sighs, and we exchange a glance. Perhaps we're both thinking the same thing. So she clarifies, just in case. "Did you think I was talking about you? I'm not so emotionally fragile that I'd be shedding tears over you, Apolo. Especially when we haven't even—" She pauses, and it's like we share a single mind. She seems to be remembering the night we hosted the party here. How she danced with me and rubbed her body against mine. This, of course, was soon followed by my drunken confession to Gregory, the night I told him that I liked her.

Silence.

Well, the easy, casual vibe we had when we started talking has clearly vanished. I rub the back of my neck and clear my throat.

"I'm not so vain as to think you were crying over me, Kelly."

"Yeah, I know. I was just kidding." She hugs the cushion a little tighter.

"So, Gregory, huh? What happened?"

"I'm confused. He and I, well, we have fun. Yet every time it feels like we're about to make things official, one of us shuts down. It's weird. It's like we can never be on the same page at the same time. Also, he . . ."

"What's wrong?"

"I think he's still in love with her."

I frown, looking puzzled.

"Who?"

"With his ex."

She catches me completely off guard. Gregory never talks about any girl. He's a gentleman and very discreet, though I think he would have mentioned an ex to me. Especially if what Kelly is telling me happens to be true and he's not over her.

"I have no idea who you're talking about."

"You see. He never mentions her. She's like his Voldemort."

"I didn't know Gregory had ever been in a serious relationship. I thought his first year in college was as wild as his second has been," I add.

Kelly sighs. "Not really. As far as I know, he'd been in college for about two months when he met her."

"What's her name?"

"Erica."

I freeze. It can't be the same Erica who happens to be the only friend I've made so far. "Excuse me?"

Eleven

APOLO

Kelly pulls out her phone and opens up Instagram to show me. On the screen is Erica's profile. Most of her photos are of fancy coffee drinks and selfies of her smiling from ear to ear. There isn't a photo where she doesn't look happy. And yes, it's the same Erica—my one and only friend in college. In retrospect, our conversation and her reaction from a few weeks ago make sense now. How she left in a huff after I said I was friends with "party monster."

"I see." I don't think sharing anything about Erica and me with Kelly will add much to the conversation. Kelly already seems sad enough. "Do you know what happened between them?"

"I have no idea. I'm not sure who left whom. But he . . . I don't know how to explain it, Apolo. Sometimes I can tell when he's thinking about her. Even when he's right next to me."

"I'm sorry, you must feel—"

"Horrible. Sometimes, yes. Then other times, I don't feel anything."

"Huh?"

"That's why I say I'm confused. Sometimes I'm bothered and hurt. Then there are other times when I simply don't care. I'm not sure what I feel anymore."

"Oh. I understand." Though, to be completely honest, I don't really understand what's going on between these two.

Kelly rests her face on the couch and watches me for a few seconds. "Are we ever going to talk about it?"

I tense up a bit. "About what?"

"About what you told Gregory when you were drunk."

Ah.

I can feel the heat rushing down the back of my neck. She's right, though, I never explained myself. I haven't given that moment much thought, and have yet to offer an apology.

"I'm sorry, Kelly. I don't know what came over me. I had a bad day and I got drunk. Truthfully, I'm really sorry I put you in an uncomfortable situation."

Kelly doesn't immediately respond. She just looks at me with an intensity that I find hard to read. "It's refreshing."

"What?" I ask, feeling confused.

"The way you are. You, Apolo. You're refreshing," she tells me. "You're always mindful that your actions won't bring any harm to others. And you apologize when you have to. I've met very few people like you."

I must admit, the way she says *you* as she stares at my lips is tempting. And this is why I have avoided her. Why I haven't wanted to deal with this at all. Because I do like her. And being here alone, like this, only makes it more obvious and impossible to avoid. I chuckle under my breath, trying to lighten the mood.

"And this is the part where you tell me I'm different," I joke, but she's not laughing.

My body tenses when she moves closer, until she's sitting right next to me and I can feel the warmth of her body mingling with mine. Up close, I get a better look at her puffy eyes and reddened nose. Regardless, she still looks beautiful. Her lips look so full and moist.

"Kelly?" I whisper.

I don't know what she's doing, but I know we shouldn't be this close. She shouldn't tempt me, which is exactly what she's done for as long as I've known her. She looks me in the eye and smiles before posing a question.

"Do you like me?"

Her hand cradles my cheek and I almost close my eyes when I feel her touch.

It's been a while since someone touched me with such gentleness and affection. And I clearly crave this type of attention. I just don't think she's the one who should give it to me.

"Kelly."

"At some point we'll have to talk about this."

"We just did and I apologized." I give her a firm reply.

Her smile fades and she lowers her hand. I almost protest.

"Oh right. It was a mistake." She clears her throat and looks away. "I understand."

She hugs the cushion again and purses her lips, looking embarrassed. At that moment, after all the times I've been told to relax, to let loose, and to stop overthinking, it finally clicks. This isn't the best time and she's definitely not the right person, but I need to kiss her. I've wanted to do it since the day I met her.

And it's Gregory's words that give me the final push.

What we have, it's not serious. But I appreciate your honesty . . . Apolo, you have to stop taking life so seriously. . . . You're eighteen, in college, and girls are coming at you in droves. Just enjoy yourself.

So I cup Kelly's cheek. She tenses slightly and our eyes meet. I swallow hard; I'm making my intentions crystal clear. Then she draws closer and lessens the space between us. Our lips brush and a warm current runs through my body. And that's all it takes to unleash my desire. Rational thinking goes out the window, and I proceed to kiss her passionately.

Few times in my life have I let myself go like this. And though I'm not kissing her hard, I'm not being gentle either. After our mouths make contact, we proceed to suck each other's lips rather awkwardly until we build a rhythm. She knows what she's doing and tilts her head to one side. She sticks her tongue in my mouth and nearly drives me wild. A few seconds of this and I can already feel the heat rushing down to my groin.

The sound of our combined breathing echoes around the room. She bites my lip. I let out a hoarse gasp and get back to kissing her again with abandon. My mouth moves more aggressively and she moans softly before draping a leg over my lap. She maneuvers herself to a straddling position and presses herself tightly against my growing erection.

My hands travel down to her hips and I give them a squeeze. She whimpers against my lips. Maybe it's because I really like her, but the feelings I'm experiencing at this moment are unlike any others I've felt in a long time. With Charlotte it was all rather quick and very quid pro quo. With Kelly, it feels more meaningful. This kiss is amazing. It's certainly driven by lust, but it's also motivated by a need to feel a connection and someone's affection. There's a warmth to the way we kiss and caress each other. Every gesture is important. My fingers move upward and brush against the hem of her shirt. That's when I make contact with the exposed skin of her waist and abdomen. We pull apart for a brief moment to catch our breaths.

"Apolo." She whispers my name as she opens her eyes, and I momentarily loose myself in her gaze, partly because I don't know what else to say.

I take a lock of her hair in my hand and tuck it behind her ear. We shouldn't be doing this. Or should we? How did I go from comforting her when she was crying over someone else to kissing her madly with her straddling me? What am I doing?

"We shouldn't." I groan when she moves her hips. I'm completely hard and have already forgotten what I was about to say. Kelly buries her face in my neck and licks it eagerly while she keeps gyrating on my lap. I let out a sigh, close my eyes, and let my head fall back against the couch. "Kelly . . ."

She continues to lick her way up to my ear and murmurs, "Stop thinking so much, Apolo."

Her breathing is heavy. I encircle her waist with my hands. I sense every movement she makes on top of me. I want her so much. So I grab her by the shoulders to pull her off me. At first, she looks confused. Then I push her shirt up, exposing her breasts. They're small and sexy. My erection jerks a little at the sight and she says nothing; instead, she just looks at me, waiting.

I can't take it anymore. I give in and lean forward. My mouth captures one of her breasts. She moans and arches her back as I lick and suck. I have waited, and been tempted, for far too long. I draw a circle with my tongue over her already hardened nipple.

She strokes my hair and her hips increase the speed of her movements. Her crotch is pressing against my erection and it's complete torture. I move to the other breast, leaving a trail of saliva across her chest. Her movements become clumsy and uncoordinated. Her moans grow louder, so I reach up with one hand to cover her mouth. I'm pretty sure that Gregory is in his room.

I can feel the warmth rising from her core. I get harder just thinking about how wet she must be and how much I would love to be inside her right now. She grabs my face and kisses me again. This time it's a desperate, passionate, hungry kiss. There is no more gentleness. We are both way too turned on for that. There's no denying we want each other badly, and are more than ready to fuck.

It's at that very moment we are startled by the sound of a door opening. The noise is from somewhere down the hallway that leads to the bedrooms. We pull away from each other as fast as we can. Kelly pulls her shirt down and moves to the other end of the couch. In the meantime, I reach for a cushion and use it to hide my visible hard-on. Our chests rise and fall quickly as we watch Gregory come out of the hallway looking disheveled. He squints one eye as he tries to adjust his focus and get a better look at us.

"What are you doing awake?" he asks as he yawns, and his hand gropes the wall, looking for the switch to turn the light on.

"Talking each other's ears off to the point of exhaustion," Kelly responds. "Don't turn the light on. You're going to chase away the little bit of sleep we've racked up during our chat."

"I thought I heard wailing," Gregory adds as he lets out another yawn.

Kelly leaps in with an explanation. "Uh—the door to the balcony is open. A car full of rowdy boys drove past. They were screaming and shouting nonsense. It's the weekend. You know how it is." I'm surprised at how easily she's able to lie. Meanwhile, I haven't been able to utter a single word.

"Oh." Gregory scratches the back of his neck and looks at me. "Are you doing okay?"

I nod. "Yeah. Just having difficulty sleeping."

"Still thinking about Rain, huh?" Gregory asks, and I tense up.

I look at Kelly. Her expression has turned somber.

Gregory keeps going. "You're obsessed with that girl. I don't blame you. Rain is—"

"Why weren't you at the party?" I cut him off, hoping to steer the conversation in a different direction. I'm not stupid enough to engage in a discussion about another girl while the girl I was just making out with a few seconds ago is sitting right next to me.

"I got kicked really hard in the last soccer match and my leg hurts. I need to take something for the pain," Gregory replies.

He walks to the kitchen. The light from the fridge momentarily floods the space when he opens it to grab a bottle of water.

He heads back in the direction of the our bedrooms, but comes to a halt and gives Kelly an expectant look. She smiles and gets up.

"I hope you manage to sleep, Apolo," she says.

She walks toward him and I stare until they both disappear down the hall. For a second I picture her going to bed with me, not him. Then I immediately feel confused, and there's a bitter feeling in the pit of my stomach. Are they going to fuck? Would Kelly be able to screw him when I was the one who just got her hot and bothered?

That's none of your business, Apolo, I remind myself.

I knew she was still with him when I kissed her. I have no reason to feel bitter. Still, I'm an idiot, so I can't help but feel weird about the whole thing. I'm having a hard time figuring out what just happened. I throw the cushion to the side and head to my room. I carelessly plop down on my bed, back first. I check my phone and come across a text message from an unknown number.

I won't be able to sleep without apologizing first. I'm sorry for the way I spoke to you. You were just trying to help. Rain gave me your number. Xan.

I lick my lips and text him back.

Me: Don't worry. It was nothing.

Xan: Tomorrow, order whatever you want at the shop, free of charge. Compliments of the house.

In the darkness of my room, I break into a smile.

Me: Great. See you tomorrow, Xan.

Twelve

XAN

One, two, three, four, five.

Ding!

The elevator doors open and I take a deep breath. I walk slowly to the door of our apartment and then briefly stand still. I pray that Vance had too much to drink at the party and is already sleeping like a log. Tomorrow is another day.

I insert the key in the door and it opens, triggering a soft ring. As soon as I step inside, I hear the sound of the television playing in the living room down the hall. Of course he's awake and waiting for me. Vance isn't one to let go of things easily. I let out a deep breath and shut the door. I take off my shoes and leave them in the foyer. Vance is pretty obsessive about keeping the place looking spotless. When he bought this apartment he renovated it: white marble floors, white kitchen . . . everything is so sterile, so it's hard to miss a speck of dust.

I walk into the living room and there he is. Vance. His black hair is tousled, his shirt is off, and he's wearing pajama pants, which hang pretty low. That toned and chiseled body has been my safe place countless times. He doesn't look at me, and takes a swig from his beer. I purse my lips. I don't know what I should do.

"Vance."

"Did you have a good time?" His voice is not warm; it's somber. My heart is racing a little. I'm worried this will escalate into an argument. But I feel somehow emboldened by the conversation I had earlier with Rain.

"I was at Nora's, with your sister."

"I know."

He picks up the remote and switches from the show he was watching to an app that has access to the closed-circuit security cameras installed at the shop.

I narrow my gaze. "I didn't know that you could watch from here."

"Does that bother you? That I can see how many times that kid has been to the shop?"

I know he means Apolo. It all makes sense now. This is the reason why Vance has been showing up at the shop more frequently lately. It's because he caught a glimpse of Apolo on camera. I'm a complete fool. Here I was thinking he was coming around a lot because he wanted to spend more time with me.

Vance stands and walks toward me slowly, his eyes searching for something in my expression. "Do you take me for an idiot, Xan?"

"No, Vance. There are a number of regulars who frequent the café every day. He's just one of many." I shake my head.

He sneers. "Just one of many? And what was that shit he pulled tonight at the party?"

"It's called common courtesy. It's how you show that you care about others. Apolo is kind to everyone. There's nothing more to it, I swear."

"Maybe there's nothing on his part—I've overheard him talk about how smitten he is with my sister—but what about you? Xan, I know you. I can tell when you're attracted to someone by the way you look at them."

"You're crazy."

"I bet you would have flirted with him more if I hadn't been coming to the shop as often to keep you company."

"Vance, we've talked about this. Stop thinking the worst of me, I've given you no reason to doubt me."

He takes another step forward and I take a step back. My back hits the edge of the kitchen island, bringing me to a complete stop.

Vance takes my cheek gently. "Stay away from him. I don't know what your intentions are, but I don't want to see him at the shop ever again."

I open my mouth to protest but he kisses me. It's a brief kiss intended to shut me up. Nevertheless, I'm overcome with a flow of emotions because I love him so much.

He pulls away. "We were doing so well, Xan. Please don't let a random guy who just showed up out of nowhere ruin everything. We're sharing a life together, and you know damn well how much work and effort we've invested in building something for the two of us."

"I'm aware."

"So what are your priorities? What matters most to you? Is it going to be a guy you just met? Or me?"

"Of course you are one of my priorities. But I'd also like to make some friends, Vance."

I try to hold on to what Rain and I discussed.

"You don't need them, Xan. Who was there for you when your mother got sick?" My silence gives him permission to carry on. "Who was there to support you in every possible way? With the bills? With your grief? And the pain from losing her?" He cradles my face with both hands and looks me directly in the eyes. "No one knows you like I do, Xan. I know my sister loves to fill your head with ideas, but she hasn't been there for you during your darkest times, and you know this very well. It's all sweet words and empty promises until the going gets tough. And when that happens, I'm the only one you can really count on."

"It's just that, meeting new people, making friends . . . it's the normal thing to do, Vance," I mutter under my breath.

"No, it's not the normal thing, Xan. Everyone pretends to be friends with others. But you have outgrown that phase in your life. You're past that naive stage in life when we believe the company of friends is necessary."

I want to say something but he kisses me again, and it's not a quick kiss. It's passionate. He roughly inserts his tongue in my mouth then encircles my waist with his arms, and moves one hand down to give my ass a squeeze. He tilts his face to one side and deepens his kiss. He peels his lips off mine and licks my neck. And I let myself get lost in the moment. How can I resist? I never thought I would love someone like this. He consumes me, and the more I allow it, the deeper he gets under my skin.

Vance has left the bathroom door open and the sound of the shower echoes through the room. I'm lying sideways on the bed with a sheet covering my naked body. I stare at the glass wall that offers a gorgeous view of Raleigh at night while keeping us discreetly out of sight from peering eyes.

Vance comes out, toweling his hair dry. He's already dressed.

"I'll be in the studio. I'm going live soon, and may not be back until dawn." He leans over and gives me a quick kiss. "Get some rest."

I don't say anything because this is our weekend routine. Vance hosts live broadcasts at night from the studio he set up at the opposite end of the apartment. He rarely sleeps with me and that is something I miss very much. This bedroom, with all its luxury and comfort, has turned into a cold and lonely place.

I watch him leave the room and close the door. Something comes to mind that makes me uneasy. Vance has never made our relationship public. He hasn't even come out to his followers. I respect his choices and decisions, but it makes me a little uncomfortable when I watch him shamelessly exploit his good looks to charm girls. I feel like he's using them and leading them on. Or perhaps I'm overanalyzing. I'm sure if he was open and honest, they would be okay with him regardless.

But then again there are the so-called "collaborations" he does with other female influencers. Those videos where there's a lot of flirting happening, or the reels featuring "relationship goals" and other lovey-dovey stuff. I understand it's all fake fluff intended to engage an audience. Still, it hurts a little when I see him pretending to do and be these things with other people and not with me. I have nothing against these girls. But for once, I would love to be the one in those videos with him. And have comments left by fans wishing us the best and all those other wonderful things they write every time he posts videos he makes with these girls.

I lie on my back, staring at the ceiling. At last, I reflect on the matter I've been avoiding all night. Apolo. The look of hurt on his face still haunts me, and I know I should apologize, which is why I asked Rain for his number. I reach for my cell phone on my bedside table, and send him a text.

> **Me:** I won't be able to sleep without apologizing first. I'm sorry for the way I spoke to you. You were just trying to help. Rain gave me your number. Xan.

I nervously await an answer that may never come. Apolo has every right to never speak to me again after the way I acted toward him outside the party. My cell phone vibrates. I rush to open the message app and my finger nearly slides to the Call button by accident.

> **Apolo:** Don't worry. It was nothing.

I inhale.

> **Me:** Tomorrow, order whatever you want at the shop, free of charge. Compliments of the house.

Vance's words of warning resound inside my head. There's nothing wrong with offering him one last drink before I ask him never to come back to Café Nora. I'm still trying to figure out how to ask that of him.

> **Apolo:** Great. See you tomorrow, Xan.

I exhale. I put my cell phone away and walk to the window, to watch the city lights. I feel so alone.

Vance claims that friends are not essential. Yet he does have quite a few, and even hangs out with them. He has fun in their company while I'm left on my own in this sparse and lonely apartment. I've never been one of those people who has lots of friends. Growing up, it was just me and my mom. I was raised outside of Raleigh, in a rural area surrounded by pretty closed-minded folks. I had to pretend I was just like the other kids. I tried to come out one time and show my true self, but I was mocked relentlessly to the point of being scarred. The memory of that experience still gives me nightmares. Still, I've always wanted to have a large circle of friends who accept me for who I am and laugh with me. Friends who would lend me their support and let me give them mine.

I feel like there's a part of me that belongs to little Xan, the kid who wants to be accepted for who he is and who wants to have the friends he never had in school. But Vance is right. Maybe all I need is just one person to be there for me. My mother was my everything, and now he's taken her place. This void that craves acceptance and friendship will be filled in time. I'm not a child anymore. I'm doing fine, and don't need anything else.

I get dressed, and decide to make myself a chamomile tea. I walk over to the studio, holding a cup in my hand. The door is ajar and I can see Vance facing the computer; he's laughing and licking his lips.

"Thank you for your contribution, rosita276. You're always so supportive. I promise I'll give you a big hug when we finally meet."

I scrunch up my face. I turn on my heel and head back to our room. As soon as I enter, I notice the screen of my cell phone is lit up.

It's a missed call from Apolo.

I swallow hard and hesitate. I close the bedroom door before I sit on the bed and call him back. "Hey, did you just call me?"

His voice sounds hoarse on the other end of the line. "Yeah. I wanted to make sure you were okay."

"I'm fine. You have to stop worrying about me."

Apolo sighs. "I can't sleep."

"And calling me is the solution?" I ask as I make myself comfortable in bed, placing the cup of chamomile tea on the bedside table.

"I'm sorry, were you sleeping?"

"No."

"Are you with him?"

"Yes. But he's working right now." Before he has a chance to say anything about Vance, I carry on. "And why can't you sleep? Are you thinking too much about Rain?"

"I think about everything excessively. It's my passion."

That makes me smile. "I've noticed that when you're at the shop. And what are you thinking about?"

"That I should stop kissing girls if I'm not sure what I want to have with them."

Oh.

"Apolo. You're a bad boy, huh?"

"Nope. It's not what you think. Everyone tells me I need to relax more and enjoy life. Then I pick the wrong time to let myself get carried away."

"So you end up screwing everything up?"

"Pretty much."

"And what's wrong with that? Welcome to life, Apolo. It's a place where every one of us is constantly screwing up."

"I don't like making mistakes. I prefer to be . . ."

"Perfect?" I finish for him. "If that's what you believe, you have a long way ahead of you filled with disappointment. You will always be frustrated if you're obsessed with being perfect."

"Xan, you're good at giving advice."

"Thanks."

"But are you good at following your own advice?"

I tense. "Not really."

"Aren't we all like that? Great experts when it comes to dishing out advice to help others but never able to do the same for ourselves."

I take a sip of my tea before I speak. "Why are we deep diving at two o'clock in the morning?"

Another sigh from Apolo. "The best conversations are had in the early-morning hours."

"Good. Then tell me about yourself, Apolo. So far all I know is how you take your coffee. Also, I know you like kissing girls and you're afraid of screwing up. Lastly, I know you have a crush on Rain."

"Where do I start?" he whispers and I smile. Then the door to the bedroom bursts open.

Vance walks in and his gaze goes straight to the cell phone against my ear. His face reddens with absolute fury and I immediately put it down, abruptly ending the call.

"Who were you talking to?" He rushes toward me and I move the cell phone out of his reach and behind my back.

"Xan!"

"Weren't you doing a live broadcast?"

He leans over and grabs my arm tightly. I wince but manage to free myself from his grip.

"Vance, calm down!"

"Who was on that call?" he shouts in my face, and pulls me by the hair, forcing me to get up.

"Vance, stop."

I struggle to free myself but his grip tightens and the pain I feel shooting through my scalp intensifies. With his other hand, he succeeds in taking my cell phone. I can see his anger push past its limits when he reads Apolo's name on the last call.

"I knew I couldn't trust you!"

Vance lets go of me, and I slam into the wall, groaning in pain. He's furious and throws the cell phone at me. I barely manage to catch it in midair.

"We just finished having this fucking conversation! And as soon as I turn my back you call him? What the fuck is wrong with you, Xan?"

"He was making sure that I got home safely, that's all."

"You really don't care about me at all."

"Vance."

"We just went over this! Damn it!"

"I wasn't doing anything wrong. I was just talking to him."

"Right after I asked you not to? You don't love me, Xan. Because if you did, you wouldn't do this to me."

"Do what to you, exactly?"

"Talk to someone I have specifically asked you to stay away from."

"Vance . . ."

He turns, puts his hands to his head, and looks directly at me. I immediately sense that I'm not going to like what he's about to say.

"This is the reason no one took you seriously before I came into your life. It's because you do things like this."

That hurts a lot. Before I met Vance, I dated several guys and even fell in love. Unfortunately, none of them were interested in having a serious relationship. I was the one who always ended up with a broken heart. Vance's words rip open an emotional wound festering with insecurities, and I don't know how to respond.

"Is this all you are, Xan? A promiscuous fuckboy?"

"No. I love you, Vance. It's you, and only you. There's no one else."

"Then prove it." His black eyes watch me intently. "Give me your cell phone."

"What?"

"Give me your damn cell phone. I won't be able to carry on with the live broadcast if I'm wondering whether you're sneaking a call and talking to him."

"Vance, you're so out of line. I'm not going to—"

"Give me your fucking cell phone right now!"

The fury emanating from him terrifies me and I give in. I don't want this to escalate any further. I don't want him to hurt me again. To make matters worse, my cell phone starts to vibrate with an incoming call from Apolo.

"He must be worried because I hung up on him, that's all."

"Answer it and put it on speaker. You're going to tell him you want him out of your life, for good."

I shake my head and Vance clenches his jaw.

"Xan."

"Vance, please."

"Do it! Or should I take care of him myself?"

That paralyzes me with fear.

"No."

"Then do as I say."

I nod and answer the call, putting it on speaker.

"Xan? Is everything okay?"

The sound of Apolo's voice makes me sad, because I felt safe and secure a few minutes ago while we were talking, and now all I feel is fear. Still, I keep my emotions under control.

"Apolo, I think it's best if you delete my number. To be completely honest, I don't have the time to make new friends right now. Best of luck to you with everything."

"Excuse me? What are you saying, Xan?"

"Please leave me alone. I don't need you to complicate my life. Don't call me anymore. Bye."

And I hang up.

The call lasted just a few seconds but it felt like an eternity. Vance stares at me for moment, then reaches over and grabs my face.

"See? That wasn't so hard, Xan. We're going to save ourselves a lot of trouble with that call. Do you want us to fight like this ever again?"

"No."

"And we won't because now he's out of the picture. We're going to be fine—it's you and me against the world. You are the most important thing to me, that's why I get like this."

He hugs me. His body used to be my warm, safe haven. Now it feels cold, just like the glass on the wall of windows overlooking the city. My chin rests on his shoulder as tears form in my eyes. The city lights become blurry spots. A deep sadness sweeps over me; it feels like it's choking me.

I think of my mother, how hard she worked and fought for

me. And how much she suffered when she got sick. She gave everything to raise me. Would she be proud of me? Or the opposite? I don't know who I am anymore, or what path to take. All I have is Vance and he seems to change every day. The sweet and serious boy I fell in love with barely comes to the surface. I rarely get any affection when we have sex without something unpleasant happening afterward, like it did just now. I constantly crave his affection, and pain seems to be the price I must pay to earn it.

Vance strokes my back. "Stop crying, it's not a big deal. Don't be so dramatic, Xan."

"I'm sorry."

"I'll make it go away."

Vance keeps hugging me. He starts kissing my neck and touching me all over. The last thing I want to do is screw, but I don't have the strength to stand up to him. I don't want him to yell at me or hit me again because he thinks I don't want to have sex with him because I'm thinking about Apolo, or any other crazy idea that pops inside his head. So I don't put up any resistance as he kisses me and takes off my clothes. Or when he turns me around and bends me over on the bed.

My body responds immediately to his rousing, mostly out of habit and familiarity, yet my mind is somewhere else. It's as if I'm not here. And I don't want to be here, so I let my mind wander and think of other things. I conjure the memory of old friends, the aroma of my mother's freshly made coffee, Rain's words, and Apolo's kind and warm smile. Tears fall and wet the sheets. I feel lonely and trapped. And in this moment, I want more than anything to have friends.

Thirteen

APOLO

"I thought you were my friend, Apolo," Erica reproaches me.

"I am."

"An incomplete? For real?"

Erica frowns as she scans my essay. I don't blame her. We worked on this social psychology assignment together, and she loved everything I told her I would write, but between us, the only one who ended up putting brilliant ideas to paper was her. I mostly contributed a few lines here and there. To be honest, it's a miracle that I haven't failed more assignments. I've had a lot of problems with concentration and motivation. Anytime I make an attempt to dig deeper and figure out the root cause of the problem, I end up circling back to that fucking night, so I immediately push it out of my mind. Not to mention I'm still bothered by what happened the last time I ran into Rain, when I met her brother and Xan asked me to stay away from him.

"What happened?"

Erica hands back my essay and folds her arms. The autumn breeze gently blows her curls. One lock of hair brushes against her nose and she pushes it away, looking slightly bothered. She is waiting for an answer. I avoid her gaze and look out the cafeteria window instead. I stare at a tree that has already lost all its leaves.

"Apolo?" Her voice is insistent.

"I don't know."

She lets out a sigh and takes a sip from her coffee.

"Ugh. We should have gone to Nora's, the coffee here is terrible."

I agree with her, but I haven't been to Nora's for over a week now. I haven't talked to Rain either. When I'm at home, I spend my days locked in my room. I'd rather not run into Kelly, and I can't bring myself to face Gregory after what happened. I feel like I don't want to deal with anything right now, but why is that?

"Apolo, are you feeling all right?" I nod, and Erica makes a grimace. "You don't look well. I get that you're not the most talkative guy, but lately you've been quieter than usual. Also, you're not—" She points to the sandwich I haven't touched. "This is the third time this week you haven't eaten your lunch."

"I suppose I'm just feeling a little demoralized."

"Or depressed?"

"No, I'll get over it."

"Missing your family?"

Now that Erica mentions it, she might be partly right. I miss my niece's angelic smile, Artemis's funny faces, Claudia's words of wisdom, and my grandpa's warm embrace. Thanksgiving break seems so far away. Maybe I can squeeze in a surprise weekend trip. I just don't want them to worry. Though I'm pretty certain that if I visit, they'll insist that I go to therapy. I understand that I need to talk about that night and go over what happened to me. Still, every time I picture myself discussing the experience, I get the chills.

"I'll take your silence as a yes," replies Erica.

Huh?

Oh yeah, the answer to the question she asked.

"I guess we're all missing our families. Aren't we?"

Erica opens her mouth, about to say something, but I give her a serious look. I don't want to talk about that. So she lets out a sigh.

"All right then. How did it go with Rain? You never told me if you managed to talk to her at the party. I lost track of you. One moment you were there, the next you were gone."

"Ah. It's complicated."

"And why is that?"

"A long story."

Erica looks at me with curiosity. "Apolo, do you really have a crush on Rain?"

"Why do you doubt that I do?"

"I don't know. A few things I came across while I was doing my research for the project." She pauses, concentrating. "Have you ever heard of the suspension bridge effect? It's a term used to describe a phenomena known as misattribution of arousal."

"Never heard of it."

"It's what happens when a person is crossing a suspension bridge and spots someone else at the other end. Their fear of falling gets their heart racing, so they may confuse this sensation with the excited beating we experience when we fall in love."

"What's your point?"

"That perhaps you're not really into Rain, and are simply

misreading what you feel due to the fact that she saved you that night. She was the light in the darkness, and kept you safe when you were afraid. She was that someone standing at the other end of the suspension bridge."

I snort. "Erica, no disrespect, but you've been pursuing this major for a little over a year, and you're already feeling confident enough to psychoanalyze me? Even worse, you go as far as denying the validity of my feelings?"

"I wasn't saying that. I was just making an observation." She shrugs.

"Let's go, Miss Observer."

We leave the cafeteria and Erica keeps talking, offering to assist me if I need help with my essays. Out of the corner of my eye I catch a glimpse of a full head of blond hair. I turn to see Rain approaching. The wind moves her hair to one side. It's hard to miss her, in the middle of the trees that have lost all their leaves. She stands out with her vibrant energy and that smile that makes my heart race. Nah. Erica has to be wrong. What I feel is the real thing.

"Apolo!" Rain is dressed all in black, wearing baggy jeans and a long-sleeved sweater.

Erica giggles next to me.

"I'm going to see if the hen has laid any . . ." she says as she starts to walk away.

"Pardon?" I ask confused.

Before making her exit, Erica points at Rain and whispers: "Ready, set, go."

I clear my throat, and smile back at Rain when she comes to a stop in front of me. "Hello," I greet her, feeling a little nervous.

"Long time no see, Apolo." She sounds excited to see me,

and I feel the urge to pinch her cheeks because she looks so cute. However, I manage to keep my emotions under control.

"Yeah. I've been a little busy"—I look down at the essay with the incomplete grade in my hand. Rain follows my gaze—"with failing out of college, I guess."

She shakes her head. "Don't worry, we all hit a few bumps at first." She shrugs. "The first term is all about adapting to a new environment, adjusting to expectations, figuring out the system and all that. Don't feel bad."

Rain's energy is so powerful that I immediately feel uplifted. It's a very strange thing. So I narrow my eyes and tease her a little.

"Are you telling me you got bad grades your first term? Wow, Rain. I didn't expect that from you."

She laughs.

"Oh me? I get As all the time." She touches her head. "I'm unbearably smart."

"So those words of encouragement only apply to poor mortals like me."

"You are not a poor mortal." Rain looks me in the eye. "Like Xan said, you're more of a Greek god."

I curse inwardly when I feel the heat creeping up my neck because I can't be more obvious. Rain raises an eyebrow.

"Are you blushing?"

"Nope."

Rain laughs and playfully approaches me. "Apolo, a Greek god."

I laugh with her. "Stop it."

"Greek goooood."

"Rain," I warn her. When she doesn't stop, I feel emboldened to take a step forward, which forces her to move one step back. I can tell from her expression that she's amused.

"Oh? Is the Greek god angry?"

I take one more step forward and she backs away again. This time she trips, and before she can fall, I catch her by the waist. That scent of citrusy perfume invades my senses and fills me with an overwhelming feeling of calm. Rain fits perfectly in my arms. Her smile begins to fade. She looks nervous and her cheeks are flushed. For a few seconds, we say nothing. We are so close, and I can see something sparkle in her eyes.

I lower my gaze to her lips; they are slightly open and I wonder what it would be like to have them pressed against mine. She clears her throat and frees herself from my hold. She finally breaks the silence.

"I should go to class."

"Okay." I smile.

"See you later, Apolo."

"See you later, Rain."

I walk away steadily but my heart keeps racing.

Two days later, I find myself walking to Nora's right after class.

I just want to make sure that Xan is fine. I let out a sigh as I push open the doors of the coffee shop. I pause for a moment to look at the customers occupying the tables. As expected, the place is crowded, but there's no one behind the bar. Then a head of blue hair comes up from under the counter. He was probably looking for something in the bottom drawers. I come to a full stop.

Xan is his usual self. He looks relaxed. His cheeks are flushed, and he's humming along to the song that's playing through the speakers. The one thing I notice that's different is the shirt he's wearing. It's a turtleneck, so alarm bells go off in my head. I take a deep breath as I make my way toward him. If I confront him, it will get me nowhere.

Xan notices me, and his eyes widen briefly in surprise. But he immediately gets back to preparing drinks, acting as if nothing is wrong. Luckily, Vance is nowhere in sight.

"Hi," I say when I reach the counter.

Xan turns to me and gives me his friendliest yet professional smile.

"Welcome to Nora's, how can I help you?"

"Xan, are you okay?"

He doesn't say anything, just stands there, waiting, as I think back to the call from a few days ago.

Apolo, I think it's best if you delete my number. To be completely honest, I don't have the time to make new friends right now. Best of luck to you with everything. Please leave me alone. I don't need you to complicate my life. Don't call me anymore. Bye.

"I'd like a latte, to go." I finally give him my order.

Xan enters the order in the system and replies.

"It will be three dollars and forty-five cents." After I pay, he adds, "It will be ready in five minutes."

He gives me his back and proceeds to prepare my drink. I stand there looking at him, partly in disbelief. Xan has never treated me like this, not even when I was just a customer and we weren't on friendly terms. He's always been warm and funny. He would make jokes when I placed my order, and that was back when we didn't even know each other.

I can't help but blame myself a little. Did I overstep? Did I make him uncomfortable? I couldn't stay quiet when I noticed what was going on between him and Vance, but was the best approach speaking up and saying something? Or should I have helped Xan figure it out gradually all on his own?

I've spent several nights visiting online forums and reading testimonials from victims of abuse. The approaches and suggestions vary from one situation to another. The most important advice shared is to be there for the person. It's important to make it clear that you are concerned about their safety. Lastly, it's crucial to be vigilant and know when to call the authorities, even when the victim gets angry and is resistant; in some cases, this becomes a matter of life and death.

Maybe to Xan I'm just a nosy stranger. To me, he's a good guy, and no one deserves to go through something like this. No one. I grab my coffee while Xan stands there in silence, then I move away and walk out.

I feel like a stalker as I sit in the dark on a bench across from Café Nora. I watch Xan get the place in order after closing time. I hope that maybe after he has locked up, we can talk. While I wait, I pull out my cell phone and send a text message.

> **Me:** If you saw me right now, you would think it's déjà vu.
>
> **Raquel:** What are you up to, Lollo?
>
> **Me:** Waiting around in the dark, for a boy.
>
> **Raquel:** HAHAHA. I wasn't expecting that.
>
> **Me:** Neither was I.
>
> **Raquel:** Is he a hunk?
>
> **Me:** It's not what you think. I'm just worried about him.
>
> **Raquel:** Sure, sure. And I used to watch Ares practice soccer because I love the sport.
>
> **Me:** If you mention anything about this to Ares . . .
>
> **Raquel:** Easy. Don't worry. Ares is thousands of miles away 😕

Me: Oh. Do you miss him?

Raquel: Always, but that's not what we're discussing. I've already made myself a hot chocolate, so tell me about this guy. Who is making Lollo Hidalgo wait in the dark?

I smile because it's still a long while before Xan is done. So I use the time to tell Raquel about everything that's happened with Rain, Xan, and Vance. I've always felt so comfortable around both Dani and her. I trust them completely and feel most at ease with them. And to think it all started because Raquel gave me a drink one night at my brother's bar. I never expected we would all become such good friends.

Raquel: Okay, information overload. I stop paying attention for two seconds and you are already making big moves at school.

Me: I know.

Raquel: Apolo, can I ask you something?

Me: Sure.

Raquel: Are you attracted to Xan?

I snort and laugh.

Me: Of course not.

Raquel: Hmmm. I think you're in denial.

Me: Come on, Raquel. I'm not. I'm just concerned about another human being who's in a difficult situation.

Raquel: Uh-huh. Sure.

I can picture her on the other end, her eyes narrowed in disbelief.

Me: It's Rain I like. You know that.

Raquel: You can like Rain. And you can also like Xan. One doesn't have to cancel out the other. Both facts can be true at the same time. Maybe I should be the one studying psychology, huh?

Me: Don't make stuff up, okay? It would be way too complicated if I was attracted to both at the same time.

Raquel: Making things complicated seems to be a Hidalgo passion.

I catch a glimpse of Xan. He puts on his jacket and a black cap, then turns off the lights.

Me: I'm afraid I have to cut short your psychobabble. I need to go now.

Raquel: Good luck, tiger. Grrrrrrrrr.

I grimace and slip my cell phone inside my pocket. I hate her.

I run toward the entrance of Café Nora and catch Xan just as he's about to lock the place up. When he turns around and finds me standing there, he jumps.

"Sorry, I didn't mean to scare you."

Xan doesn't reply, and starts walking away, so I follow him.

"Xan, I wanted to apologize if I made you feel uncomfortable. I was only worried about you."

He shoves his hands into the pockets of his jacket and stops when we've walked a fair distance away from Nora's. He shoots a quick glance in the direction of the shop, and there's a look of fear in his eyes that disappears as he turns to face me.

"Apolo, you don't need to apologize. You haven't done anything wrong, okay? Just go home."

"If I haven't done anything wrong, then why won't you talk to me anymore?" I hate how needy I sound.

"My life is complicated, Apolo. I wish we could be friends, but it's not in the cards at this moment. Okay? Maybe we can try again, in the future."

"Did Vance forbid it?"

Xan grimaces at the mention of his boyfriend's name. "No, it was my decision."

"It was your decision? Just like that, out of the blue? Xan, we were having an easygoing conversation that night and all of a sudden you hang up on me. And when I call you back, you tell me that you don't want to talk to me ever again. It's way too obvious that you're not the one calling the shots."

"Why don't you just leave it alone? If someone doesn't want to talk to you, let it go."

His eyes avoid mine.

"If I was one hundred percent sure that this was your decision, I would leave you alone without hesitation."

"What do I have to do to prove it to you? Swear it? And why do I have to explain myself to you? You just came into my life and have no say in it."

Very rarely in my life have I felt this angry. Xan knows exactly what to say to frustrate me. I take a step toward him, and his composure cracks a little. He looks at me nervously.

"What are you doing?"

I stop right in front of him.

"Look me in the eye and tell me you never want to speak to me again."

His blush deepens more, and he looks away. "I don't have to do anything."

I don't want to fluster him, so I back off.

"Anything you need. Whenever. I'm here for you, Xan. I'm not going to push or force you to talk to me. I just want you to know that he has no right to choose who you can be friends with. He shouldn't be controlling your life to this extent. I think you know that, you're smart. Good night."

And I leave him because it feels like I'm talking to a wall. I can't force him to be my friend.

As I walk away, there's a pounding in my chest. Shortly, I realize that it's my heart racing. I smile like a fool. I believe my sweet, crazy Raquel is right: making life complicated is indeed a passion of the Hidalgos.

Fourteen

RAIN

I can't stop thinking about him.

It's ridiculous and shouldn't be happening. How many times have we met? Four? Five? Not enough to have him repeatedly pop up in my head. Even in my mother's novels people don't fall in love this quickly. *Fall in love? Ugh. Rain, you need to rein yourself in.* Damn it. It's his fault for looking so hot, being kind, and having a sweet smile. I'm just another victim falling for the perfect package also known as Apolo Hidalgo. It's a little crush and nothing more. It's normal. Quite normal, indeed.

"What did that notebook do to you to make you torture it like that?" Gregory asks me, pointing.

I look at the state of my notes and they're a mess. I've stuck the pencil in so hard that it's ripped the paper in several places. I plaster an angelic smile on my face and play dumb. "I'm exploring my artistic talents."

Gregory raises an eyebrow. "By slaughtering the pages of your book? You never cease to amaze me, Rain Adams."

"Shut up."

He raises his palms, making a gesture of surrender.

"Did you come to go over your notes or to decimate your notebook?" Gregory takes a sip from his energy drink, then sets it on the island in the kitchen.

His kitchen.

That's right. Here I am in Gregory's apartment because the crush I have is totally normal. The same apartment I happen to know Gregory shares with a certain guy I can't seem to get out of my head.

Very subtle, Rain.

"Let's get to work," I propose.

I turn the page I destroyed and flip to the ones where I have my notes. My eyes keep darting from the entrance to the hallway that leads to the bedrooms. I purse my lips, and Gregory follows my gaze.

"Apolo isn't here," he informs me, as if I had asked.

"Great, thanks for letting me know even though I didn't ask."

Gregory leans back in his chair and folds his arms.

"You remind me of someone . . . you're not being very subtle, Rain."

"Subtle?"

"We both know that your average far exceeds mine. You don't need my help for this exam. You're here looking for a certain someone with Hidalgo for a last name."

I laugh, and it's way too loud and exaggerated. "Gregory, please!" I let out a snort, and roll my eyes. "You're imagining things."

He watches me, amused.

"I've never seen you like this before," he says, smiling. "You never appear restless or nervous, and are always so chill. He's really gotten under your skin, huh?"

I open my mouth to challenge him, but we hear the sound of the front door. I freeze on the spot, and have a mini–panic attack.

What will Apolo think when he sees me here? Will it be weird? Will it be too obvious, just like Gregory said? No. It shouldn't be. Gregory and I met before Apolo started at the university. This isn't the first time I've visited Gregory either. Everything should be fine.

Apolo makes his way in but stops in his tracks when he sees me.

"Oh. Rain," he says, looking surprised. Then he looks at Gregory. "I didn't know we had company."

I stare at him because it's been over a week since I last saw him. We haven't talked or texted. No contact whatsoever. I'm cursing internally because he's just as hot as ever. Today he's wearing a white T-shirt and jeans, and his hair is messier than usual. I notice dark circles under his eyes and he looks tired. Going by appearances, it seems like he's still having a hard time adapting to college life.

"Oh, yeah, I came to go over some notes with Gregory," I reply, and hope the tone of my voice doesn't give away my nervousness.

Apolo walks past me to the fridge and retrieves a bottle of water.

I watch his profile as he throws his head back and takes a swig. Even his neck is sexy. I look away and find Gregory staring at me, a mocking expression plastered on his face, and I want to slap him so hard. Apolo finishes his drink and takes a seat next to Gregory on the other side of the island.

"What are you studying for?" he asks.

Gregory looks at me. "Yes, Rain, what are we studying today?"

I give him a murderous look because I can't actually recall which notes I brought along for us to review, or what exactly we're supposed to be preparing for.

"I believe it's anatomy, Apolo. We could use some volunteers," adds Gregory.

I'm ready to throw something at him when Apolo asks, confused, "Anatomy? For your engineering degree?"

"He's kidding." I let out a nervous chuckle. "You know how he is."

"Now, this tropical sweetheart is feeling tired." Gregory stands up and stretches out his arms. "I'm going to take a nap."

"Okay." I stand because that's my cue to leave, but Gregory raises his hand and points his finger at me. "No, you don't have to leave. Actually, it's movie Thursday, and I'm feeling a little under the weather."

"You were fine this morning," Apolo reminds him.

"Not anymore. Apolo, you know how these things can change. Life is a never-ending cycle of turmoil and desire," he explains with a serious expression.

"What?" Apolo still looks confused.

"The fact is you owe me a favor, Rain. So you have to stay, watch tonight's movie, and keep Apolo company. It's a horror movie and those scare him." Then he nonchalantly turns to leave. "Bye-bye."

And just like that, we're alone. Gregory may be many things, but subtle isn't one of them.

We remain silent. I'd like to say that it's not awkward at all, but I would be lying. Apolo didn't expect to find me here. And I'm not sure what my intentions were when I decided to come over. Apolo scratches the back of his neck, his eyes looking everywhere except at me.

"How have you been?" I ask, hoping to ease the discomfort. "You look stressed."

"I think it's an accumulation of everything. I miss my family, and classes are hard, you know how it is."

That piques my curiosity. "What is your family like? I only know that they're wealthy and very well-known."

That's not entirely true, because I know much more than that. I've searched for information about his family: he has two brothers and his parents are separated. It's very easy to find details when there are newspaper articles.

"We're a normal family, I guess. Artemis, my eldest brother, is married. I have a beautiful niece named Hera. The middle brother is Ares, who is studying medicine. He has a girlfriend he's been going out with for two years, and she's one of my best friends. My father is, you know, like every other parent. And my mother—" He pauses and purses his lips before speaking again. "I also have a grandfather, whom I adore. I give him credit for having turned me into a decent human being."

"Is that the opinion you have of yourself? A decent human being?"

"I like to think I am."

"I think you undersell yourself. To me you're a pretty amazing human being." I give him my most honest opinion.

From the moment we met Apolo's behavior has been exemplary. What I appreciate most about his character is the way he stood up for Xan, even though they'd just met and despite how stubborn "Mr. Blue Hair" happens to be.

Apolo blushes as usual; receiving compliments is something he seems to struggle with, which blows my mind. Going by external appearances alone, I bet he's received compliments throughout his life. Why does he have such a hard time accepting them?

"And how are you?" His question makes me sigh.

"Tired and . . ." *Thinking about you all the time, while checking my cell phone, waiting for a message from you. Also, confused because I thought we were at least friends, and it feels like you're ghosting me.* "And . . ."

Apolo waits for me to finish, but when I fail to do so, he takes over.

"And?"

We stare at each other. The direct eye contact helps put me at ease, just a little.

"I missed you." I blurt the words out unintentionally, and cover my mouth. Apolo is just as surprised as I am. We both turn red immediately. "What I meant is I missed talking to you."

"I'm sorry. School has kept me busy."

"You don't need to explain yourself to me," I clarify. "I understand."

Argh. I hate this. I don't often find myself in such a vulnerable position. People don't rattle me that easily. I guess I've underestimated this boy with the warm gaze, and the effect he has on those around him. Well, the effect he has on me in particular.

Apolo points to the couch. "Time for a movie?"

I nod and make my way to the couch. I sit down and get comfortable. I feel much better. This is the Rain that I'm used to, uncomplicated. Apolo puts a bag of popcorn in the microwave and brings some drinks, which he places on the table in front of the TV.

"I didn't know you and Gregory had this tradition," I say.

"It was Kelly's idea," he replies and then pauses as if remembering something. "And we got in the habit."

"Kelly is Gregory's girlfriend. Right?"

Apolo hesitates then nods before going back to the kitchen to get the popcorn. We're all set, and he sits at the other end of the couch, leaving a fairly large space between us. I get that he doesn't want me to feel awkward, but I think this is a bit extreme. But I don't say anything about it.

"What are we watching?"

Apolo reacts with a shrug. "It's your choice."

I raise an eyebrow. "Are you sure?"

I think of several options. If I were to suggest a romantic movie would it be too obvious? I bite my lip and glance at the sliding glass door leading to the balcony. The lights of the city are visible on the other side.

"Rain," he says, and I turn my gaze to him. "Honestly. It's your pick. Whatever you feel like watching, I won't judge."

"Okay," I reply.

I choose *Love, Rosie*. It's a very emotional movie about two best friends who share this impossible love, and life is always putting them in difficult situations that prevent them from being together, which doesn't happen until the very end. It's one of my favorites.

Apolo turns off the lights and starts the movie. He sits up, stretching his arm across the back of the couch with his hand nearly reaching where I sit. I notice how his white T-shirt rides up a little above his waist, and I sneak a peek of skin. From where

I'm seated I can see his profile. The TV screen reflects on his skin, giving it a multicolored glow. I stop staring at him and focus on the screen, keeping my hands folded on my lap. My dress was a great choice for studying while sitting on a chair at a table; however, it's not ideal for a couch as it keeps riding up, so I have to pull it down constantly. Apolo notices what I'm doing and turns my way at the exact moment that I happen to be looking at him. His eyes move down to my thighs, where I happen to be tugging at the hem of the dress, and his lips slightly part. I smile at him and let go of the hem. I don't want him to get the wrong idea and think that I'm doing this in an attempt to seduce him.

"There's a—" He clears his throat and reaches for something on his side of the couch, then hands me a blanket. "It's clean, I swear."

I reach for it with a smile. "I believe you."

I cover my legs with the blanket and we carry on watching the movie.

We're almost halfway through the film when it happens: the sound of thunder outside. Apolo tenses visibly, and I look at the balcony window to see raindrops beginning to fall heavily, wetting the balcony floor and the glass. It's hard to concentrate when I see him looking this tense. His hands have become balled fists, the veins in his neck and arms are slightly bulging, and his jaw is clenched.

My mind revisits that night. I recall the fear I felt when I found him lying half dead on the ground, soaking. I can't begin to imagine what the rain does to him. I don't know what to do or say. I feel the same way I felt that night. For a few minutes, I hesitate, and reconsider so many things. Then I open my mouth, hoping to say something, but nothing comes out. So

I grab the blanket and drag it with me as I slide next to him. I wrap us both under it, moving my arm behind him to give him a side-hug. Apolo rests his head on my shoulder, but doesn't look at me.

"Everything is going to be okay," I reassure him as I stroke his hair.

With each passing minute, I feel the tension in his muscles disappear as he relaxes. He rests his hand on my leg. Even though there's a blanket in between, the gesture makes me acutely aware of every inch of his body pressed against mine; the same goes for his scent and his warmth.

Apolo turns his face. His nose brushes against my neck and I stop breathing right away.

"Your scent, Rain. It helps calm me down."

His breath caresses my skin. I drag my tongue over my lips. I'm tongue-tied. Every nerve in my body is set off by his words. We are sitting too close—extremely close.

When the movie ends, the darkness of the credits and the sound of the rain elevate the moment, turning it into something that's hard for me to explain. Apolo moves again, and this time it's not his nose that brushes my skin. I feel the touch of his lips, moist and soft. Though the contact is brief, it quickens my pulse. Apolo stops. He seems to be giving me time to react so he can assess whether I plan to refuse his advances. I do the opposite. I allow him more access to my neck, hoping the gesture is a clear enough answer for him.

His lips open and close on my skin, between my shoulder and my neck, kissing and licking. I struggle not to let out a whimper. At what point did things take a turn? I went from soothing him to this? Why does it feel so good?

His mouth moves up to my ear. The sound and sensation of his agitated breathing against my skin makes me weak.

"Apolo . . ." I whisper.

He pulls away just enough so we can look into each other's eyes. I wasn't expecting the expression I see on his face. It's a combination of desire and need. His gaze drops to my lips and we don't need any more words; we both know exactly what we want. So there on the couch, with the rain echoing outside, Apolo Hidalgo kisses me.

Fifteen

APOLO

A kiss . . .

The girl I've been searching for since that night is here in my arms. Her lips brush languidly against mine as we figure out a rhythm that works for both of us. It's not a passionate kiss, not the kind that leaves you breathless. It's a gentle kiss. One of discovery, probing and exploring. And I enjoy it, maybe too much, because I become acutely aware of every touch and the warmth of her breath. I completely forget that it's raining outside.

Rain invades all my senses. I slip my arm around the side of her waist to pull her a little closer. She gently nuzzles my neck and tilts her head as we kiss. This escalates things further. My breathing quickens as my body reacts to the closeness of her breasts, her scent, and the brush of our tongues. If this keeps up . . .

She pants a little as she pulls away. Her eyes meet mine and I lose myself in them for a few seconds.

"This is—" She starts but doesn't finish, wetting her lips with her tongue.

I don't know what to say either. Holding her this close, I can read every emotion revealed by her expression. The same goes for any doubt she might have about what to say or do next. It's the first time I've seen this vulnerable side of Rain and it's beautiful.

She looks down at my arm, which is still wrapped around her, and I immediately pull it away.

"I'm sorry."

"There's no need to apologize." She moves a few inches away from me, widening the space between us. "But I think I should go home."

What?

"It's still raining."

She stands up. "It's okay, I'm not made of sugar."

"Rain . . ."

She makes her way to the door, and I follow her in a hurry.

"Wait." I intercept her. I'm still feeling worked up from the kiss. "Did I do something wrong?"

"No, Apolo. Of course not. The kiss was incredible, it's just that . . ."

I give her time to explain. But when she fails to continue, I take over.

"Rain." I take a step closer to her. She licks her lips and her eyes fall to my mouth. "What's the matter?"

She sighs, and hesitates again for a few seconds. Then she wraps her arms around my neck and crushes her lips against mine. It catches me by surprise, but I quickly kiss her back.

"The problem is that if I stay here," she whispers against

my lips, "if I keep kissing you like this, I'm going to want more, Apolo. So much more."

I spin and press her against the wall.

"And that's a problem?"

She nods and bites my lip. "Yes."

"Why?"

My hands move down the curve of her body until I reach her ass and I give it a lustful squeeze. I'm not exactly sure how we got to this point. She's acting as if what we're doing is something forbidden, and it's turning me on.

The way Rain is kissing me now is more aggressive than the way she kissed me on the couch. Her hands slide under my shirt and she caresses my abs. Her touch makes every one of my muscles tense. Meanwhile, there's another very specific part of my anatomy that's getting hard. Our breathing is labored, and I let myself get carried away by a myriad of sensations. Our tongues are entangled, adding to the already built-up desire. I rub my hips against hers, pressing and grinding.

"Apolo," she moans softly. I leave her lips to kiss her neck, my hand awkwardly caressing one of her breasts. Rain turns around, giving her back to me. She brushes her ass against my erection. I don't waste time and kiss her neck, as my hands squeeze her breasts. She grips the wall, panting. "I want you to touch me . . ."

I don't need to be a genius to figure out exactly what she means. My hand sneaks inside her dress and my fingers caress her over her panties. I can feel how warm and wet she is.

"Rain." I say her name in a whimper that slips out of my mouth as I touch her.

I pull her panties to the side. My fingers slide easily inside her because she's so wet. I rub my thumb against her to wet it, then use it to stimulate her. She moves her hips in sync with the rhythm of my touch. My erection is pressed between her buttocks. The constant rubbing combined with all the sensations I'm experiencing are pushing me over the edge.

"Apolo." She whimpers as I increase the speed of my thrusting fingers and cover her mouth with one hand to stifle her moans.

I rest my forehead against the nape of her neck. In this position, I can see everything: her ass pressed against me, my hand thrusting inside her hiked-up dress as her hips rock sensually. I can see the wet spot forming on the front of my jeans and I'm not shocked. I don't know how much longer I can keep myself together. Rain stifles a loud moan and her movements become clumsy. I know she's about to come, so I enhance the stimulation by sucking on her earlobe while my hand intensifies its thrusts inside her dripping center.

Her moans become continual and my penetrations become deeper; all the while my thumb keeps working its magic on her. Rain finishes with a stifled moan, and I can feel the contractions around my fingers. Her core keeps squeezing them, which makes me even more excited. She hasn't even caught her breath when she turns around to kiss me passionately as she unbuttons my jeans. Part of me remembers that we're in the hallway, but I soon forget when she pulls my jeans and my boxers down and kneels in front of me.

"Rain." I gasp as she takes me in her hand.

She puts me in her mouth. I put both hands against the wall, afraid that my legs won't be able to keep me up. This is going to end much too quickly. Her mouth is warm and wet, and takes me in lustfully. She sucks and licks me with incredible skill.

I make the mistake of looking down to watch her. Then we make eye contact, and that's all it takes.

"I'm going to—" I warn her and give her time to pull me out, but she doesn't stop. The pressure rises and rises; the pleasure is too much for me and I empty myself inside her mouth with a grunt, hands clenched in fists against the wall.

Our labored breaths can be heard throughout the hallway. Rain stands, wipes her lips, and swallows. I pull up my jeans and have barely finished buttoning them up when the door to the apartment bursts open. Rain adjusts her dress and I freeze.

Kelly walks in, whistling, and comes to a stop when she finds us standing in the dark hallway. Our expressions and appearance seem to blow our cover because she immediately looks away.

"I didn't know you had a guest."

Rain clears her throat. "Um, I was just leaving." She runs out the door before I can stop her.

Kelly stands there staring, just for a few seconds. Then she walks past me and makes her way to Gregory's room. I'm left processing what just happened. I lift my fingers, which are still marked with Rain's wetness, and let out a sigh.

That was incredible.

Sixteen

RAIN

Rain, Rain, Rain . . . what have you done?

I don't mind the rain that falls on me and soaks my clothes in a matter of seconds. Maybe I need this to cool off the overheated Rain who seems to come out to play too easily, especially when she happens to be around Apolo Hidalgo. I was supposed to comfort him on the couch, I was supposed to . . .

Instead, we kissed and . . .

We pleasured each other.

What happened in that hallway will go down in history as one of the hottest things I've ever done in my life. And given my track record, it's hard to top that list. Sweet mother of . . . ! The way his fingers work. It's like he knew exactly the right combination needed for me to reach my climax. I'm getting all hot and bothered just thinking about it.

How did I go from comforting him to coming all over his fingers, which was quickly followed by me giving him head?

I feel like I should be kicking myself. This is not how I imagined things would unfold with Apolo. We were just getting to know each other. Sure, I'm no prude and enjoy having sex, but I would have liked to have spent a little more time talking before taking things further. But do I regret it? Not at all, because it was incredible.

I take an Uber home. When I get out of the car, I step in a puddle and immediately swear. Then I look up, and I'm surprised to find someone sitting on the front sidewalk. I narrow my eyes as I move closer, trying to figure out who it is.

"Xan!" I exclaim, as I come to stand in front of him.

He's soaking wet. His blue hair is plastered to his face. But that's not what catches my attention; it's the cut on his lip and his swollen eyes and nose. He's been crying.

I lean over him.

"What happened? Are you okay?"

"No. I've got nowhere to go, Rain. I'm sorry, I—"

"Hey, hey." I shake my head. "I'm here. I'm here," I repeat, as I take his hand in mine. "Let's go inside, you're freezing."

"I don't . . . I don't want your mother to see me like this. I—"

"Don't worry. At this hour, my mother is busy writing in her study. We'll go straight to my room."

"If he finds out that I came here . . ." I know he means Vance, and the fear is palpable in his voice.

"He never drops by during the week, so don't worry." I help him up. "Let's go, Xan."

We sneak inside the house quietly and carefully. We go upstairs to my room, and I hand him a towel. Then I give him an oversized shirt and a pair of shorts. While he's in the shower, I use the bathroom in the hallway and change into my pajamas. I wish I could say this is the first time I've seen Xan in this state. It's definitely the first time he's come to my house. Things must have gotten really ugly with Vance, and I can't stop myself from feeling hopeful. Maybe this is the moment that finally opens Xan's eyes. He towels his hair dry as he sits on my bed.

"I'd rather not talk," he says before I can ask anything.

"That's fine," I assure him. "You don't have to."

Pestering or badgering him will not help. Still, I need to check that he's not injured.

"Are you hurt though?" I inquire. Xan shakes his head. The cut on his lip speaks for itself. "Do you want something to eat?"

He nods. That's when I realize that Xan has lost weight in the last few months. My insides boil with rage when I recall a comment that Vance made about Xan putting on a few extra pounds. My brother is tearing apart the boy in front of me in so many different ways. Helplessness and guilt course through me once again.

"Make yourself comfortable, I'll be right back."

In the kitchen, I make him a sandwich. I'm pouring orange juice into a glass when my mother comes in to grab a cup of coffee.

"Oh, I didn't know you were back. It's a fine downpour out there tonight. It lives up to your name."

She kisses the crown of my head and walks over to the coffee-pot. The dark circles under her eyes give her away. Though we all like to pretend, I know life hasn't been easy for her since it happened.

"You don't look well, Mom."

"Neither do you." She points to my hair, which is still dripping at the ends. "Did you get caught in the rain?"

"A little."

My mother takes a sip from her coffee and stares at me briefly. "Everything okay?"

I run my tongue over my lips, and hesitate. The trust I have with her is huge, but I don't know how much I can unload about myself, or if I should share someone else's secrets. Xan could become exceptionally closed off if I try to get outside help. He tends to deny the abuse is happening at all, and makes it look like I'm making things up. Vance also hasn't come out to our parents. And despite how shitty my brother happens to be, it's not my place to out him. The loyal yet stupid sisterly part of me respects his choice in this matter. I know my mom would take it well; my dad is a different story.

"Xan stopped by for a quick visit. He had a rough day." That's all I'll share. My mother knows who he is. I've taken her along with me to Café Nora a few times so she can write there. Still, she has no idea that Xan is dating Vance.

"Oh. Things not going well at the coffee shop?"

I sigh. "Something like that."

"Let him know that if he needs me to organize a book club or an event at the shop to help draw a crowd and increase its popularity. I'm willing to help in any way I can."

My lips curve into a smile. My mother is the kind of person who is always ready and willing to help.

"I'll pass on the message." I exhale, and scrunch my face. "Mom, a friend of mine shared something about a friend of hers. The friend is a guy who's in a toxic relationship with another boy, who has gone as far as getting abusive. We want to help him, but nothing has worked so far. It's as if this boy doesn't want to see what's really happening in front of his very eyes. We can't pull him out of it, and it's frustrating."

My mother puts her coffee cup down.

"The boy can see, Rain. Just as spiders spin their webs, abusers spin their manipulations in the victim's mind, one thread at a time. Yesterday it was a comment, today a gesture, tomorrow it will be an action. The abuser is methodical, and will isolate a person from everyone else so that he can become everything. When he is certain that his strings are tightly knotted and in place, that's when he delivers the first blows. Then he'll make promises that it won't happen again. He will say that it was you who made him angry. He will tell you that he gets angry because he loves you and cares about you so much. He will rationalize it and claim that if it wasn't 'love,' then he wouldn't snap. And you will stick around or keep coming back because you have no one else, or at least that's what he'll have made you believe." My mother gives me a sad smile and pats me on the shoulder. "My sweet daughter, he knows and sees what's happening. He's bound by thousands of invisible threads."

My gaze turns to the kitchen window. Raindrops slide down the glass. My mother's words echo in my head. I picture the blue-haired boy sitting on my bed, bound by all these threads that Vance has spun around him, and think of different ways I could cut them once and for all.

Seventeen

APOLO

WELCOME TO THIS YEAR'S FALL FESTIVAL!

The banner is huge and hangs precariously on the wall of the university's main building. The letters are red and black, the colors of the university. This is what they call the warm-up to the main event, leading up to tonight's game. It's also intended to raise funds for the scholarship program and to repair some equipment.

The weather is not cooperating much; it's cloudy and the gusty, bitter wind blows in our faces every now and then. I'm glad to be on grill duty, in charge of cooking the burgers. I'm stationed right next to the heat.

When Erica told me this would be my job, I complained a lot, but now I see it wasn't such a bad idea. As for my friend, she took up the role of guide for parents and anyone stopping by who wishes to partake in the festivities. Even though the sky is mostly cloudy, there are a bunch of white canopies set up all over the grounds. It appears someone didn't check the weather. We students have red shirts on to identify ourselves, though they don't help much since we're all wearing jackets.

Erica appears next to me, with a big smile and her hair pulled back in a high ponytail. Wavy strands hang loose, adorning her face.

"How's your first university event going?" she asks.

"The hamburgers are selling well."

"And we could boost our sales if you would smile just a little more," she says as she pats me on the shoulder. "You need to use your charm, Apolo. Why do you think I gave you this job?"

"Because I'm good on the grill?"

She rolls her eyes. "Now, now. Give us a smile." She cradles my face with her hands. "Come on, you can do it."

I lift the corners of my mouth slightly and give her a fake smile. Erica grimaces and doesn't look amused. "Forget it. Now you look like a serial killer."

She gives me a hand flipping patties on the grill.

"What's up with you?" she asks directly. "You've been more absent-minded than usual."

"I'm fine."

She raises an eyebrow, so I put down the tongs and wipe my hands with paper napkins before sitting down at one of the picnic tables.

"Well . . ." I let out a long sigh. If there's one thing I've learned with her, it's to not beat around the bush. "Let's just say that something went down with a certain someone. I've sent her a couple of texts, and have yet to receive a reply."

Erica folds her arms.

"Do you mean something like sex?"

"Erica!"

"Relax, you're too old to be sugarcoating the facts."

"We didn't screw, but we did get each other off. And I was left with the impression that it was as good for her as it was for me. Yet she's not answering my messages. So now I'm second-guessing myself, and maybe I just imagined that we both enjoyed it."

"It was Rain, wasn't it?" I don't give her a reply. "Maybe she's processing, Apolo. The last time I talked to you, you were just friends who were flirting a little, and now this has happened. Maybe she's taking her time to take it in."

"Or maybe she regrets it, or didn't like it and doesn't want to have anything to do with me."

"Why am I not surprised that you are as pessimistic about love as you are about life."

I open my mouth to challenge her, but then Erica's face turns pale. She's looking at something over my shoulder. I turn and see Gregory making his way over. He jokes and smiles, greeting half the crowd, because of course he knows almost everyone on campus. When I look back at Erica, the warm and chatty girl is gone. She's just sitting there, her body tense and her expression icy.

"At some point, you have to tell me what happened between you two," I say frankly.

"He's my ex, that's all." Even her tone has changed.

"Apolo!" Gregory exclaims when he reaches our side, his smile lingering when he sees her. "Erica."

"Gregory." She nods her head in greeting.

"What do we have here? Are you the cook? Does that mean I get a free burger?"

I sigh, and stand up. "Don't be cheap. It's only five dollars. Seven, if you want the combo."

"For him, it's ten dollars," Erica interrupts. Gregory and I exchange a look. "He just spent ten dollars at the lemonade stand and he didn't even drink it. He can afford to give us ten."

Gregory bites his lower lip. "Someone has been keeping a close eye on me. I thought you wanted nothing to do with me."

"I'm a businesswoman. My job is to observe all potential customers and keep track of how much money I can squeeze out of their pockets."

Gregory snorts. "Great. Then how about I give you twenty and you join me for lunch." He points to the picnic table.

"I'm not for sale."

"I didn't say you were, I'm just interested in your company."

Erica lets out a fake laugh. "Company should never be a problem for someone like you."

"Aww. Feeling jealous, my darling Erica?"

She blushes, though I'm not sure whether it's from anger or embarrassment. "Don't call me that."

"Why? Does it bring back memories?"

Erica turns even redder.

"I'm going to check on the burgers," I say to no one in particular, because neither of them looks at me as they carry on with their banter.

There's a lot of tension there. And it piques my curiosity. *Why did they break up?* I focus on my work, and when I look up again, I catch a flash of blue hair approaching in the distance. It's Xan. This is the first time I've seen him since we talked outside his café.

And why do I have to explain myself to you? You just came into my life and have no say in it.

His words still sting a little. As much as I want to help, and have the best intentions, it's his life. and I'm just the new guy in town. I need to remind myself to respect his boundaries.

Xan walks through the crowd of students. He is dressed warmly in a black sweater under a denim jacket. As usual, his cheeks look slightly flushed. I notice a cut on his lip, which looks swollen. I curl my hands into fists because I'm certain that was no accident. When Xan sees me, he raises a hand to wave. I do the same, although I'm confused because the last time I saw him he didn't want to talk to me again.

"Hi." He greets me from the other side of the grill.

"Hi."

"Do you recommend the burgers?" He licks his lips and seems nervous, but maybe it's just my imagination.

"Not really. I mean, they're okay if you're hungry and want to make a contribution to the university's fund."

"Do you have any meatless options?"

"Hmm. How about the bread, lettuce, and tomato?"

"Okay, then. I'll pass." He scratches the top of his ear where he has a few piercings. I've caught him doing that a couple of times at the café when he's restless.

"How are you doing?"

"I'm well. How about you?"

"I'm good."

Silence.

It's strange. It's as if there's something hanging in the air that we haven't cleared up. Xan takes a deep breath.

"Apolo, listen. I know I haven't been . . . Well, the truth is—" Another heavy pause. "I wanted to apologize. You were trying to help and I acted like a jerk. My life is complicated. But that doesn't give me permission to treat others poorly."

"Xan . . ."

"I was rude."

"Xan, it's fine. I understand." I speak candidly.

I know he's not a bad person or intentionally rude. I suspect that when he feels cornered or vulnerable, he closes off. He looks away, but I manage to catch something in his eyes. Fear. I think he's afraid of a few things he hasn't shared with me. He's also afraid of one person in particular: Vance. Yet here he is, apologizing. That takes courage, because I'm sure Vance asked him to stay away from me.

"How's the café? Still making the best latte close to campus?" I change the subject; Xan is too tense.

He shakes out his shoulders. "Nope, my new specialty is matcha."

"Really? I'm not into green-colored drinks. I was traumatized by the smoothies Clau used to make me at home when I got sick."

"Clau?"

"My sister-in-law."

"Oh, that's right. You have brothers. Rain mentioned something about that."

I pretend to be unaffected. "Have you seen her?"

"A few days ago." His expression darkens. "And today we were supposed to meet here, but I don't see her anywhere.

"She's inside at the booth selling hot chocolate," Gregory replies, joining us. He glances at Xan. "The coffee shop guy."

Xan smiles. "The very same."

"What brings you here?" Gregory rests a hand on my shoulder. "I hope it's not Apolo's burgers, because they're awful."

"Shut up." I push his hand off.

"What? I can't let you kill the guy who makes the divine coffee drinks that keep me energized and get me get through college."

"You haven't even tried my burgers."

"I don't have to, Apolo." Gregory shrugs. "I just have to look around me. Look at all the plates left on the picnic tables. What do you see?"

I do as he says, and notice several plates with abandoned burgers that have been left almost whole.

Ah. Fantastic.

"Erica said they were good." It's all I can say.

Gregory pouts and pats my head dramatically. "Awww. Erica lied to you, Apolo. I know, the real world is cruel and merciless."

Xan smiles, and I let my gaze linger on him for a few seconds. When our eyes meet, he turns his gaze to Gregory.

"Apolo is too good for this world," adds Xan in a joking tone.

I roll my eyes. "Awesome. Now there are two of you against me."

"We just want to protect you." Gregory rubs my head again and I push his hand away.

"Okay. I'm going to see if I can find Rain inside." Xan waves good-bye and leaves.

Gregory and I make ourselves comfortable at the picnic table. I've prepared enough burgers to last for a while, though I doubt anyone else will buy any more since apparently they're so bad.

"Where has Erica gone?" I ask to get the ball rolling, because one of them has to tell me something. And Gregory is one of my best friends.

His cheerful disposition evaporates. "I don't know."

"Uh, Greg. What went down between the two of you?"

My friend sighs and scratches the back of his neck.

"We were very different. I wanted to party all the time, while she . . . well, you know the type of person she is. She doesn't like to socialize that much. Then I met Kelly, and she was like a female version of me. We would go out together, get drunk, have fun, and for a moment, I thought Kelly was exactly who I needed to be with. Our personalities were so similar. So I broke up with Erica so I could date Kelly."

"You're an idiot."

"I know. I'm not proud of what I did, okay? The first few weeks with Kelly were great. We went from party to party, and had crazy sex. It was everything I thought I needed. But then, whether I was partying or just going about my life, at night before going to sleep I started feeling like there was a void I needed to fill, an emptiness inside me. I found myself staring at the ceiling, feeling bad because the parties and the fun were great, but I craved something deeper. I needed more in my life."

"Let me guess, that something more was what Erica brought to your life."

"I know—I'm a basic, superficial guy who realized too late that he made a mistake. I began to miss it all. Even the simplest things I would do with Erica brought me fulfillment. Like watching a movie together curled up on the couch. Or fighting over the last doughnut. Or her look of excitement as I listened to her new favorite song." A sad smile forms on his lips. "I love her, Apolo. And she wants nothing to do with me. And rightly so."

"Wow. I don't know what to say, Greg. I don't think I've ever heard you speak so profoundly."

"I may look like jerk, but I'm not one, Apolo. I'm a crazy extrovert, but I have a heart."

"Does Kelly know all this?"

"I haven't told her directly, but I think she knows. What we have has always been casual and very on the surface. It's like we need each other for parties and a good time, but there's nothing more than that."

"I—" I clear my throat. I need to be honest about what happened the other night between Kelly and me. "She and I—"

"Did you make out on the couch the other night?"

"How did you know about that?"

"Bro, you couldn't have been more obvious."

"Oh."

"No sweat. It's all good. Remember, I told you what the deal was between me and Kelly. It's nothing serious and she is free to do whatever and whomever she pleases."

"Yes, but still—doesn't it bother you?"

"Does it bother you?"

I shake my head, and he keeps talking.

"Now, it would be a different story if you said you had a thing for Erica, because in that case I would definitely beat you up, just a little."

"She's not your girlfriend anymore."

Gregory's expression tightens. "Are you into her?"

"No, of course not."

"Good."

We remain silent for a few seconds. In the distance we see Xan and Rain coming out of the building with cups of hot chocolate in hand. Rain is wearing jeans with a heavy blush-pink sweater that reminds me of the one she was wearing the day we met at Café Nora. Her blond hair is loose and parted, framing her face perfectly. Walking side by side with Xan, it's quite noticeable that she's taller than him. And my mind flashes back to what happened in the hallway; her moans, my fingers inside her, the feeling of her body pressed against mine, her mouth . . .

"Well, hello you?" Gregory pulls me out of my lustful reverie, following the direction of my gaze. "What happened with Rain?"

"It's complicated."

As if the universe also wanted to chime in, we hear a commotion at the main entrance of the event. Vance walks in, smiling as if he owns the place. Everyone greets him and asks for a photo.

I furrow my eyebrows. I'm confused.

"What's that about?" I ask.

Greg sighs.

"I suppose you know about him. That's Rain's brother. He's an extremely popular video gamer and host of a live stream. He hardly ever comes around campus, it's rare for him to be here. Maybe he came to hang out with his sister."

"He's here for Xan."

Greg raises an eyebrow.

"Huh? Why would he be here for Xan?"

I feel like punching myself in the mouth right at that moment. I assumed everyone knew about their relationship status. Apolo Hidalgo, you careless moron!

"Because he works in Xan's coffee shop. Maybe they've agreed to meet here."

"Oh yeah. You're right. I have seen Vance at Nora's."

Vance turns to Xan and Rain and starts talking to them as if nothing has happened. It seems unfair that two people as warm and sweet as they are have a negative shadow like Vance hovering around them.

"Ooh, Apolo," Greg whispers.

"What?"

"With that lost-lamb look on your face. I think you're right."

"I'm right? About what?"

"That whatever is going on between you and—" He points to Rain and the group she's with. "It's ridiculously complicated."

Eighteen

APOLO

They really taste awful.

I try one of the burgers only to spit the chunk out of my mouth. Gregory is right: they taste like cardboard. In my defense, the meat was prepared in advance; I was just responsible for cooking them on the grill. Still, I feel so guilty about the people who came through my stand and bought one. They must have been disappointed.

I begin to tidy up my area. It's getting late and dusk is falling rapidly. Not that it makes a big difference from earlier since the entire day has been cloudy and gray. However, the evening chill is less bearable now that darkness is slowly creeping in and blanketing this part of campus, which has no streetlights.

I sigh and turn my gaze to the entrance of the building where Xan, Rain, and Vance disappeared inside. I need a distraction, and cleaning the grill feels like the right task to keep my mind occupied.

As for Gregory, he's currently lying on top of a picnic table, occupied with his phone, his fingers making quick swiping and tapping motions on the screen.

"You could give me a hand, you know."

Greg turns to look at me and smiles. "Nah. It's the least you deserve for committing a crime against food by serving those atrocities."

"I didn't prepare the meat. I was only responsible for grilling it."

"Sure, sure. Whatever you say."

"You should help me. It's your fault Erica isn't here." I throw a rag at him.

"My fault?" He shakes his head and sits up. "Okay. I'll help you, but under one condition."

I have a feeling I'm not going to like it.

"What?"

"Tell me what happened with Rain."

"I don't know what you're talking about."

Greg arches an eyebrow. "I could be of help, you know. I can give you some advice. I am very wise, Apolo."

I let out a snort. "Sure you are, given the exemplary way you handled your relationship with Erica. I should give your performance five stars, Mr. Cupid."

"Now, that's a low blow. You're in a bad mood today. It's not my fault that your burgers—"

"Shut up, Greg. If you're not going to help me, then do me a favor and stop talking."

"Wow. I make the most amazing homemade meals, and this is how you repay me?"

He lies down again. Out of the corner of my eye, I notice

something moving close to the entrance of one of the buildings. Then I see Rain. She's the first to exit and is soon followed by Xan. Vance comes out last. To my surprise, he walks in our direction. He wears a look of disdain on his face, and his hands are shoved inside the front pockets of his jeans. I tighten my grip on the cooking utensils that I'm cleaning.

"Oh no. I guess I'm too late for a burger." Even the tone of his voice sounds condescending. Greg sits up the second he becomes aware of Vance's presence. "Party monster," Vance greets him before shaking his hand.

"Streamer boy," Gregory replies.

Rain and Xan walk up. They both greet me but avoid making eye contact. The Xan of earlier in the afternoon is no more. The smile has vanished and his eyes look dull. Meanwhile, Rain seems mortified and keeps looking everywhere except at me. Why? I don't understand what's happening. It's like Vance's negative energy stifles their spirits. This makes me hate him even more. He sits next to Gregory at the picnic table and the atmosphere becomes heavy and oppressive.

"How's your first semester in college going, Apolo?" Vance asks as if nothing ever happened between us.

This son of a . . .

My gaze moves to Rain. She licks her lips before saying quietly, "Vance, it's late. Let's go."

"Why?" He smiles at her. "I asked you a question, Apolo."

I look at Xan and at the cut on his lip. My mind conjures an image of that jerk laying his hands on him. I can't imagine the fear Xan must feel when he's with Vance. Immediately, rage courses through my body and my muscles become stiff.

How can you be so shameless, Vance? How can you stand here, smiling and joking around, after hurting Xan like that? Who the fuck granted you impunity to behave like this?

Vance cocks his head to one side and stares at me. "What's the matter, Hidalgo? Cat got your tongue?"

"Go fuck yourself, Vance."

The words fly out of my mouth freely and without hesitation. Vance may have some control over Xan, and maybe even Rain, but he has no power over me. He's delusional if he thinks his shameless attitude is going to sway me. Gregory stares at me, puzzled.

Vance gets up. "What the fuck did you just say to me?"

"What you heard, you cowardly piece of shit."

I've never acted rude or aggressive in my life, let alone behaved impulsively. But I can't keep this rage boiling inside me under control. It originated the night I was attacked, and it's been festering and growing ever since. I've tried to ignore it, but it's hard when I'm around Vance. He certainly knows how to push the right buttons. Right at this moment, all I want to do is use my fists to wipe that damn arrogant expression off his face.

"Apolo?" Gregory's alarm bells go off as soon as he notices my clenched fists.

"Are you calling me a coward?" Vance takes a step closer to me.

Rain jumps in front of him. "Vance, let's get out of here."

"Why?" He keeps his eyes locked with mine. "C'mon, kid. Say it to my face."

I walk around the grill but Gregory quickly steps in front of me.

"Hey, hey. Calm down, bro."

"Move out of my way." My voice sounds cold and determined.

"What's going on?" Gregory asks.

"You know me. I'm only doing this because he deserves it," I reply, and Gregory steps aside.

Vance shoves Rain out of the way.

"Okay, show me what—"

I punch him. Hard. My knuckles feel like they're on fire. Vance straightens and spits blood to one side. My attack caught him by surprise, so I advance and deliver a few more blows before he can fully recover. Fury radiates off my limbs and takes over. I lunge forward and land on top of him. I rain punch after punch on him. In my head, the lines have blurred. The night in the alley and this moment have overlapped. And I can't bring myself to stop.

"You fucking abusive piece of shit!" I shout.

Vance tries but fails to get away from me. He manages to sneak in a punch but it hardly does any damage. I'm blinded by rage.

A pair of arms grabs me from behind to pull me off Vance. I'm forced to take a few steps back, while he remains crumpled on the ground.

"That's enough! Campus security is heading here." Gregory's voice sounds far away. My chest rises and falls rapidly, and my eyes are pinned on Vance. He groans in pain and sits up, blood dripping from his nose.

"Is this the worst you can do?" Vance grins, showing blood-stained teeth.

I free myself from Gregory's hold and try to jump him again. Then a flash of blue comes into view. Xan stands in front of me. He has a firm grip on my shirt and is shaking.

"Please stop," he begs. I look into his bloodshot eyes.

"Violence is not . . . You're not like him, Apolo. You are not like him," he repeats.

I look at Vance, who is holding his nose with one hand. My knuckles are a bloody mess, and I feel a stinging pain. That's when I come out of my rage-induced trance. My eyes travel to Rain, who hasn't moved a muscle or said a word. Then I become aware of a crowd of students watching us from a distance.

"Apolo, we have to leave before security arrives," Gregory warns me.

Xan is about to let go of me when I place a hand over the one he has on my chest. I give it a squeeze, pleading.

"Don't go with him, Xan."

I blurt out the words, unable to control my emotions. The despair I feel makes me less hesitant and more decisive. Xan stares at our joined hands, his lips trembling. Then he slides his hand from under mine.

"I'm sorry, Apolo."

He turns around and goes to Vance. He helps him up and they leave together.

My shoulders slump forward in defeat. I'm at a loss and look at Rain. I had no clear expectations or outcomes in mind, but I never imagined that Xan would choose to leave with Vance.

"We can't force him to face the truth, Apolo," she says, her lips forming a sad smile. "The only thing we can do is be there for him the moment he asks for our support."

"This is bullshit."

"It'll be a worse pile of shit when campus security arrives. So can we go now?" Gregory starts walking to the parking lot.

Rain steps closer to me and takes my hand.

"It's time to go."

I study our joined hands.

"I thought you would hate me. I just beat the crap out of your brother."

"Even though violence is never the answer, he had it coming." She lets out a sigh, and her face is etched with sadness. She's right. Vance deserved what happened.

Nineteen

XAN

"That fucking little shit!"

A glass flies by and crashes against one of the walls in the apartment. My face twists into a grimace as the shards scatter all over the living room floor. My body is still shaking from what just happened.

"I'm going to destroy him, Xan. I'm going to finish him off."

Vance paces back and forth while I keep myself at a safe distance. When I get near him when he's in this mood, it never ends well for me.

"Let me tend to your cuts and bruises." I try to distract him because I'm terrified of what he might do to Apolo.

"No, no." His lips form a sinister smile, and my panic grows. "I'm going to report him, Xan. He hit me first, and look at the mess he made of me. This is assault. He doesn't even have a scratch on him. I'm sure I can find a few witnesses on campus." The sound of his laughter is unsettling and echoes throughout the room, turning my stomach with disgust. "Can you imagine the humiliation for his illustrious family? I'll make sure to leak every detail to the press."

My stomach turns at the thought. No, he can't do that to Apolo. Vance goes to the bedroom and returns with his phone. It had been charging since we got home.

"Come on. We have to go to the police station. You can be one of my witnesses."

I watch him head to the door. Though I'm petrified, I manage to summon the courage and speak in a whisper.

"No."

Vance turns around, and I'm not sure whether he heard me. Then I notice his expression contort with rage.

"I beg your pardon?"

"I'm not going with you. And I won't be one of your witnesses."

"Xan, I'm not asking you to lie for me. I just want you to tell the truth. He attacked me first, and you only need to relate what you saw, period."

"No. And you're not going to report it either."

My voice is shaky and my tone sounds uncertain. Somehow, I draw strength from the rage I saw in Apolo's eyes, as well as the disappointment, before I turned my back on him. He tried to help me. Maybe it wasn't the best way, since violence is never the answer; nonetheless, he was seeking retribution for some of the pain Vance has inflicted on me.

"What the fuck did you just say?"

Vance moves toward me. Anger radiates from every one of his pores. I'm taking a stand that is risky and makes me vulnerable. However, it's one thing to allow him to hurt me, and quite another to let him ruin the life of someone who has been nothing but caring toward me.

"You're not going to report him, Vance."

"Huh. Is that so?" His voice sounds icy and menacing. "And how are you going to stop me?"

This time, I won't let fear make me back down. It's likely that what I'm about to say could make Vance furious and turn me into the target of his rage. Yet I summon all the courage left in me because I'm tired of witnessing those around me rushing to my defense.

"If you file charges against him, I'll do the same to you." I'm firm and clear.

Vance narrows his eyes, and looks completely taken aback. He wasn't expecting this from me. Neither was I. And I feel like something in me was set free the instant the words rolled out of my mouth. This is the first time I have admitted out loud that there is something unhealthy about our relationship—that what we have between us is not right.

"You're going to do what?" Vance is quite perplexed, so instead of attacking or yelling, he studies me closely.

"You heard me. I swear to you, if you report Apolo, if you do anything to him, I'll go to the police, Vance. And you'll never see me again."

"Xan." Vance's tone softens. "You know there's nothing to report. We've had a few misunderstandings, just like any other couple. But we have overcome those challenges and moved forward. I thought we were both on the same page about that."

"Look at yourself," I tell him. "You've left me in a similar state so many times. And what did you say just now? That this is the definition of assault? Correct? I guess it only counts as assault when you happen to be the victim, right? But what about me?" I point to the cut on my lip.

"Xan." He gently cups my cheek. "It's been a hard night. You're right. Even though it was Apolo who attacked me, it's not worth pursuing it." His lips curve into a smile. "I'm sorry for putting you in a difficult position."

I run out of the strength or courage to push this further. Instead, I choose silence and clean his injuries.

Once I'm done, Vance carries on as if nothing ever happened. He jokes around, cooks my favorite dish, and suspends tonight's live stream to spend quality time with me.

Later, while we're in bed, my back is to him as he holds me in his arms. I allow him this physical closeness because I'm emotionally drained and lack the energy to push him away.

There's a part of me that came to grips with a painful truth tonight when I confronted Vance and threatened to go to the police. I had readied myself for shouts and blows. Instead, he gave in without a fight and showered me with his attention. And while he was pampering me, I had a powerful realization that broke my heart into a thousand pieces: Vance gave in to my demands because I have something to report—because something is definitely wrong about our relationship. Today, he defined with his own words the meaning of assault. In the past, I have stared at my battered and bruised self in the mirror. Contrary to his opinion, that's not something that happens in every relationship. It's not normal and it's not right.

I feel a dull ache in my chest. And here, as I lie in his warm and comforting arms, I no longer feel safe. Tears roll down my cheeks.

I can almost picture my mother's face, smiling at me. She prepares coffee while I explain to her that I'm attracted to boys.

Are you sure you're okay with that?

My mother places a cup of coffee in front of me.

The only thing that matters is that you find someone who loves and values you. Isn't that what love is all about, Xan? What does it matter if it's a boy or a girl? If he loves you and makes you happy, that's enough for me.

I run my tongue over my lips, and try hard to keep the rest of my tears from falling.

I'm sorry, Mom. I don't know how I ended up here. And I'm not sure how to break free either.

Twenty

APOLO

Rain tends to my bruised knuckles while we sit on the couch. Gregory takes a swig from his beer and lets out a deep sigh of relief.

"Whew, I really needed this." He sits on the other end of the couch. "Does anyone else want one?"

Rain shakes her head and I keep quiet because I'm at a loss for words. My body is still coming down from the adrenaline rush triggered by my angry outburst. I feel numb, and my mind is in a daze. I'm having a hard time recognizing myself. There's a dissonance between who I am and who I became tonight when I used my fists to brutally punish another human being.

All my life I have played the role of peacemaker—the person who firmly believes that violence is not the answer. I've never even had a heated argument with someone. My actions from this evening are inconsistent with my beliefs and personality. I think back to the many arguments I've had with my brothers, who often prefer to solve their problems with their fists. I used to believe I was more mature and evolved, often better than them, simply because I never used force like they did. And now look at me, sitting here with my knuckles bruised and bleeding.

Agh. If my grandpa ever finds out . . .

The last thing I want is to disappoint the people I care about the most. Rain finishes up, lets go of my hands, and gets off the couch.

"You should put on an ice pack, it will help with the swelling," she suggests, and goes to the sink to wash her hands. The air feels thick and heavy, polluted by the lingering tension from the altercation with Vance.

"All right, then, how about we lighten the mood with some gossip?" Greg says as he stretches on the couch. "So I talked to Erica today."

Rain dries her hands and looks surprised. "Oh really? Now, that's a miracle."

I furrow my eyebrows. "Did you know?" I look at Rain and wait for an answer.

"Of course. They were quite the item on campus," Rain explains, leaning against the side of the kitchen island. "You know how popular Gregory is. And he would brag about her everywhere he went and to everyone he met."

That sounds out of character to me because he's never done the same with Kelly.

Gregory grimaces. "Although I made a most heartfelt plea, she still hates me with the fiery passion of a thousand burning suns. And with very good reason." Then his face lights up. "Wow, that first line rhymes. Doesn't it? I'm quite the poet."

Rain snorts and I shake my head.

"Anyway." Rain turns to me. "They were the living embodiment of 'couple goals.' Everyone idolized their relationship. They were much like the king and queen of the prom."

"Oh, my sweet thunderstorm, I could argue that you're stretching the truth a bit." Gregory smiles. "But I won't, because we were quite the item indeed. What can I say? It's what happens when so much magic comes together, you know."

"Still, that didn't stop you from acting like a complete ass, did it?" I sound snarkier than I intend to. But Greg isn't bothered and narrows his eyes, looking at me in a playful manner.

"I don't need a reminder of my misfortune. Okey dokey, how about we talk about someone else instead?" Greg points at Rain. "Let's see. . . . So, Rain, have you told Apolo about all the obsessed admirers chasing after you?"

Rain gives him an eye roll. "I'm pretty sure Xan has already brought him up to speed. I mean, he never stops complaining about their incessant visits to the café in hopes of running into me."

"Aren't you a popular girl?" I tease her. "I suppose we should consider ourselves lucky to have you grace us with your presence this evening."

"This one may look sweet and angelic, but she's dangerous. Don't let those warm eyes and that bright smile fool you," Greg warns me.

"Sure, I guess. Though her appeal may explain a few things, it doesn't help me understand why she hasn't replied to any of my texts. Are you too busy for me, Rain?"

The mood in the room shifts. The friendly vibe fades and an awkward silence settles in. Rain doesn't have a response. And I haven't a clue why I brought it up. It seems I'm still pissed.

Greg and I exchange a knowing glance.

"I'm going to"—he takes one last sip of his beer and gets up while placing the bottle on the small table next to the armchair—"the washroom."

My good friend makes his exit, leaving us alone. Rain is still leaning against the kitchen island. Her arms are folded across her chest, and her eyes avoid mine. I replay in my head our kiss and the moment we had out in the hallway. Maybe it's not the right time, but I've sent too many texts and have yet to receive an answer from her. I would like to know where she stands and find out if I did something wrong.

"Rain."

"Apolo," she replies with a smile.

"I'm sorry about all of this. This is so unlike me."

"Impulsive? Violent?"

I'm embarrassed when I hear those adjectives because they accurately describe the way I behaved tonight.

"I guess."

Rain sighs and sits down on the couch, occupying the spot recently vacated by Gregory. She looks comfortable and at ease. The pink sweater she's wearing looks good on her. She tucks her hair behind her ears. The slow gesture feels intentional, as if she's working up the courage to speak.

"Apolo, what happened the other night—"

"Was it a mistake?" I interject.

My inner pessimist takes over. In the past, my luck hasn't been the greatest when I've pursued someone I happen to like. She stays quiet and I take that as a confirmation because her silence doesn't come across as a definite *No, it wasn't a mistake.* She purses her lips and rests her clasped hands on her lap.

"Rain, I guess I'd rather not have this conversation right now," I tell her, looking straight into her eyes.

I'm at my limit for tonight. I'm not in the mood for a rejection, nor do I want to hear an explanation, if that's her intention. I can't help but read her silence as an indication that rejection is where this is heading.

"Do you want me to leave?" She sounds defeated, and gets up off the couch.

Intuitively, I do the same and move closer until I'm mere inches away from her. Our gazes meet and I reach out to gently caress her cheek. I want to say something, but I fear the instant I open my mouth and start talking, the magic of this moment will disappear. So I take a chance and lean forward until my lips brush against hers. Then I pause and wait for her reaction. She wraps her arms around my neck and draws me into a gentle yet passionate kiss, very similar to our first. She pants heavily when she finally breaks away.

"Apolo, I—"

"Shhh."

And I kiss her again. Because it feels right. Even if tonight was for the most part a complete disaster, this moment drives away the negative thoughts that have been circling inside my head since the fight. We kiss until we run out of breath and our lips throb from the exertion. I pull away and gasp for air. Then she cups my face with her hands and looks directly into my eyes with great intensity.

"Only for one night."

"What?"

"Should we move to your bedroom?"

This sudden turn takes me by surprise. I nod and take her

hand, leading the way. Although my brain is still stuck in a kiss-induced high, I experience a brief moment of lucidity as we make our way down the hallway. Rain kisses me again when we enter the bedroom. As she moves her hands inside my shirt, I internally chastise myself for having an intense personality. I can't stop replaying those four little words: *Only for one night.* What does she mean? Is that all she wants? A one-night stand?

We reach my bed and fall in a heap. Rain lands on her back and I end up on top of her. She lets out a giggle, her expression one of sheer joy. I place both hands on the bed at the sides of her head, keeping my weight off her so I don't crush her.

I stare at her with a look of awe.

"Rain."

"Yes?" She brushes away the hair that hangs over my forehead.

"Just one night?"

Her smile fades. "Yes."

"Yes, what?"

"This. You and me. It can only happen one time."

"Is that what you think I want?"

"No, I just assumed that maybe you would be interested in something casual, with no strings attached."

I move off her. I sit on the bed and stare at the wall. Rain rises and sits next to me in silence.

"I don't sleep with people just for the sake of screwing, Rain. I'm okay with fooling around, making out, and anything else along those lines. But sex means something to me, and I'd much rather do it with someone I care about. I like you, a lot. And I'm dying to sleep with you. But I'm not looking for a one-night stand. I'm an all-or-nothing kind of guy, the type who gives his all and expects the same in return."

Rain looks away. "I know."

"Then, why?" I finally ask what I've been dying to know for days. "Why didn't you answer my messages? Why did you avoid me? Was it because you don't want anything serious or complicated?"

Rain opens her mouth as if she's about to say something but stops herself, not meeting my gaze. I take this as my cue to keep talking.

"Rain, you can be honest with me. I won't fall apart if you tell me exactly what you want to get out of this."

This, of course, is a lie. I happen to like her a great deal. And sure, if she's not interested in getting involved with me, it might break my heart a little. However, my high hopes aren't clouding my judgment and preventing me from reading the signs. Something definitely feels off. We had a very intimate moment the other night. There was chemistry and desire. So the last thing I expected was her avoidance and evasion.

"That's exactly what's wrong, Apolo." I arch my eyebrows. "I haven't been completely honest with you—I didn't want to spend any more time with you and pursue something without being completely honest."

Something is very wrong here. Her body is stiff and her hands are tightly clasped. She keeps biting her lip and seems anxious. I have a feeling that I won't like what she's about to tell me, and that it might hurt me. So I inhale deeply and brace myself for her confession.

Twenty-one

RAIN

So here we are.

I've avoided this for too long. It's the main reason I put off meeting up with Apolo in the first place. I had hoped to ignore my obligation to share this crucial information with him.

This story began a few months ago at an expensive and elegant cabin located on Lake Lure. My mother owns a beautiful lakeside property in the area. She goes there sometimes to write, away from the city and my father. On occasion, my little brother, Jim, and I would tag along. Vance would only come up in the summer. He loved to swim in the lake and would take advantage of the nice weather. In the winter, it was just my mother and me who would visit. We shared an appreciation for the melancholy of our surroundings, spending our time close to the frozen lake, drinking hot chocolate, and sitting by a blazing campfire.

My father wasn't a fan of the cottage. Eventually, he caved after we begged him nonstop and agreed to come along with the family. Then one visit turned into two. Soon, he was going to the lake every other week. However, his strong dislike for the outdoors and anything nature-related had not changed. But I didn't think much of it at the time. Shortly after, my father would take trips to the lake alone. Although this change in him raised some suspicions, I stopped myself from making any assumptions. One cool summer night, the neighbor living on the property next to ours invited us to a party she was hosting at her home. My mother had owned the cottage for many years and was acquainted with almost every resident in the vicinity, except for this one neighbor.

This woman was very distinguished and elegant. She was also cold and didn't smile much. Apparently, it had been only two months since she'd moved into her lake house and she was still settling in. So our whole family decided to attend the party. It was a beautiful property. The interior was designed in all white with gold accents, which included the stair railings, the lampshades, and fixtures. The house exuded luxury, and it stood out in a neighborhood where folks opted for a more rustic look for their vacation properties—an aesthetic that was the polar opposite to this woman's style.

"Ugh. Who throws a black-tie party at their cottage?" Vance stood next to me and complained as he loosened his tie. I had decided to wear a strappy green summer dress.

"Everyone is free to do what they want, Vance. Especially people who spend a couple of million dollars on renovations."

Vance gave a snort. "I'd wager it was more like three. And I bet even that is way off the mark," he said as he pointed to a gold candlestick. "That's pure gold, sis. Definitely not fake."

"Of course, because now you're the expert." I took a sip from my drink. What was the flavor? Orange, maybe? To be honest, I was having a hard time guessing the flavor of the cocktail I was drinking.

My mother excused herself early and went home to bed. Mingling at parties was not really her thing. She preferred solitude and was easily worn out by this type of social activity. Jim left with her, while Vance and I stayed along with my father. A handful of neighbors remained, drinking and talking with the hostess. When it was finally time to leave, Vance and I couldn't find our father, so we walked out the front door and headed home. We assumed he'd taken off without telling us. Our father is not the most thoughtful man in the world, and leaving us behind would be in character.

As soon as we arrived at the house, we realized that he was missing. I will never forget the look on Vance's face as he put two and two together. My brother has always been quite perceptive, good at noticing the little details that the rest of us often miss. Vance sprinted out of the house and headed back to the party. I followed him and was a short distance away when I saw him slip back inside the lady's house.

Then there was silence.

That lasted for a few minutes. Suddenly, there was shouting and absolute chaos. Vance was walking away from the house; he looked like a raging bull. Our father was running after him. And a feeling of cold dread settled in my gut as I watched them come closer.

My father reached out to grab hold of him but Vance brusquely freed himself from his grip.

"Don't touch me!" he shouted. My brother looked furious.

"Vance," I said when he got near me. "What happened?"

Then I noticed the blood on his fists and the bruises on my father's face.

I was completely horrified. In all my life, I would have never imagined that my brother could physically hurt our father.

"Son, listen to me. Lower your voice."

Vance was about to attack him again when I placed myself between them and demanded an explanation.

"What the hell happened back there?"

"Tell her, Dad," Vance dared him. "Come on. If you have the balls to pull that shit, then you need to man up. Go ahead and tell your daughter what a complete piece of garbage you truly are."

My heart was about to leap out of my chest as I stared at my father. "Dad?"

"Vance, don't do this," my father pleaded.

"Dad?" I addressed him again, searching for an explanation.

"Of course you don't have the guts," Vance mocked him. His tone sounded bitter and hurt. "Dad's screwing the new neighbor."

That's when my world came to a complete stop, and I felt something break inside me.

No, no.

My parents had been married for over twenty years. This was not possible. My father wouldn't do this. He wouldn't destroy his family and hurt us like this. I lowered the hand that I had laid on Vance and locked eyes with my father.

"Dad?"

I waited for his rebuttal or an explanation. I needed him to tell me that it was all a big misunderstanding, and that Vance was wrong. But my father cast his eyes to the ground and stayed quiet. And this hurt. It burned. And it stung.

Words can harm us. But a silence like this one has the power to destroy everything.

"Please, don't . . . don't tell your mother. I—"

"Fuck you," Vance spat.

My father's face became blurry. That's when I realized I was crying. I wiped my cheeks and struggled to stay on my feet.

"You have until tomorrow to tell her," I instructed him, my voice slightly breaking. I held back my anger, the disappointment, and everything else I felt in the moment. I don't remember exactly when I started doing this, but I tend to repress my emotions the second my instinct for self-preservation kicks in. "If you don't, we will."

I turned and walked away. I couldn't stand to look at him or be near him.

My father had no choice but to tell my mother the very next day. She was shocked and truly devastated. Yes, their relationship had been far from perfect, but they at least had trust and many years spent in a committed relationship. In the end, they decided to stay together, but nothing was the same between them. My mother sought refuge in her writing and my father buried himself in his work.

Vance was enraged. I don't think he found a healthy way to process and deal with the anger. I tried to help him, but nothing worked. He allowed the hatred to fester and the contempt to grow. This contempt he felt was not only directed at my father; it also set its sights on the other person involved in the affair. Her name was Sofia Hidalgo.

One day, Vance found out that the son of this woman was about to start college. I had a feeling in my gut that he was planning something, though I didn't know exactly what. I tried to get him to understand that what had happened wasn't the son's fault, and that he was as much a victim in this mess as we were. But like before, I couldn't get through to him.

Then one rainy night, he called me. He was drunk. From the noise I heard in the background, I figured out that he was at a bar.

"I need this, Rain. I have to hurt someone."

"No, Vance." I panicked when I heard those words. "Where are you now?"

"I saw him. He's the only son who still visits her after her divorce from Old Man Hidalgo. This boy is the chink in her armor. He's within my reach, Rain."

"Vance, listen to me. Don't do anything stupid." There was no response. "Vance!"

Then he hung up.

I jumped out of bed, put on some warm clothes, and grabbed an umbrella.

I used my phone to check Vance's Instagram stories. He had posted from a bar in downtown Raleigh, just a half hour from where I was. So I jumped in an Uber. But when I got to the bar, he was nowhere to be found.

No, no. Shit.

I ran outside. My feet were wet from the rain. I tried to use my umbrella to shield myself from the downpour. I had a feeling that Vance had not gotten very far, so I searched for him. I checked every bar and every corner.

I was passing through an alley when I found Apolo.

I broke down in tears right after the paramedics took him away. Someone was hurt. I'd had the power to stop it but didn't. I felt like the worst person in the world when I gave my statement to the police and held back the identity of the attacker. My actions went against everything I believed in. I hated myself for keeping this secret, but Vance was my brother. My mother was having a difficult time getting along with my father as it was, and I doubted my family had the strength to withstand the likelihood of Vance going to prison.

I was selfish. I acted like a shitty person, and put Vance's welfare ahead of everyone else's, even though he nearly beat someone to death. And I did it simply because he is my brother. There is no justification for what I did.

This is why I avoided Apolo at first. I didn't want to meet him or get to know him. I couldn't bring myself to look him in the eye when I had the answers that could bring him the justice he deserves. I couldn't bring myself to tell him the truth.

Same goes for me when you stop meddling in my business, Rain.

I don't know what you're talking about.

Yes, you do. I hope you're smart enough and keep it together . . . I would never hurt you, however—I wouldn't be too sure about those close to you.

And I failed to keep it together. I let my emotions lead the way to Apolo. And the more I get to know him, the worse I feel about everything he's been through. Maybe a part of me was hoping he'd turn out to be a horrible person. Then I would feel less shitty about what I did. But nope, Apolo is warm, kind, and caring. So I'm eaten up with guilt over letting things get this far between us while holding back the truth. But not anymore. It stops now.

Once I'm done with my confession, I wait for his response. Apolo is rooted to his seat. His eyes are wide open and his hands are tightly balled into fists. He remains still and quiet. I don't blame him. I've given him a lot to digest. Meanwhile, I feel like I'm dying inside.

"Apolo."

His gaze avoids mine. He looks like he's still processing.

"Leave."

Ouch. His request stings, but it's justified. I deserve it.

"Apolo, I just—"

"Get out." He raises his voice and I jump. I'm startled. I wasn't expecting this reaction. "I need to . . . Just leave, Rain."

I simply nod and get off the bed. Before I leave the room, I turn my head and catch one last glimpse of him over my shoulder. He hasn't moved an inch. Anger and disappointment are clearly etched on his face. That's when I realize that this thing between us is over before it had a chance to start, and the thought breaks my heart.

I'm so sorry, Apolo.

Twenty-two

APOLO

I need to go home.

It's what I need after the week I've had.

The Hidalgo mansion welcomes me with its imposing stature and massive windows. I haven't had a wink of sleep. I left my place in Raleigh early, and arrive just as the sun is rising. The family is likely all together in the kitchen having breakfast, and certainly not expecting to see me. Although this is my home, for some odd reason I feel like a stranger at the moment.

I open the main door with my key, and hear voices spilling down the hallway. I want to go straight to my room and shut everything off, but I need my family. I find them in the kitchen. Claudia wears jeans and a red sweater that complements the fiery shade of her hair, which is pulled back in a high ponytail. She holds Hera propped on her hip. Artemis has black workout clothes on, and is drinking his latte. And my grandpa is chopping vegetables for the sauté that will be served with the fried eggs.

"Hello," I greet them, sounding tired.

Everyone looks up, and I can tell they're more than surprised to see me.

"Dodo!" Hera exclaims. The sight of her little face is a welcome balm, temporarily soothing my wretched mood. "Dodo!" She stretches out her arms.

"Princess." I reach out and grab her. She immediately hugs me.

"Are you all right?" Claudia asks softly, staring at my swollen knuckles.

"We weren't expecting you, son. But what a nice surprise." Grandpa hugs me from the side opposite to the one where I hold Hera. "You look—"

"Go ahead. You can say it," I encourage him.

Artemis clears his throat. "Shouldn't you be in class?"

"Artemis," Claudia scolds him. "I'm sure there's a valid reason why he's here. What did we say about trying to be, you know, more sensitive?"

"I wasn't—" Artemis exclaims. "I'm just concerned about him skipping class."

"I'm not a child, Artemis. You don't have to act like my father anymore."

My older brother stands and puts down his cup. He grimaces and exchanges a look with Claudia. Then he walks over to where I stand.

"What are you doing?" I ask.

Artemis gives me a hug. It's quick and no words are spoken. I suppose this is his attempt to be more expressive and sensitive.

"It's good to see you," he tells me with a smile. He pats my back.

Grandpa watches me intently. Out of everyone here, he knows me best. So I'm not surprised when he fishes for more information. "What do you need, son?"

Claudia scoops Hera up again. I wave my hands, hoping the gesture will get him to drop it.

"Help me with getting breakfast ready," Claudia says, and gives me a warm smile. "That's what I need right now."

"Great."

Grandpa gives me instructions and we get to work. Our combined efforts result in a grand family breakfast. The smell of coffee, the freshly cut vegetables, the heated oil in the pan ready for the eggs, the sound of Hera's adorable laughter, and my grandpa's jokes. Every little thing about this moment brings me comfort and makes me feel at home.

This is exactly what I need right now.

Later on, I sit by the swimming pool and stare at the crystal clear water. The sight is enticing enough for a dip, and deceiving in this cold weather. The sun shines on the horizon. It envelops me in its warmth and brings me some calm.

I hear slow footsteps approaching behind me.

"You are still really bad at spying, Grandpa," I joke, and help him to the seat next to me. He is carrying two cups of hot chocolate and hands me one.

"It's the old age. My slow steps and creaking bones give me away."

His answer makes my lips curve into a smile. And the wrinkle lines on his face deepen when he smiles back at me.

"Ahhh, I guess you really are your father's son," he says, taking a sip from his cup.

"What do you mean?" I ask with a frown.

"Back there when you came into the kitchen, you reminded me so much of your father," he tells me. "Anytime something wasn't right in his life, with the company, or even Sofia, Juan would show up at my door. He never said much. Instead, he would help me cook or fix things around the house." He smiles and looks nostalgic. "And it warmed my heart because it meant that no matter what happened in his life, my son knew he had a safe place where he could take refuge when the world wasn't kind to him."

My vision blurs as I listen to the story. I take a deep breath and try to keep my emotions under control. Grandpa puts his hand on my shoulder and gives it a squeeze. "This place will always be your refuge, Apolo."

"I know."

"I don't know what happened, but if you need to talk about it, I'm here for you. Claudia is also here. And Ares is only a phone call away."

"What about Artemis?" I joke a little, and Grandpa lets out a sigh.

"He would be my last option, if you ever need to discuss your feelings."

I laugh.

"What about Dad?"

"He's not even on my list of options."

"Grandpa!" I exclaim, laughing even more.

"What? If there's one thing we Hidalgos possess, it's our penchant for brutal and complete honesty."

My smile fades. "Ah. Honesty. A small fraction of that would have come in handy. It would have spared me from so much."

"Seems like it would have at least prevented you from

wrecking your knuckles." Grandpa takes my hand and inspects it. "I must admit that this is the last thing I would have ever expected to see. Violence—"

"It's never the answer, I know." I pull my hand away from his close inspection. "Trust me, no one was more surprised than I was to find me in this position."

"Did he deserve it?"

"Pardon?"

"Son, I've watched you grow up. I was there when you cried for two hours the day you accidentally stepped on one of your puppies. I know you. Something must have set you off. The person you hit, did he deserve it?"

I stare at the water in the pool and everything I've been through replays in my head: the alley, Rain, the excitement of meeting her, the smell of coffee at Nora's, Xan and his rosy cheeks, Vance and his provocations, the bruises on Xan's arms, the argument outside the party, and the fall festival. I watch myself on top of Vance, hitting him with all the rage I had buried deep inside. And then the scene switches to Rain sharing her confession. This memory triggers another chain of thoughts: my mother's involvement with a married man, Vance's thirst for revenge, and Rain's efforts to hide from me the fact that her brother was my attacker. Vance could be in jail now, and Xan would be safe. The power has been in Rain's hands all along, and she chose to do nothing. She looked me in the eye after having witnessed what Xan went through, and did nothing.

"Apolo?" Grandpa puts his hand on my shoulder again.

My fists are clenched tightly and my jaw is tense.

"I—" I turn to look at my grandpa. "I have . . . I am . . . Grandpa, I have so much anger bottled up. It feels like it's eating me up. Ever since the night of the attack, I have a heaviness in my chest. Because these dark and negative emotions were never a part of who I am. The world sucks, and I knew that. But now—"

"Now you've been out there and have witnessed it with your own eyes." He sighs and strokes my hair. "I worried as I watched you grow up, Apolo. I felt that you were too good for this world. I worried that the pain that the real world would inflict on you would be greater than what it would inflict on the rest of us."

"And you were right."

"No." He shakes his head. "No. I was so wrong, my son. Being a good person does not make you weaker than the rest. You are an incredible human being, and I don't want you to stop being this amazing person because you feel anger or frustration and happen to make the wrong choice. There are no bad feelings, Apolo. Our decisions are influenced by our emotions, and they can be good or bad. But the emotions we feel are valid."

"It's like an avalanche—I'm overwhelmed so I push back and block everything. Then I find myself unable to cope with all the bad I've been through, with everything in my life."

"It's because you're experiencing the real world away from your family in a strange city where you are on your own. So you've come back home to reconnect with yourself, your roots, and your family. But you'll have to go back out there. And you'll get knocked down again. Eventually, the day will come when you won't need to come home to rediscover who you are, because you'll have a stronger sense of self and a better handle on your emotions."

"Grandpa, you should have been a psychologist."

"Aren't you the one studying psychology?"

I sigh. "Look at me. Do you think I'm capable of helping anyone else with their mental health?"

"Of course not, you've just started your studies. But you are undoubtedly the most empathetic guy I know. In time, this quality will benefit anyone who seeks your assistance."

"I don't know how to move forward."

"You do know how. And have known for some time. So what's stopping you?"

"I'm ashamed, Grandpa."

My grandpa dissolves into a fit of boisterous laughter. I'm startled and jump in my seat. Then I let out a chuckle; the sight of him laughing soothes me.

"Ashamed?" He coughs a little and keeps laughing. "Why do you feel ashamed, Apolo?"

"I don't know. As a student of psychology, I'm afraid that I'll be judged for going to therapy."

"So according to this logic, if Ares were to get sick or injured, he shouldn't seek assistance at a hospital because he's a medical student?"

"When you put it that way, it does sound foolish."

"You are not a fool, son. You just need clarity. As I told you the night of the attack and on many occasions after, you need professional support to process the repressed emotions brought on by such a traumatic event."

"That's the other reason why I don't want to go. I'm terrified of what might come out."

"And you think that by keeping it all bottled up it will eventually go away just like that, without any help? Every emotion you feel is justified, and it's crucial that you experience every single one of them."

"I feel good when I talk to you, and—"

"No. I'm not a therapist, Apolo. I'm just an old man who's lived long enough and has been at the receiving end of my fair share of knocks, someone who's still figuring out how to navigate this brave, new, technologically advanced world." He lets out a deep breath. "Believe me, stepping out of my comfort zone hasn't always been easy. But if I can figure out how to play that sniper game so I can spend more time with my other grandkids on PartyChat, you can surely figure out how to navigate therapy."

"Are you talking about Uncle Jamel's kids? Wait, have you been playing *Fortnite*?"

Grandpa puffs out his chest proudly.

"Every time I play, I manage to stay alive longer," he says. "Last time, I lasted a whole three minutes."

I smile at him because it's too adorable.

"What about Uncle Jamel?"

"He's the same, aloof," he tells me with a hint of sadness in his voice. "But I'm too old to get stuck in petty grievances with my children. I'm deeply aware that their inheritance is the main reason they keep in touch. However, my grandchildren are a different story. They're innocent bystanders, and I'm doing my part to nurture a connection with them. It's why I bought that console from hell. Now we video chat every Saturday. And in two weeks, I'll see them in person when I visit." Grandpa gets up. "So. Go to therapy. Or your grandfather will drag you there, Apolo Hidalgo."

"Yes, sir."

I watch him go back inside the house. He's slow on his feet and takes small steps. I adore this old man with the white hair and boisterous laughter. He plays an important role in my life, always imparting wisdom and insight. Today, it was not just the advice he gave me, but the story he shared that shed some light. His other children forced him into a nursing home. They pretty much abandoned him. And what does he do? He chooses to move forward, and does his best to maintain a connection with them. He puts wisdom ahead of pride or any bitterness he may feel. And why? Because he's a good person through and through. And no harm or rejection thrown at him has changed that.

I guess the time has come for me to take charge and do what's long overdue. This is something I should have done immediately after I experienced my first bout of panic—the first time I felt uneasy when it rained. Back in the days when I spent my days living like a zombie, doing my best to repress the red-hot anger— the same rage that was unleashed during my altercation with Vance. Maybe once I put myself back together, I can think clearly and figure out what to do with the information that Rain shared with me. For the time being, I need to focus on myself.

It's okay to ask for help, Apolo.

The time is now.

PART TWO

XAN

PART TWO

Twenty-three

APOLO

It still very difficult for me to talk about what happened that night.

It's no wonder that I'm emotionally drained and feel wiped out after my second appointment with the therapist. I'm back to feeling like a zombie. For the past two weeks, I wake up and go to class. Then I come back to the apartment and go to bed. Every day is rinse and repeat. I even stopped running in the mornings.

Gregory has tried to interrupt my routine by extending invitations to socialize, including parties and movie nights. Erica makes a few attempts of her own whenever I happen to see her on campus.

I steer clear of Café Nora. I don't think I can look Xan in the face without telling him that his boyfriend is the attacker who nearly killed me. And then there's Rain—I try hard to push any thoughts about her out of my mind.

I've discussed her with my therapist. We have identified what it is about her that unsettles me most. We agreed it is the deception on her part and the feeling of betrayal it lodged in me. I can't deny that I'm also angry with her because she refuses to do the right thing by not coming clean about Vance. Still, the fact that she lied to me from the very beginning is what stings the most. It hurts when I think back to the times we spent together and all the opportunities she had to tell the truth.

I can't forget my mother and the role she played in this mess. Then there's me: the only child out of three who still visits and spends time with her.

"Come in, Apolo." My mother greeted me with a big smile the last time I was over at her place. "They just put those curtains up. What do you think?"

"They look nice." I don't particularly care about luxuries or interior decor. My mother, on the other hand, lives for these things. She was accustomed to a high standard of living and certain comforts when she was married to my father, and the settlement from the divorce has permitted her to keep the same lifestyle. My father agreed to a generous alimony as long as she gave up her company shares.

"So when do you start classes?"

"Next week."

"Oh." She walked around the kitchen island and put on an apron. Then she got to work on the pancake batter. "Sit down. I'll make your favorite kind. With strawberries and bananas, right?"

I nodded. I didn't expect her to remember that. And it was the first time in my life I had ever seen her cook.

"Are you nervous?" she asked as she beat the mixture.

"A little. You know that . . . well, making new friends is not my strong suit."

My mother shook her head. "It'll be fine, you'll see. Next time you come visit, you'll have a ton of stories to tell me about all the friends you've made."

I let out a snort. "Of course."

A silent pause followed and she licked her lips. I watched her closely and could read what was on her mind.

"They're doing fine, Mom."

She looked a little crestfallen. "Good. I follow Claudia on Instagram; she posts beautiful pictures of Hera."

"Yes, she does."

She got back to working in the kitchen. When she was done, she presented me with a stack of three pancakes topped with fruit.

"Thank you. This looks amazing."

She nodded and smiled as she wiped her hands on her apron. But the sparkle in her eyes was gone. It vanished the moment she mentioned Hera. And I couldn't help but feel bad for her. Yes, she is mostly to blame for the estrangement from the rest of the family, but she is still my mother.

"Give them time, Mom." I spoke to her with honesty and sincerity. "Artemis and Ares . . . well, they were deeply affected by what happened between you and Dad."

"I know. I deserve this. It's just—" She let out a long exhale as she looked out the window. "I'm very lonely, Apolo."

"I'm sorry, Mom."

"There's no need for you to feel sorry. I brought this on myself. I wish I had the clarity of mind then that I possess now. Perhaps I would have realized sooner how my actions were hurting you. Juan and—" She paused and licked her lips. "Living here on my own and spending my days completely alone—well, I've had lot of time to reflect, look back, and realize the gravity of my mistakes. Though I fear it may be too late, Apolo."

I reached across the island and took her hands. "I'm here for you, Mom. I can't speak on behalf of my brothers, it's up to them to sort out their feelings and figure out their own timeline. Still, I'm a firm believer that it's never too late to face one's mistakes, make amends, and move forward."

My mother circled the island and gave me a hug. "I love you."

Right then and there, I believed every word she said. I really thought she had changed.

And now I've found evidence to the contrary. Is there anyone who can be trusted anymore?

I've been holed up in my room since class ended today. I need to shut my mind off. I can only hope that sleep will help put a stop to my racing thoughts as I close my eyes.

"Apolo." A hand shakes my shoulder. "Hey."

I groan, roll over, and give my back to whoever this is. I don't want to wake up.

"Apolo!" Though my name comes in a whisper, the tone is urgent. As the drowsiness from sleep dissipates, I realize the person trying to wake me is Gregory.

"What's going on?" I mumble with my face half buried in the pillow.

"Wake up, we have a situation."

Greg shakes me harder, and I groan in frustration as I reluctantly sit up. "What's wrong?" I rub my eyes and squint, my sight adjusting in the darkness and giving me a clearer look at his face.

"It's Xan."

Alarm bells go off in my head, and I'm wide awake the second I hear his name. This can't be good.

I look at the clock on the wall. It's four in the morning. And Greg's worried expression gives me a bad feeling. "What happened?" My heart is pounding hard in my chest.

"He's here."

"What?"

"Well, he's at the door. He didn't want to come in. He asked me to get you."

"But why?"

I jump quickly out of bed and, wearing only pajama bottoms, make a beeline for the door, where I find Xan waiting. He's trembling and has his arms wrapped around himself. His hands keep rubbing his arms. His hair is a mess and his eyes look puffy, like he's been crying. I spot fresh bruises on his face, and the skin around his neck looks red, like it was . . .

"God, Xan. What happened? You're hurt and—"

"Sorry. I'm sorry for coming here at this hour. I don't know why, but I didn't have anywhere else to go. Rain gave me your address a while back. I wanted to apologize for the way I treated you at the party. I don't even know how I got here. I've been walking for a while . . . hours."

I look down and notice that he's barefoot. Suddenly it hits me that it wasn't his intention to end up here. He's definitely running away. He coughs and winces. And his neck—I'm pretty certain that Vance is responsible for the red marks around his neck.

"I'm sorry, Apolo."

"No, no. You don't have to apologize for anything. Come in."

"No. It's not a good idea. I don't want to drag you into this mess, I—"

"Xan, come in, take a break, and have something to eat. We can help you figure out your next move after."

He hesitates. "I'm so embarrassed, showing up at your door like this. But I was so scared." His voice breaks. "I just took off without much thought or a plan."

"You did the right thing, Xan. Now come inside."

I hold out my hand. He's reluctant at first, but gives in and takes it. We walk to the kitchen, where Gregory is waiting. Xan looks at the floor. I remember my most recent visit to my family, and what I needed most at the time. When we are at our lowest point, the last thing we need is an inquisition. Xan hugs himself and his gaze remains downcast.

"I'm truly sorry. I shouldn't have shown up here like this, it's very late, and I—"

"You want your bread toasted?" I interrupt him, and walk to the other side of the kitchen island. Xan lifts his gaze and looks perplexed, so I keep talking. "Today, breakfast will be served extraearly. As my grandpa loves to say: everything is better on a full stomach."

I give Xan an understanding smile and his eyes turn slightly red.

"Toasted," he mutters.

"Excellent choice." Gregory joins in and points at me. "Okay, Apolo. Take out the eggs and chop the vegetables. I'll get the frying pan. And, Xan, please sit down."

The boy with the blue hair sits down on a tall chair next to the island while Greg and I get cooking. Well, Greg is the one who does most of the cooking. I simply follow his instructions. I'm terrible at cooking, so I'm grateful that he's in charge.

"Not like that!" Gregory scolds me. "God, how can you not

know how to make bacon? It's not rocket science, Apolo. You only have to flip it and cook each side."

Xan doesn't say a word as he watches us intently. He seems quite entertained by our back-and-forth. This is exactly what I hoped would happen. At this moment, Xan doesn't need to deal with questions or probing from anyone. He'll talk when he's ready. And when the time comes, I'll be around to listen.

We eat our food in silence and thoroughly enjoy our improvised breakfast. The meal turned out great, even for Gregory. His culinary skills never cease to amaze me. It's still dark outside. I look at the clock and it's almost five. Greg lets out a yawn, and says good-bye.

I hesitate for a moment. I'm unclear as to what I should do next. I have a feeling that Xan doesn't want to be alone. So I take him to my bedroom, which is spacious and has a big, comfortable couch. Once we're inside, he stands rooted next to the door. All the lights are off except for the lamp on the night table. It casts a warm glow over us.

"Can I use your bathroom?" he asks.

His voice sounds despondent, and he looks absolutely wrecked. His battered appearance mirrors his broken spirit. The cheerful Xan who smiles at me when I drop by Café Nora is nowhere in sight. I hate Vance for hurting him like this.

"Of course."

When Xan comes out of the bathroom, he stands still for a few seconds. He looks tentative and unsure.

"You can sleep in my bed," I offer, as I sit on the couch.

He licks his lips and wraps his arms around himself again.

"Xan," I say and he looks at me. "You are safe."

He nods and lies down on his back, face to the ceiling.

"You don't have to sleep on the couch," he whispers. "Your bed is big enough. You can lie here too. If you don't mind."

"Of course I don't mind," I reply, and move to the bed.

I lie down and mimic his posture, resting on my back with my face up. The dim light coming from the lamp casts soft shadows on the ceiling. The silence in the room is comfortable and peaceful. I hope Xan finds the comfort he needs to process tonight's ordeal.

"I—" Xan begins, but stops himself and keeps quiet.

I place both hands on my tummy and turn my face to him.

He keeps his eyes glued to the ceiling. Tears roll down his cheeks and his lips tremble.

"Xan, you don't owe me an explanation. Take all the time you need."

"How . . . how did it come to this? How did I let it get this far? How can I still love someone who can do this to me?"

"This isn't love, Xan. What you had with Vance possibly started out as love, but that's no longer the case."

"Then what is it?" He turns his face to look at me. "Because I feel like I can't go on without him, and at the same time, I feel trapped."

"This is all his doing. He set you up and made you feel this way so you wouldn't leave him."

"He wasn't like this before. It hasn't always been this way. When we're good, everything is perfect." He looks at the ceiling and breathes through his stuffy nose. "He promised me that he would never do this again. But tonight he—I thought he was going to kill me, Apolo. I was—" He breaks into sobs and shuts his eyes. "So afraid."

I cautiously reach over from my side of the bed, searching for his hand. "You're safe, Xan." I give it a gentle squeeze. "Rest now."

He sobs inconsolably for a while. I hold his hand and try to do my best to be there for him.

Eventually, Xan falls asleep. His long eyelashes brush against his cheekbones and his mouth parts. I let go of his hand and sit up to tuck him in. Xan shudders but doesn't wake up. He turns on his side in his sleep, facing me. His blue hair hangs over his forehead. The bruises on his face and neck have changed color and are more visible. I stare, debating what to do next. One thing is for sure: someone has to stop Vance. As time passes, it's become abundantly clear that I'm the person who has to step up and make that happen.

Twenty-four

XAN

I don't want to wake up.

If I do, I'll have to face my reality and deal with what happened. I'll have to think about him.

Besides, I feel well rested. I haven't slept this deeply and soundly in months. I don't know what time it is. When I look out the window I notice the sun is up, so it must be late. Apolo is nowhere in sight so I get up to use the bathroom before venturing out of the bedroom. The apartment seems empty when I come down the hallway. No one is in the living room or the kitchen. However, I find a note on the island counter.

Xan, I'm off to class, I'll be back after 2. I've left waffles in the microwave. We have other options in the fridge if you feel like eating something else. Please wait for me to come home.

I feel warm in the pit of my stomach as I read the last sentence. How does he know me so well? The first thought that popped into my head when I came out of his room was to leave. As the remnants of sleep fade, I begin to doubt my decision to come here. Maybe this was a mistake. I can't deny that this was a welcome respite and I feel safe here. Still, I don't want to get Apolo entangled in my mess. I don't want to take advantage of his kindness. Last night I came to his door because I had nowhere else to go. The truth is Vance is my entire life. He's my home, my job, my one and only relationship, and so much more. Without him, I'm pretty much on the street and on my own.

This is all his doing. He set you up and made you feel this way so you wouldn't leave him.

I hear Apolo's words, and have a hard time believing that Vance would do that to me. Who would do something like that to another human being?

He's my brother and he's not a good person.

Now it's Rain's voice that plays inside my head.

I take a deep breath, heat up the waffles, and pour myself a cup of coffee. As I sit at the kitchen island, I stare at my phone, which is currently turned off. I gather the courage and turn it back on. My palms are sweaty and I wet my lips with my tongue. I get a sinking feeling as soon as Vance's texts start to show up.

1:04 a.m.

Vance: ANSWER THE PHONE!

1:05 a.m.

Vance: XAN, ANSWER ME RIGHT AWAY.

1:06 a.m.

Vance: Where did you go?!?

1:06 a.m.

Vance: Xan, I swear that if you don't answer me . . .

1:07 a.m.

Vance: Why aren't you returning my messages? Have you turned off your phone?

In addition to the texts, he's left a total of nine messages in my voice mail. I decide not to listen to them. Instead, I focus on the texts that keep showing up one after the other on the screen. The first batch of texts sound angry and are full of threats. Eventually, he appears to calm down. As usual, the last text has a tone that's completely different from the first ones.

Vance: Xan, I'm so sorry. It's already dawn and I'm worried about you. At least let me know that you're okay. Please, it's all I ask from you.

I debate whether it's a good idea to let him know that I'm okay, but as soon as I flash back to the events of last night, I'm paralyzed with fear.

We were watching a movie at home. Then a call came in and he moved to the studio where he hosts his live streams. I stayed on the couch with the bag of popcorn on my lap, and waited for a few minutes. When he came back to the living room, he said we'd have to watch the rest of the movie another day because he needed to go live. And that was the beginning of our argument.

One thing led to another, and I broached the subject of our closeted relationship. I brought up the fact that he flirted with everyone he engaged with on social media and in real life, meanwhile he kept me hidden away, like a dirty little secret. As always, Vance tried to use sex to fix the problem, but when I didn't give in, he was furious. Next, we were both shouting, and neither of us was listening to what the other had to say. And that's when he lost it.

This time was different. He didn't stop. He pressed me hard against the wall and proceeded to choke me. The grip he had around my neck was so tight I nearly fainted. When he finally let go, he looked enraged. His shoulders kept rising and falling rapidly. He screamed at me but all I could hear was a never-ending screeching sound. That's when my survival instinct kicked in and I acted purely on impulse. I fled the apartment and ran to the elevator. Then I left the building and ran down the street barefoot, in a daze. I didn't stop and kept going, hoping to get as far away from him as possible.

For hours I wandered aimlessly through the deserted streets of Raleigh, shivering in the autumn chill. I thought about going to Rain's house but decided against it when I recalled previous incidents of a similar nature. It would be at the top of Vance's list if he came looking for me. And that led me to the door of the boy with the warmest smile: Apolo Hidalgo.

Never in a million years would I have imagined finding myself right here. As expected, Apolo has shown me nothing but kindness. He's a good person. It's exactly the impression I got the first time he walked into the coffee shop. The same day he was waiting for Rain. He was nervous and easy to read. As time went by, my assumptions were confirmed. He is, without a doubt, an incredible guy. I hate that he knows the twisted details of my relationship with Vance, and that he's witnessed some of the ugliness between us. I'm also flustered by the emotions he stirs in me. These are feelings I shouldn't entertain.

My phone rings. It's an incoming call from Vance, and I have a hard time swallowing. I know that sooner or later I'll have to face him. Still, I'm not ready at the moment.

The front door opening makes me jump off the chair. Apolo walks in, dressed in jeans, a sky-blue sweater, and a hat in the same color. He carries a backpack over his shoulder, and there's a look of relief on his face when he realizes that I'm still here.

"You waited for me," he says, with a reassuring smile that makes me believe that everything is going to be all right.

I want to kick myself. I should not let my thoughts get carried away. My life is in shambles, and my head is a mess. The last thing I need at this point is to be crushing on a straight guy.

"The waffles presented a very convincing argument," I answer, though I have hardly touched the food on my plate.

Apolo puts his backpack on the counter and takes off his hat. His hair is ruffled. He walks over to where I sit. I'm a bundle of nerves when he touches his hand to my face.

"I think the bruises will heal soon."

My throat tightens and I swallow hard. "Yeah."

He doesn't move away. I look at him and can't help but wonder: *Does this guy have no concept of personal space?* He's standing so close to me. The chair is high, so my knees are elevated, almost brushing against him. When he takes a step back, I feel like I can breathe again.

"What are you planning to do?" he asks as he pours himself a glass of water.

"I don't know." I sigh. "I have to open the coffee shop soon. But it's likely that he—"

"—he'll be there. Do you want me to come with you?"

"No, you've done more than enough. I have to figure this out by myself."

"Xan."

"Thank you very much, for everything."

"You have nothing to thank me for," he replies, and his expression is etched with concern. "What are you going to do after you close the shop tonight? Where do you plan to go?"

That's a good question. My only option so far is crashing at the café.

"Don't worry, I'll be fine."

"You can stay here as long as you want, Xan. This apartment is big enough, and Greg won't mind."

"No, I don't want to take advantage of your generosity. You've already done enough for me."

"It's not a big deal, I swear. He and I are great roommates."

That puts me at ease, and I smile. "I don't doubt it. I had no idea Gregory was such a good cook."

Apolo lifts his chin. "And I'm very good at baking desserts."

"I'll have to try them someday. Though I will be the one preparing the coffee because this right here is awful." I point at my cup. "No offense."

"Well, do forgive me, Mr. Coffee Expert, for insulting your taste buds with our humble offerings."

I laugh, and Apolo stares at me.

"What?" I ask.

"Laughing looks good on you, especially after what you've been through."

"Thanks, I guess? No need to worry about me. I'll survive."

"I hope so." He leans on the counter. "I'm serious, Xan. You can stay here with us."

"Do you expect me to share a bed with someone who commits these awful crimes against coffee?" I joke, and raise my cup. "That goes against my beliefs."

"If sharing a bed is a concern, I don't mind sleeping on the couch. We can also put a bed in the living room."

"Apolo." I roll my eyes. "I'm just kidding."

"I know you are. I just want to make sure you're comfortable."

I don't know why I get nervous all over again. "But are *you* comfortable with this arrangement?" I ask him.

Apolo gives me a smile. "Sharing a bed?" he asks. I nod. "Yeah, it's fine. In fact, Greg and I shared a bed for a month when we were waiting for mine to be delivered."

"Yes, but you guys have been friends for years. You and me, on the other hand . . ."

Apolo waits for me to finish, and I want to kick myself.

Why are you making everything awkward, Xan? Of course it's normal for him to share a bed with a friend. You need to stop overanalyzing everything. Stop being neurotic.

"Yes, you and me?" Apolo presses me to elaborate but I take a few seconds to think carefully before I give him an answer.

"You and me, well, we've been friends for a very short time."

He furrows his eyebrows. He seems puzzled by my argument but doesn't pick it apart.

"It doesn't bother me, Xan."

"I should get ready and go to the café."

"Can I lend you some clothes?"

"Are you saying that I smell bad?"

He laughs. "Nah."

"Okay. And thanks," I say with utmost sincerity. "Thank you, I really appreciate it."

An empty Café Nora welcomes me with a still and serene silence. Immediately I'm struck by sadness. This coffee shop is much more than a business venture for me. This place is my life and my dream. It sounds simple and modest. Even my mother scolded me for having few aspirations. Yet I never saw anything wrong with turning this passion into my career—making my life's work the creation of a space where people could gather and find solace while surrounded by the rich aroma of brewed coffee.

I'm not even surprised when I notice a figure sitting at a table in the corner. Vance looks like he hasn't slept. His shirt is wrinkled and there are dark circles under his eyes. I clench my hands into fists to keep them from shaking. Vance stands, and I'm scared by the surly look on his face. Perhaps I made a mistake when I declined Apolo's offer to come along with me.

"Where were you?" His voice is cold and restrained.

I struggle to keep my head up. "What are you doing here? I have to take over the afternoon shift."

"Xan, where did you spend the night?" He inspects the black sweater and jeans that I'm wearing. They're loose since Apolo is a lot taller than me. "Whose clothes are you wearing?"

"Vance, you have to leave."

"Answer me!" I'm startled by his shouts. "I haven't slept all night! Meanwhile you seem like you had a great time, all set in someone else's clothes."

"Have you lost your mind?" I ask in a serious tone. "Do you

think you have the right to ask me these questions and make a scene after what you did to me last night?"

"Xan, don't provoke me, and answer the damn question!"

"No!"

Vance grabs my arm and drags me behind the counter.

"Let go of me! Vance! Let go!"

Then he throws me to the ground and climbs on top of me.

No, no.

"If I don't get an answer from you, then I'll have to check for myself."

"Stop it! Stop it! What are you doing?" I freeze when he starts to unbutton my jeans. Then he slides a hand inside, rounding the swell of my ass. "No, no, Vance."

Tears flood my eyes when he inserts his fingers inside the crack, probing and searching for evidence, looking for fluids from someone else. Once he's completed his examination and is satisfied, he gets off me and stands up while I lie still on the floor. I feel broken and shattered. What he just did to me hurt more than his blows from last night.

"Well, then," he adds in a confident tone, "I'll be back at closing time. Don't you ever scare me like that again, Xan." He issues his warning then leaves.

I'm unable to move and stare at the ceiling. My eyes are teary and my vision is blurry. The lights hanging from the beams are on, giving off a warm, soft glow. I chose them for this very reason. I wanted to create a mood in the café that made people feel safe and welcome.

I eventually manage to sit up and get off the floor. I button my jeans up with trembling fingers and fight the urge to vomit.

Then I wash my hands. I splash my face with water, and get ready to open the doors of Café Nora.

I don't want to think about what just happened. I just want to focus on preparing delicious coffee drinks and fill the place with the aroma that makes me feel at home. I want to reclaim the feeling of being wrapped in the warm embrace of my mother, and away from the clutches of a beast like Vance. The time has finally come for me to face the truth: Vance Adams is a monster.

Twenty-five

APOLO

We need to talk.

I hit Send and slip my phone inside the front pocket of my jeans. I can no longer avoid her. Sooner or later, I have to talk to Rain. Weeks have passed since our last encounter. She's texted me a bunch but I haven't responded. I needed time to process what she told me. I didn't want to be stuck in a place of anger the next time we spoke. However, Xan's ordeal last night has sped up this process. Vance has to be stopped.

I head to Café Nora, and when I arrive the big white neon sign is still on. I had a bad feeling in my gut I just couldn't shake, so I show up two hours before closing time. Ever since Xan left the apartment for work this afternoon, I have been sick with concern. Vance doesn't appear to be the type of guy who gives up easily, and he knows that Xan won't miss work. What is there to prevent Vance from coming to the café looking for him?

I look through the shop's window and spot Xan. He smiles at

a customer as he hands him a latte. He's wearing a scarf around his neck that he didn't have on when he left for work. The bruises are likely more apparent. It makes me sad to see him like this, acting as if everything is fine and carrying on despite the trauma of last night. I push open the glass door and the little bell rings, catching everyone's attention. Several tables are occupied, and Xan waves in my direction when he notices me. I return the gesture and approach the counter.

"A latte, please."

"You really should give matcha a try." He shakes his head as he prepares my drink.

"No, thanks. Nothing green for me."

Xan frowns slightly, playfully conveying disappointment.

"I believe this friendship has come to an end."

"Oh really. So we were friends?" I joke with him, and he narrows his eyes.

"And roommates."

I smile from ear to ear. "Does that mean . . . ?"

"I accept your offer to stay"—he pauses and clears his throat—"at your place. It will be temporary while I find something else more permanent."

I can't stop smiling. This is a huge breakthrough for Xan. Only by staying away from Vance will he be able to gain perspective and clarity. I'm impressed by Xan's willingness to take this very important step.

He hands me my latte and wipes his hands on his apron as he comes around the counter.

"I'll sit with you for a minute."

At the table that's closest to the counter, we sit, and Xan shakes his hair. That's when I notice that his roots are past an inch in length, displaying the dark pigment of his natural hair color. They're confirmation that I've known him longer than I realized.

"Does this table bring back any memories?" he asks with a twinkle in his eye.

"Of course. This is where you first spoke to me."

"Yeah. You looked so smitten with Rain."

I tense up a bit. "Hmm, and I was just one more name on a long list of admirers. You made that very clear to me that day."

"Nah. You could never be one of many, Apolo."

The ease in his voice when he makes that statement catches me off guard. I look into his eyes and the red on his cheeks deepens as he keeps talking.

"What I mean is that you're a Hidalgo. So of course, you'll always stand out."

"Simply because of the last name or is it something else?" I feign deep concentration. "What did you tell me that night at the party? Oh yeah, that I look like a Greek god."

Xan looks down and lets out a chuckle. "I was hoping you wouldn't remember that."

"It's not every day that someone says something like that to me."

He snorts. "I don't believe you."

"Do people come up to you every day and tell you that your cheeks always look rosy and adorable?"

Xan sits very still. And it's my turn to clear my throat and take a sip from my latte.

What the hell was that, Apolo?

"Adorable?" Xan laughs. "Not the adjective you want to hear from someone who is—" He stops abruptly and purses his lips.

"Someone who is what?"

"Nothing."

I tilt my head to one side and Xan avoids my gaze. He looks quite nervous.

"Xan."

"What should I bring home for dinner? I'd like to take a turn and show my appreciation for your hospitality. Chicken wings? Or do you want pizza?"

"Pizza is fine." I look at him carefully and give him a reassuring smile. "Your coffee is amazing, and I'm no longer offended by your critique of mine from this morning."

"I make a living preparing coffee. It would be a disaster if I sucked at it, don't you think?"

"What other things do you do well?" I probe, and Xan looks a bit stunned.

What the hell is up with me?

"I'm sorry." I quickly recover. "Listen to me, getting comfortable and being cheeky with you. Clearly, living with Gregory has rubbed off on me."

Xan licks his lips. "It's all good." He appears to be thinking about what to say next. "To tell you the truth, I'm only good at making coffee."

"Which is great, because you look the happiest when you're standing behind that counter," I add, hoping to distract him from the implication of my innuendo. "When did you know this was your thing?"

Xan smiles wistfully. "I remember the smell of coffee filling my home from the time I was a child. My mother was very passionate about it. At first I thought my interest stemmed from my connection with her. Then I realized that I truly enjoy making it.

And most important, I take pleasure from watching the look of joy in people's faces after they have the first sip of a great cup of coffee. It quickly turned into an addiction. Fast-forward and here we are."

"Your mother?"

"She passed away last year. She was around long enough to experience some of the joy this place has to offer." He draws invisible circles and lines on the table with his finger, and as I watch I see that he's tracing the name Nora. "She was happy and liked Vance very much. She died thinking that she was leaving me in good hands, and that I would be fine. And that was the case for a while, until he started . . . acting up."

"I'm sorry."

"I'm comforted by the fact that she died without worry, you know."

"That makes sense." I study his crestfallen expression. "Do you miss her?"

Xan lets out a long exhale. "Every single day." He wiggles his head and shoulders, hoping to shake off the sadness. "What about you? Do you get along with your mother?"

Every muscle in my body becomes tense and I clench my jaw. I was the only one who gave my mother a chance. I thought that as a single and independent woman she could finally be happy without hurting anyone. Instead, she ended up messing around with a married man.

"I'm closer to my grandfather. My parents are not . . ." I struggle to explain.

Xan studies me for a few seconds. "It's complicated, isn't it?" he asks. I nod. "My father was never around. It was always my mother and me. So I get it."

"It's always the parents," I joke, recalling one of my lectures.

"Where would we be without parental drama?"

We laugh and look into each other's eyes, sharing a comfortable silence. Then Xan lets out a sigh and looks around.

"I think I'm going to close now."

"There's still an hour to go."

"Vance has cameras installed to monitor the café Apolo. He probably already knows that you're here and is likely on his way. I don't want to see him ever again."

I raise an eyebrow.

"Again? Did he come by already?"

"Yes. And he is still furious. So if it's possible, I'd rather avoid him."

"I understand. I'll stick around and wait for you."

Xan proceeds to tidy up while I remain seated at my usual table.

My phone beeps, notifying me of an incoming message.

Rain: Yes, we need to talk. Text me the time and place.

I stare at the message but fail to reply. I replay in my head the memory of Rain in my room; she's sitting on my bed and spilling her guts. And I can't help but feel disillusioned, which I guess is an improvement from the anger I felt at first. Now that I've had some time to process and digest the truth, all I'm left with is disappointment.

I've been debating whether I should tell Xan. I watch him while he puts a few things away. After he's done tidying up, he pulls his apron over his head, which messes up his blue hair. He's careful and makes sure the scarf stays in place. Xan is already dealing with a lot and doesn't need one more thing on his plate. This is not the right time, and it wouldn't be of any help. What matters is that he's finally left Vance.

Once he's done, we head home together.

"Sacrilege!" Gregory cries when he sees us come in with a box of pizza.

Uh-oh, I completely forgot.

"What's wrong?" Xan asks, placing the box on the island's counter.

"How dare you bring fast food to the home of a chef, Xandwich?"

I press my lips together, trying to contain my laughter. Xan stares at him, looking confused.

"Ss-xandwich?"

"That's what you are. You get a nickname for disrespecting me like this."

Xan looks at me, pleading for my support. I respond with a shrug. "How could you, Xan?" I stir things up. He gives me a murderous look.

"Apolo didn't tell me anything," he protests.

"C'mon, it's common sense." I play dumb.

"What's going on here?" Kelly asks as she walks in.

She catches me off guard. I haven't seen her around the apartment in weeks. She has a backpack over one shoulder and is pulling a suitcase with the other hand. Wait. Are Greg and Kelly—is she leaving for good?

"This xandwich over here brought pizza for dinner. Can you believe it?" Gregory fills her in, still sounding offended.

Xan clears his throat and wipes his hand on his jeans before offering it to Kelly. "My name is Xan."

"Kelly," she responds, after releasing his hand. "I was on my way out."

"Do you need help?" I offer, gesturing at her bags, and she nods. She says good-bye to Greg and Xan, and we go downstairs. Outside the building, I give her a hand loading the bags into her car.

"All good?" I ask.

No matter what happened between us, I've enjoyed her company, and her presence in the apartment.

"Yup." She closes the trunk and rests her hands on her hips. "It was inevitable. Greg and I were bound to break up."

"I get it."

"Apolo, I'm sorry I got you involved in my drama. I shouldn't have provoked you. Or—"

"Kelly," I cut her off. "It's okay. You didn't force me to do anything I didn't want to do."

She offers me her hand. "Are we good?"

I accept it. "We're great."

She turns and gets into her car. Then she rolls down the window before starting the engine. "You're a good guy, Apolo Hidalgo."

"I get that a lot."

She smiles and takes off.

When I return to the apartment I find Gregory sitting on one of the high chairs and Xan standing next to the island. They're both eating pizza while they talk about their plans for Thanksgiving. Xan looks a little pale. My clothes are a little too big so he looks smaller, almost frail.

Or maybe it's my imagination. He's been through a lot and I may be overthinking.

"I thought you were insulted by the pizza," I tease Greg. I walk over to Xan, hoping to help myself to a slice.

"What can I say? This xandwich is charming."

I turn to look at Xan, who smiles and gives me a shrug.

"When you're hungry . . ." He stops talking when I move my arm next to his waist, reaching for a slice, then jumps out of the way. I give him a puzzled look. "Sorry, I wasn't expecting that," he says.

"It's okay." I try to apologize. He's likely to be hypersensitive following his latest ordeal.

Gregory is watching me with a stupid grin on his face.

I gesture a *What?*, and he moves his fingers across his lips as if he's zipping them shut.

Before bed, Xan and I take turns using the shower. I lend him clothes to sleep in. He apologizes yet again for putting me out, and promises to collect his stuff soon. Although no one is rushing him, he seems to think that his presence is an inconvenience, which is far from the truth.

I stand by the bathroom door wearing only pajama pants, toweling my hair dry as he gets into bed. He slowly lifts the covers and tucks himself in. He looks relaxed and self-assured. He rolls to his side and his eyes land on me. He looks at my face first, then lowers his gaze. He stares at my abs then quickly looks away. I remain silent. I toss the towel away, move to my side of the bed, and slip under the covers. The bed is huge, so there's a lot of room between us. I hope he doesn't mind that I sleep shirtless. I don't want to assume so I ask him.

"Would it bother you if I sleep without a shirt?"

"No," he whispers.

"What a day," I comment, and let out a deep sigh. I rest my forearm over my closed eyes.

We keep still and quiet for a few seconds. Then Xan breaks the silence with a whisper.

"Apolo."

"Huh?"

"I'm afraid."

The words that come from Xan are few yet powerful because he's taking a huge step by voicing this fear. A flood of warmth settles in my chest at the realization that he chose me to hear his admission.

"I'm here for you, Xan. I promise you that very soon Vance won't be able to hurt you, or anyone else for that matter."

I take the arm that was resting on my face and stretch it, hoping to reach his side. Cloaked in darkness, I cup his cheek and feel the warmth of his skin as his breath caresses the palm of my hand. The contact feels intimate, and maybe not what I intended, but he doesn't seem to mind.

"I don't know what I'm going to do, Apolo." Every time he speaks, his breath caresses my skin. I wet my lips and swallow with difficulty.

"One day at a time, Xan." I speak under my breath and do my best to ignore the sensation provoked by this light contact. "You've already done the hardest thing. You've admitted there is a problem and removed yourself from an impossible situation."

"You probably think I'm stupid, right? How could I let it get this bad?"

"Xan, none of this is your fault." I move my thumb up and down, hoping to stroke his cheek. But my finger moves lower and ends up touching his lips.

A shiver runs up my spine and I attempt to pull my hand away. I don't want Xan to think that I'm making a move while he's being vulnerable and opening up to me. But he grabs hold of my wrist, pressing his cheek firmly against my palm.

"It feels good," he murmurs. "I've forgotten what a gentle and caring touch feels like."

I listen to his soft sobs while his tears run down my hand. On an impulse, I inch closer to him and embrace him sideways. Xan buries his face in my bare chest and weeps inconsolably. I rest my chin on the crown of his head. His hair is soft and smells like my shampoo.

"Everything is going to be all right, Xan." I repeat this like a mantra several times while I hold him in my arms.

And that's how we fall asleep.

Twenty-six

APOLO

Here I am, again.

I wait at the usual table, steeped in a sense of déjà vu. It seems like only yesterday when I first saw Rain enter through the doors of Café Nora. She smiled at me, and I was overwhelmed. I was a ball of nerves and my heart was racing. Many weeks later, I sit here and wait for her, feeling sad and disappointed.

And just like that day, Xan sits across from me and sighs.

"You practically live here," he chastises me, shaking his head.

"As if you don't enjoy it."

He arches an eyebrow playfully.

"You are many things, Apolo. But conceited is definitely not one of them."

"What? Are you fed up with me now that we're roommates?" I joke. Xan has been staying with us for a week and we've gotten more comfortable around each other. Truth is, I enjoy his company a lot. He's very organized, quite funny, and somewhat naive at times.

When I first asked him to stay with us, I was a little worried that it would be awkward. After all, it's not every day that you have to share the privacy of a bedroom with a brand-new friend. But it turned out better than expected, and we already have a routine in place. Gregory is in charge of breakfast and Xan looks after dinner. And what do I contribute to the mix? I wash the dishes.

"You're a great roomie. I'll give you that," he admits with a smile.

I've noticed that as the days go by, Xan's personality keeps blossoming. I suppose his separation from Vance has given him the space he needed to be himself. He's no longer quiet, withdrawn, or hesitant. He's actually the opposite.

Neither of us has brought up the night we fell asleep in each other's arms since it happened. It's like we entered into a silent agreement: he needed someone to lean on and I happened to be there for him. That's all there is to it.

So why do I keep thinking about the feel of his soft hair against my skin? Or the way he fit so perfectly in my arms? Or his breath blowing on my chest and the warmth of his body against mine? Argh. I feel terrible for having these feelings at a time when he's vulnerable.

That's enough, Apolo.

"So tell me, what's new today?" Xan asks with a hint of excitement in his voice. "You always have juicy gossip for me."

"Hmm, today—"

I'm interrupted by the sound of the bell echoing throughout the room. We watch as she enters the shop.

Rain.

She wears baggy jeans and a pink sweater. Her blond hair looks shorter than the last time I saw her. She waves to me and I do the same. Xan's gaze jumps from her to me, and his excitement fizzles.

"Oh. You didn't drop by to see me." He gets up, and something feels off. He attempts to cover up whatever is bothering him with a forced smile. "You're here on a date."

"Xan."

He turns around, waves at Rain, and heads back to his spot behind the counter.

"Apolo Hidalgo!" Rain exclaims as she takes a seat across from me.

"Rain Adams."

"It's quite poetic that you suggested Café Nora, the place where we had our start." Her eyes look dull and sad. "This must be the end, right?"

I feel a slight tightness in my chest. She's someone I would have loved to get to know better, even if what we had is permanently wrecked. Who am I kidding? I was close to jumping into a serious relationship with her.

"Ugh, this is more uncomfortable than I expected," she says.

"It doesn't have to be." I soften the tone of my voice. Despite what happened, I don't want her to feel bad. "I want you to know that I understand your reasons for doing what you did, Rain. It took me a while to reach this place, and that's because I was angry and disappointed."

"I understand. And I'm very sorry about that."

"I accept your apology," I say frankly.

One important lesson I learned from my grandpa is to not hold a grudge. Ultimately, when we hold on to the anger we feel, we hurt ourselves more than those who wrong us. In some cases, in order to forgive we must let go.

"You're too good." Her expression shows relief.

However, there is a big difference between letting go and not holding someone accountable for their actions. So I take a deep breath and look her in the eye.

"You made a decision then, but I need you to do the right thing now. It's the only way we can ever be friends."

Rain furrows her eyebrows. "Do the right thing?"

"Give your statement and report Vance."

She pales and her jaw drops in shock. I'm surprised by her reaction. Was she truly not expecting this? Did she think it was going to be forgive and forget?

One thing that's become blatantly clear is that Vance needs to be stopped. And for that to happen, Rain has to testify against him. I sought legal counsel from my family's lawyer and Rain's testimony is crucial. In the statement I gave I told the truth: I didn't see the face of my attacker and have no idea why I was assaulted. I can't lie all of a sudden and change my statement when I already said that I couldn't see anything that night. It doesn't sound credible, and would be no help to my case. I know it was Vance because Rain told me. She has to make a declaration.

She says nothing and runs a hand over her face.

"I'm going to get a coffee, do you want one?" I offer, hoping to give her time alone to consider my request.

She nods and I head to the counter. The smell of coffee grows stronger the closer I get. I've grown fond of it. It's the aroma that permeates the air in the apartment when Xan comes home from work in the evenings. The boy with the blue hair stands by, waiting for me to place my order. His hands are on the cash register and his fingers alternate between tightening and loosening their grip. It's something he does when he's nervous.

"Welcome to Nora."

I give him an *are you kidding me* look, but he remains professional and serious.

"What would you like to order?"

"A cappuccino and a matcha."

"At last, you dare try our delicious green option."

"It's for Rain."

Xan narrows his eyes. "She doesn't like matcha."

I blink and realize that I have no idea what Rain likes. Did I used to know and have forgotten? Xan watches me closely.

"I'll make her a caramel macchiato," he concludes, and begins to prepare our drinks. He glances at me over his shoulder while he operates the machine. "So, Rain, huh?" I watch him draw something on the foam. "It's been a long time since I've seen you two together."

"We've both been busy with school," I lie to him.

Xan hands me the cappuccino and gets to work on the other drink. "I bet you've missed her," he comments, and stares at me.

I don't give him an answer. Instead, I stretch out my hand and hand him my card so he can process the payment for the two drinks.

Xan stops me. "No, it's on the house."

"Xan."

"You're letting me stay in your apartment, Apolo. The least I can do is offer you free coffee." He gives me a smile that doesn't feel genuine. Or maybe it's just my imagination. "Now go back to your girl."

He waits for an answer and once again, I don't respond. I make my way back to Rain without saying another word to him.

"Thank you so much," she tells me when I hand her the coffee. "My favorite. You remembered."

I press my lips together and give her a smile. We take a sip from our respective drinks and our gazes meet. Rain clears her throat. The time has come to discuss the elephant in the room.

"I know I made a mistake, and that it's wrong of me not to report him. Everything may seem black and white, Apolo, but sometimes there are shades of gray in between." She inhales deeply. "You probably already know that Xan left Vance. I seized the opportunity and had a heart-to-heart with my brother. He decided to seek therapy and enrolled in an anger management program. He's making an effort, Apolo. How can I testify against him when he's trying hard to change?"

I keep my tightly clenched fists on my lap. "What about me and what I'm going through because of him?"

"I get it, Apolo. I'm not—"

"Rain, your brother did not make a tiny mistake that can be easily corrected with promises and attempts to get better. He committed a crime that deserves a jail sentence. And I'm just talking about what he did to me. But we both know what he's been doing to Xan. Why do you think he left your brother?"

"I know!"

"You know, yet you're not processing the information adequately," I chastise her, annoyed. "He almost killed me, Rain. You were there, you found me half dead. If you hadn't come when you did what do you think would have happened to me? And if I had died, would you still be protecting him? Because—"

"He's my brother!" She raises her voice and the other people in the café stare at us, Xan included. Rain bows her head and mutters, "I'm sorry, but he's my brother. I know it's not a justification for his actions, but I can't report him without giving him a chance, Apolo."

"So the rest of us can go fuck ourselves. He almost killed me, but that doesn't bother you. And he nearly strangled Xan, but you don't give a damn about that either. What kind of person are you, Rain?"

Tears fill her eyes. But I don't care anymore if I hurt her feelings because she obviously doesn't care about anyone else except for her deplorable brother.

"I'm really sorry, Apolo."

"Bullshit." Rage and impotence build up inside me. "If you were sorry, you would do the right thing. You would report him and let him deal with the consequences of his actions, so he can't do the same to someone else. You understand what you're conveying to your brother with your actions, right? You're letting him know that he can nearly kill someone and never have to face consequences. Therapy, you say? That's great. I believe in it. However, his actions have ramifications. You're certainly not helping him if he gets aways with what he did to me with total impunity. You'll be doing the opposite."

I stand up. Then I look at her. Any feelings I may have harbored before I became aware of the truth have completely vanished. I watch her as she stays rooted to her seat and firm in her decision to protect her brother. And I can't fathom ever being friends with her.

"The next time he hurts someone, I hope you'll be able to acknowledge that you had the power to stop him but chose not to. Good-bye, Rain."

I feel the rage emanating from my body and make my way to the door. Xan comes out from behind the counter and follows me. He looks worried.

"Apolo?"

I walk past him.

"I'm fine," I answer and leave.

Good-bye, Rain Adams.

I take a sip of whiskey and the furrow in my brow deepens. I don't know why I keep trying to stomach this drink.

All the lights are off in the living room. I look like a ghost. Or worse, I feel like one, as if I don't exist. Maybe it sounds melodramatic, but today I felt like Rain minimized Vance's actions and the impact they had on me. The nightmares I've had, the therapy I receive, and my aversion to the rain—all that and more weren't enough to convince her to do the right thing. Maybe I'm being selfish because I refuse to put myself in her shoes. But I won't do that. Vance almost killed me, and my mental health suffered; I have the right to be selfish.

I hear the main door open. It's followed by the sound of someone turning on the kitchen light. In a matter of seconds the aroma of coffee spreads throughout the apartment. Xan walks in and comes to a stop next to the kitchen island.

"Apolo?" he asks tentatively. "What are you doing sitting there in the dark?"

"Having a drink." This sounds very unlike me, and doesn't go unnoticed.

Xan comes closer and stands behind the couch, facing me.

"Are you okay?" I look up and he appears concerned. "Rain was inconsolable. I don't know what went down between you two and she wouldn't tell me, but if you need to talk about it—"

I shake my head. "I've done enough talking for today."

"Okay."

Xan leans on one foot, then shifts his weight to the other and waits, silent. I let out a sigh, set my glass down, and stand.

"Let's go to bed."

I won't solve anything if I keep drinking. Xan turns and I follow him. We walk down the hallway that leads to our bedroom. I stare at his hair, his neck, and his back. I pay close attention to the fit of the jeans he's wearing. They look good on him. I wonder what it would feel like to hug him. I let my impulses taken over when Xan reaches for the doorknob, and wrap my arms around his waist from behind. I feel his body tense the moment I press my forehead to the back of his neck. His scent pulls me in and invades my nostrils. It's a blend of coffee and a light fragrance.

"Just for one minute?" I ask, holding him.

Xan relaxes in my arms. He places his hands on the backs of my arms, and lets me have this moment. My heart is racing. It's been a while since someone made me feel this way with just a hug. It's different from the night we were in bed and I held him in my arms. The intensity is stronger, and the embrace feels good and so right.

I rub my nose against the back of his neck, then I move upward and bury it in his hair.

"Apolo." He gasps, tightening his grip on my arms.

"You're so warm, Xan."

"And you've had too much whiskey."

"Nah. I just had one glass—I'm not drunk."

I lower my gaze and manage to get a peek of his naked back under the collar of his shirt. I kiss him right on that spot, acting impulsively. He shudders in response.

"What are you doing?" he murmurs.

I don't exactly know what I'm doing. I fail to give him an answer, so he turns around in my arms. This is a big mistake. Now that our faces are inches apart, I notice his fiery blush and rapid breathing. I can't help myself and stare at his lips.

"I'm not sure." I'm being honest with him, but my answer comes up short and isn't good enough.

"If you're not sure, then let go of me." He slips out of my embrace. "The last thing I need right now is for you to confuse me even more by using me to satisfy your curiosity."

I frown. "Excuse me?"

"Let me make something very clear, Apolo. I'm not here to be some straight guy's experiment. Okay?"

I smile as I take a step closer. "I don't know where you got that idea from," I whisper, looking straight into his eyes. "But I'm not straight, Xan."

Twenty-seven

XAN

What? Apolo isn't straight?

I'm at a loss for words. This is the last thing I expected to hear. Maybe I was wrong to assume his sexual orientation. Still, I never thought he would . . . I mean, he seemed so taken with Rain. And when I first told him I liked guys, he failed to share this very important tidbit about himself. Without a doubt, my gaydar failed me this time.

What were you expecting, Xan? Since when do people have to go around declaring out loud their sexual preferences?

I don't know what to say and can't look at him. I'm still processing this new development. So I walk away from him and slip inside the bedroom.

"We should go to bed," I suggest, heart hammering in my chest as he walks closely behind me. "Tomorrow is another day."

Apolo remains quiet as he goes to his side of the bed. He sits down and takes off his shoes. I catch a glimpse of the muscles of his back flexing while he performs this task. But I quickly look away. I try hard not to get my hopes up and rein in my wishful thinking after what just happened out in the hallway. Not so long ago I thought Apolo wasn't an option because I was under the impression that he was straight. And now that my assumption has been proven false, there's a glimmer of hope in my heart and I can't help but feel elated.

I get under the covers and lie on my back. He sighs and does the same. A deep silence settles in the room and all I can hear is the desperate beating of my hopeful and foolish heart. Then he speaks first in a whisper.

"I'm sorry, Xan. I never meant to make you feel uncomfortable."

Is that regret I hear in his voice? "You didn't make me feel uncomfortable at all," I tell him.

"I shouldn't have grabbed you like that, without your consent. I just needed a hug."

I roll over and rest on my side. I place my clasped hands on the pillow right under my cheek, and stare at him.

"It's okay, Apolo. I understand. You were there for me the other night. I know what it's like to need a hug."

Apolo turns on his side and faces me. The fiery glint in his gaze cuts through the near darkness, and I have a difficult time swallowing when I look at him. His hair looks messy and hangs over his face. He's incredibly handsome. There's really no other way to describe him. Though his physical appearance draws me to him, what I find most attractive is his energy and his personality. It's the way he's supportive and helpful without hesitation. I take the liberty of staring at his lips. The memory of his embrace out in the hallway stirs emotions in me that I shouldn't entertain.

Apolo slides one hand over the covers, and I take one hand from under my cheek and reach out to meet his. Our fingers lightly touch, moving in an awkward and clumsy manner. We stare into each other's eyes and I'm overwhelmed by my emotions. I think back to the first day I saw him walk in the café. I remember his smile, the warmth in his eyes, our conversations, the look on his face when he defended me from Vance, his pleas the night of the fight when he asked me to stay, his hospitality, and his support these past days. Everything that's happened makes it blatantly clear that I'm a fool if I think that a friendship with this boy holding my hand is all I can ever have. That is not enough.

I want more from him. Much more.

Maybe it's wrong of me to give in to these feelings. I just came out of a long and toxic relationship and I'm still recovering from its aftermath. This is the worst time to explore these emotions. But they're hard to ignore now I know there's a slim chance that he feels the same way.

Apolo moves closer and I hold my breath. He stops when we're nose to nose. The gap between us is small and his scent—one of expensive cologne and whiskey—is strong.

"That wasn't just a hug, Xan. You know that, don't you?"

I don't answer. The hand that was holding mine moves to my face and gently strokes my cheek.

Friends don't touch each other like this. They don't share this intimacy. And they don't stare at each other this way. His thumb lightly rubs the corner of my mouth and I try to keep my breathing under control. His touch is soft, and so different from everything I've experienced these past months. It's not right to compare. And it's wrong of me to indulge in this respite—this touch and this closeness. Nevertheless, I'm powerless, unable to resist when his face is mere inches away from mine.

I close the gap and press my mouth to his. A whimper escapes my lips at the sensation. This is all the encouragement that Apolo needs and his mouth becomes desperate and demanding. He kisses me with the intensity of someone who has been holding back for too long and whose need has reached its breaking point. Our kiss gets wetter and hurried. It's the type that takes your breath away. I can't stop. Then he inserts his tongue in my mouth and I welcome the invasion, wondering what he would feel like inside me.

He pulls away and our ragged breaths mingle. We make eye contact for a quick second and kiss again. This time our lips meet with more urgency and desire. I feel like we are entering a silent pact to let go of our inhibitions. I act on instinct and press my body against his. I get hard after a few hungry kisses, and he is affected in the same way. Soft moans escape our lips when the physical evidence of our arousal makes contact.

"Xan." He pants and murmurs my name against my lips.

I keep kissing him and shudder when his fingers lightly touch my waist as they slide down to my ass. He squeezes one buttock while pressing his erection to mine. This is getting out of control. Apolo pulls his mouth from mine. He moves his lips to my neck where he plants clumsy and fevered kisses, licking and sucking passionately. He pants as he rocks his hips back and forth, rubbing his hard member against mine over our clothes.

This change from the boy who is often hesitant and self-controlled is a turn-on. I'm aroused by the thought that I may be the cause of his undoing. And that his desire for me and me alone is the sole thing occupying his mind at this moment. I wonder if it was the same for him as it was for me. Did he feel this attraction from the very beginning? His passion is consuming and overpowering; it certainly doesn't feel like it is sudden and brand-new.

I reach down to undo the fly of his jeans, feeling impatient. He grabs my wrist and stops me. He takes his face off my neck and looks at me.

"Xan, if you touch me—"

I understand what his eyes are silently conveying. If I touch him, there will be no turning back. We can have some control over our urges while fully clothed, but it'll be a different story once we make skin-to-skin contact. I doubt we'll be able to stop ourselves from unraveling. And truth be told, I want to feel him inside me right now. I want to forget and let go. I want to lose myself in these emotions and let my senses take over my mind and body.

I look into his eyes while I unbutton his jeans. He watches me intently.

"Are you sure?" he asks, sounding out of breath.

"Yes."

I slip my hand inside his jeans. Apolo closes his eyes and lets out a low groan. I take his member in my hand and stroke it slowly. We kiss again and I swallow his moans into my mouth. He moves the hand that was on my ass to my waist. He removes my pants in one rough pull, nearly tearing the fabric. My underwear gets the same treatment. Once he frees my erection, I use it to rub and masturbate his. The sensation is intense.

We continue to touch, rub, and French kiss until we reach a lustful frenzy and are reduced to a whimpering and wet mess. Apolo bites my lip and pulls away.

"Turn around."

His words send a shudder down my spine. I know what comes next and I want it badly. I obey, turn around, and expose my naked back to his gaze. His fingers tentatively circle and graze the rim of my entrance. Apolo lubricates his fingers with saliva in preparation. He begins by inserting one finger to get me ready and the intrusion is uncomfortable at first. However, the slight sting feels familiar and goes away once my body adjusts to the sensation. I'm surprised by how skilled he is. On top of not being straight, it's obvious that he's also slept with other guys. And here I thought I would be his first, though I don't mind who and what he's done before me. At this moment, what I care about is how amazing all of this feels. Apolo licks my ear as he strokes my erection with his hand and adds a second finger to his penetration. I'm out of breath, struggling to cope with all the stimulation.

"You have no idea how much I wanted this to—" I blurt between gasps.

"Really? You wanted me?" The tone of his voice is flushed with desire.

"Yes, so, so much."

He runs his tongue over my neck.

"I've fantasized about you too," he admits as he keeps stimulating me with his fingers. "I've fantasized about doing things . . . to you."

He pulls his fingers out and I hear the sound of plastic tearing. He's opened a condom wrapper. This is really happening. Then I feel the head of his member teasing my entrance. I can't wait any longer so I pull my buttocks apart and wait. Apolo rubs the hardened tip against my hole, then grabs me by the hips and moves forward. He slowly eases himself inch by inch inside despite my initial resistance. I roll my eyes backward and break into desperate moans. This is just the beginning, and I feel like I'm on the edge of my release.

Apolo delivers one final thrust and fully sheaths himself inside me. Then he starts to move in and out at a furious pace that brings me pleasure.

"Xan." He moans my name in my ear over and over again, working me into a frenzy.

The hand that was holding me by the hip moves to my groin and jerks me off in sync with his punishing thrusts. I feel full, and every nerve ending in my body is throbbing. He has turned me into a quivering mess of liquid pleasure and lust.

His movements become clumsy, unrelenting, and desperate. I can feel that he's getting close, just like me. The desire we secretly had for each other is too great. I place my hand on his and help him speed up the strokes. I want us to climax at the same time. That's when everything spirals out of control. We are already reduced to a bundle of moans and grunts when I feel the throb before his release. I amp up the intensity of our hand strokes and come at the same time, panting heavily. Apolo lies very still, resting his forehead against the back of my neck. His ragged breath tickles my skin. And I feel my heart beating a tattoo inside my chest.

That was incredible.

My mouth is dry from all the moaning and whimpering. I run my tongue over my lips, trying but failing to produce more saliva.

Apolo leaves my body, moves off the bed, and quietly heads to the bathroom. I'm speechless and as shocked as he is. I listen to the sound of the water running. I lie on my back with my eyes fixed on the ceiling, still processing what just happened. The wet, sticky drops on my lower abdomen serve as reminders of what we just did. I just had sex with Apolo Hidalgo. So what happens now?

Twenty-eight

APOLO

What have you done, Apolo?

I lower my head as the water drizzles over me, dripping from the tips of my hair. Even the cold shower fails to turn down the heat coursing through my veins. I needed to get out of that bed. I wanted to keep fucking, even when I had already found my release.

I had to clear my mind and get this lust under control. Who am I? And what have I become? I always thought I had more self-restraint, but tonight I couldn't stop. I managed to pull back when I was with Rain. Why is it different with Xan? I don't even know what this thing between us means. I'm not the type of person who has sex without having a heart-to-heart or figuring out where I stand.

It's obvious that I like him. From the very beginning, I found Xan and his rosy blush endearing. I didn't make a move at first because Rain and Vance were in the way. And now that they're no longer in the picture, my attraction has taken a feverish turn. Since he moved in, our friendship and rapport has evolved. There are times when I've found myself paying close attention to him, noticing little things.

Now that we've been intimate, I realize that everything about the boy with the blue hair drives me wild. His smell, his skin, his moans, and how it feels to be inside him. But this attraction isn't purely physical. Xan and I enjoy each other's company; we share a friendship and a connection.

After putting on a pair of pajama bottoms, I exit the bathroom. Xan is already dressed. I feel the need to say something, but I can't find the right words. He avoids my gaze and walks past me, heading to the bathroom.

Well, that was awkward. But what did I expect? We went from budding friendship to unrestrained passion right there on that bed.

I decide to get a glass of water from the kitchen and find Greg pouring himself a glass of orange juice.

"Did you just come home?" I ask, and he shakes his head, holding back a smile. "What?"

I open the refrigerator and its bluish light briefly brightens the kitchen. Gregory leans against the island and folds his arms across his chest.

"It finally happened, huh?"

I give him a puzzled look and play dumb. "What do you mean?"

"The walls are thin in this apartment, Apolo. You can hear almost everything."

You've got to be kidding me.

"I have no idea what you're talking about."

Greg smiles and pats me on the shoulder. "It was about time. The tension was palpable."

Then I hear the door to my bedroom. My eyes open wide, and I immediately turn to him with apprehension. "Not a word out of you, Gregory."

"Relax." He takes a sip of his juice. "Your secret is safe with me. Although I must confess, this is unexpected. I thought Rain was going to be the one."

"It's complicated."

"I see."

Xan walks in, wringing his hands in front of him.

"I came to get water," he informs us, heading to the refrigerator.

Greg looks at me. "I bet. One can get dehydrated after . . . exercising."

Xan ignores the insinuation and remains quiet. He drinks from his glass as he watches Gregory and me.

My crazy friend opens his mouth, yet again. "Xan, I talked to my family lawyer about what you told me. Since you covered seventy percent of the down payment, you own the larger share of the property and have the option to buy Vance out."

"Can I still do it if he refuses to sell?" Xan asks.

I'm attentive. I had no idea that Xan asked Gregory for his advice.

"Ideally, it would be best if you both could reach an agreement. A legal battle for sole ownership could be lengthy, and may cost you a pretty penny."

Xan sighs.

"I didn't know that Vance was part owner of Café Nora," I say.

He nods, but avoids my gaze.

"Yes, he is. My mother helped me out with her savings, but it wasn't enough. Since the café is close to the university campus and in a prime location, the price was more than what we'd estimated—"

"So Vance helped you out," I finish for him.

Of course that jerk helped him. It was just another way to exert his power over Xan. He knew how much it meant to Xan to open his own coffee shop. It's everything Xan ever wanted and needed in his life. It's his dream. And in the words of my grandpa, it's also his safe place.

"I don't know where you two have left things, Xan." Greg intervenes. "Honestly, if he were to refuse your offer, a legal fight would be long and very expensive. Your best option is to negotiate and reach an amicable agreement."

"And what if I sell?"

I narrow my eyes. "Xan," I protest but he ignores me.

"Let's say I sell and give him thirty percent of the profits. That would conclude our partnership, correct?"

Greg scrunches up his face, thinking. "Sure, that's another option. However, from what you told me, Café Nora is quite profitable and it's in a prime location. A retail coffee space nearby a college campus is always profitable, so they're always in demand and easy to rent. I doubt you could find anything quite like it anywhere else."

Xan's expression becomes duller. "I know."

Greg and I exchange a glance. I wave my hand at him, gesturing to let Xan be.

"Fine. It's your decision, Xan." Greg pats him on the back, then heads to his bedroom, leaving us alone in the kitchen.

The silence is uneasy and awkward. Xan avoids my gaze at all costs. And I don't know what to say. It's hard to believe that only a little while ago we were having sex. I tense up when I think about our encounter, so I try to push the memory out of my head. I need to think clearly and forget about the pleasure I experienced in his arms.

I circle around the island and approach him with a great deal of caution. It's hard to keep my urges under control when Xan is too close, so I make sure to keep a safe distance between us. I stop and face him. His eyes meet mine briefly, then he lowers his gaze to my chest.

"Xan."

"It's late, we should turn in. Good night, Apolo."

He walks past me to the bedroom.

I turn around, lean forward on the counter, and close my eyes. I want to stop him, talk to him, try to reason with him and sort out this thing that happened between us. But I also don't want to be pushy and force him to talk when he's not ready. So I keep these questions to myself and join him in the bedroom.

I find Xan already tucked under the sheets. He's covered from head to toe. I get into bed and let him be. At first I struggle to fall asleep in the same bed where we pleasured each other earlier, but eventually I manage to doze off.

"Earth to Apolo!"

Erica waves her hand in front of my face.

"I'm sorry," I respond, pulling myself out of my daze.

The picnic table on the university lawn is in the same spot we set up during the fall festival. The same place where I hit Vance back when I wasn't privy to the full truth. At the time, I was still figuring out my feelings toward Rain and trying to protect Xan. But I was also lying to myself, making up silly excuses to justify my attraction to him.

Xan is not the first boy I've slept with. Last year, Daniela invited me to a college party where she introduced me to my first. She knew I wanted to explore and served as my guide. To be honest, she probably knew what I wanted and needed before I did. The fling with that boy was nothing serious, but it opened a door to those who came after.

Then I met Rain, who led me to Xan. In the beginning, I suppressed what I felt anytime I looked at him. I made up excuses in order to avoid admitting my true feelings, but I can no longer do that. Our night together was proof that letting an attraction build up over time eventually leads to an explosive unraveling. I have rarely let myself get carried away like I did last night.

"Are we going to finish the assignment or what?" Erica asks, sounding worried.

I don't blame her. We both want to leave school for our Thanksgiving break without any assignments hanging over our heads.

"Of course. I'm sorry. A lot has happened lately."

She looks at me with an arched brow. "Is it Rain?"

"Something like that."

"Something like that?"

I take a deep breath and let out a long exhale. "I did something I shouldn't have. Something that was out of character for me."

Erica lifts her eyebrows even more. "Apolo, we're friends, so you don't have to beat around the bush. Okay?"

"It's about Xan."

She gestures for me to carry on.

"Xan is crashing at our apartment."

"I know," she says matter-of-factly, so now it's my turn to look at her with a frown.

"And how do you know that?" I ask.

Erica looks away and clears her throat. "We were talking about *you.*"

"Last night . . . we did it," I murmur, sounding slightly mortified.

"Did what?" It takes her a few seconds to process. "Oh . . . ooh . . . *ooh!*"

"Yes," I repeat, because she looks baffled. My cheeks feel warm.

"That was . . . unexpected," she whispers.

"I know."

"And your head is in the clouds because . . . ?"

"Because Xan is brushing me off. I understand that he's going through a really tough time right now. Still, I'm not the kind of guy who screws someone and moves on. As much as I try, I need to know what this means to him. Was it a one-night stand or does he want something more with me?"

Erica exhales and shakes her head. "Why are you so intense, Apolo?"

"I don't know!" I exclaim, running my hand through my hair. "I don't want to put any pressure on him because it's the last thing he needs right now, but—"

"It's eating you up."

"Exactly. It hasn't even been twenty-four hours, Erica. Literally. It just happened last night."

"First, you need to relax a little. Okay? You slept together once, Apolo. It wasn't a marriage proposal. It happened, you enjoyed it, and that's great. Not everything needs a label or has to have deep meaning. And I get the type of person you are. But you also need to think about Xan. I'm sure you'll have this conversation when you're both ready and feel comfortable."

"And in the meantime, what do I do? Should I act normal, as if nothing happened?"

"I suppose."

"Erica, I can't look him in the face without thinking about . . . you know, everything that's happened and what I want to—"

"Do you want it to happen again?" I nod. "And have you tried anything?"

"No, no, of course not. I don't even know why it happened the first time. I don't think I can handle it if it becomes a pattern without figuring out what we mean to each other."

"Apolo." She reaches across the table and takes my hand. "Don't make things more complicated than they have to be. Breathe, for god's sake."

I exhale then place my hands on the back of my neck and stretch a little.

"Fine, I'll relax." Erica narrows her eyes. "I promise."

"Maybe Xan isn't ready for an intense discussion at this moment, Apolo. What if he just wants to feel something with you and that's all? And if you really want a repeat of what happened, then flirt with him. Words are not the only tools for seduction at our disposal. Our bodies"—she moves her eyebrows up and down suggestively—"they can be used to communicate our desires in more creative ways."

"I'm not sure. Anyway, while we're on the topic, how did you find out about Xan? Are you talking to Greg again?"

Her expression changes and she looks weary. "We're back to being friends."

"Greg and you?"

"That's right. He begged me and I decided to leave what happened in the past, move forward, and accept his friendship."

I remember Kelly leaving the apartment. Is Gregory getting his hopes up? Is this the reason why he broke up with Kelly? Does he think he can win Erica back?

"You know that he still has feelings for you, right?"

She nods. "This is his punishment." Her voice sounds weary and melancholic. "To have me as a friend and be near me but not in the way he wants."

"Erica."

"I know, it's cruel. But this is what he deserves after what he put me through. He broke me like no one else had ever done in my life, Apolo. Imagine loving someone with all your heart only to have this person leave you for someone without any warning or any explanation. Suddenly, you're forced to see him with her popping up everywhere you go, and all over your social feeds, showing no remorse or regret. I was the laughing stock of campus. So, yes, he deserves to endure this torture for a little while."

"Do you think you'll ever be able to forgive him?" I ask. Personally, I believe that true forgiveness means letting go. However, there are wounds that take a long time to heal.

"I've already forgiven him." She smiles at me and I know she's being sincere. "That doesn't mean I still love him. Or that I don't love myself enough and would get back with someone who didn't value and respect me enough the first time we were together."

"I feel bad for him," I admit. "I know it's not my place, but he figured out that you are the one he loves, even though it was too late. And he does love you, Erica."

"I know."

"Ah. And here I was thinking that college would be less complicated than high school."

"Dream on, buddy. Now let's finish this up so you can head home and make out with Xan."

I laugh with her, and give the assignment my full attention.

Still, every now and then my mind wanders. I think about all the different ways I can try to get closer to Xan when I see him again. Then I shake away these thoughts. Maybe he's not interested in a second round and what happened last night was a onetime thing. I'm saddened by the possibility, because I do want more from Xan.

Much more.

Twenty-nine

APOLO

Nothing happens.

Xan is very good at avoiding the subject. And just like I promised Erica, I try my best to play it cool, which is the total opposite of my usual self. But I have a gut feeling that if I don't bring it up soon, he won't ever. How long can we go on living like this? Pretending we didn't have sex a week ago? Ever since, the atmosphere before bedtime has been awkward. We both do our best to ignore the tension and leave the matter alone. To be honest, the situation is complete torture.

Am I the only one who can't stop thinking about that night?

It's the week of Thanksgiving break already. Tomorrow is Wednesday so I'll be heading home to have Thursday dinner with my family. I'll go shopping on Black Friday, and head to the lake on Saturday. I won't be back to the apartment until Sunday. I'm eager to go home and spend time with my family. However, I can't bear the thought of going away before I have an honest conversation with Xan. I don't want to spend my holiday obsessing over him. I hate it when I can't fully partake in special moments with my family because my mind happens to be somewhere else.

So I've decided that tonight is the night we're going to have our talk. To be fair, I've given him enough time and space. I have acted as normal as possible around him. But I have my limits.

I feel confident and determined after my shower, and head to the kitchen. I didn't think a bare torso is the most conducive look for a serious conversation so I'm fully clothed, wearing pajama bottoms and a T-shirt. Xan stands over the stove, his back to me. There's a pot on one of the burners and he stirs its contents with a spoon. I clear my throat and he turns, bringing the spoon to his mouth for a taste of what he's cooking. It smells like pasta sauce.

"It's almost ready," he informs me before turning his attention back to the pot, adding salt and pepper to the mix.

I sit on one of the chairs next to the island. I rest my elbows on the counter and watch him work. The blue of his hair looks more radiant. His hair is growing fast and no longer shows the black roots of a few weeks ago. He must have dyed it recently. Maybe today?

"What made you pick the color blue?" The question rolls out without thinking, and I kick myself. We're supposed to be having a serious discussion and not make small talk like we've done these past few days.

"My mother had beautiful blue eyes." There's a tinge of longing in his voice. He turns to look at me as he washes his hands in the sink. "As you can see, I didn't get that from her."

"You don't need to. Your brown eyes are very pretty."

"Thank you," he replies, looking down at the sink.

And there it is. The fucking tension that's consuming us. This torture is unbearable.

"Xan."

"Do you want me to serve now? You must be hungry."

My gaze follows him as he moves around the kitchen. He sets plates of spaghetti and tomato sauce sprinkled with cheese on the kitchen island.

"With extra cheese, just the way you like it."

"Thank you," I reply, with a forced smile. The last thing I want to do right now is eat.

I use the fork to wind up the spaghetti, but I can barely eat a bite. So I get up from my chair and circle the kitchen island. I'm leaving tomorrow and can't afford to waste any more time. I stand in front of Xan and catch him off guard. He's startled and takes a step back.

"Do you need anything else? Water?"

"Xan, we can't go on like this. Sooner or later, we have to talk about it."

He removes his apron. "It's late. You should finish your dinner. I'm going to bed."

I gently grab him by the wrist, trying to stop him. He doesn't turn around and stands sideways, staring in the direction of the hallway.

"Xan."

He faces me. We're silent for a moment. My hand around his wrist serves as the only physical connection between us. Maybe it's just my imagination, but I can almost feel the throb of his pulse. I don't know exactly where to begin. I need to choose my words carefully because I fear that whatever comes out of my mouth next will determine the course of this conversation. I've been obsessing over getting everything out in the open, but perhaps I rushed into something I'm not ready to tackle.

"Xan, what happened—"

I stop midsentence when Xan leans in for a kiss. He cradles my face with his hands and urgently moves his mouth over mine. I'm stunned and lose my focus. The taste of him and the familiarity of his kisses are all-consuming. They swallow the words I was about to say, making me respond with the same passion and urgency. I encircle him in my arms and gently press him against me. This guy is undeniably a great kisser. It only takes one kiss from him to turn me on and put my head in a daze. The last thing on my mind right now is talking. All I want is a repeat of the night we spent in each other's arms.

When his back makes contact with the edge of the island, I peel my mouth off his. I crouch down and wrap my arms around the back of his knees. I lift him up and put him on the counter. Then I wedge myself between his legs. I resume our kiss and slip my fingers inside his shirt, hoping to make contact with his skin. I caress his waist, his back, every inch of him that I can reach. We work ourselves into a heated frenzy of wet kisses and ragged breaths.

"Xan," I murmur against his lips, experiencing a brief moment of lucidity. "This was not what . . . what . . ."

"I know." He bites my lip and whispers, "We don't have to talk, Apolo." And we lock lips again. Our tongues brush and tease each other, then he pulls away momentarily. "We just need to feel."

"Oh, trust me. There's nothing that I would rather do than feel all of you one more time, Xan. But—"

I become stiff and let out a gasp when I feel the touch of his hand over the fabric of my pajama pants. He caresses and kisses me at the same time. This is definitely leading to sex. If I let lust lead the way, I'll spend my Thanksgiving break agonizing over all these unanswered questions.

I fight my urges and pull away from his arms. I take a step back while Xan remains seated on the counter. His shirt is rumpled and the rosy blush on his cheeks is deeper than ever. My breathing is labored, causing my chest to rise and fall rapidly. I don't have to look down to confirm that a specific part of my anatomy, encouraged by our make-out session, has grown in size.

"I can't, Xan. I'm a very intense person," I tell him, out of breath. "I know. I know. But I'm not the type of guy who sleeps around."

Xan uses his hands to push himself off the island, then leans forward and plants a kiss on my lips. I wish I could hold back but I can't resist him. The part of me that would rather feel than overanalyze takes over, desperately wanting to be with him one more time. The past few days have been sheer torture. I've shared a bed with him, and during the entire time I've reminisced about our night together and hoped for another chance.

"We'll talk. I promise," he whispers against my lips. "Not now, Apolo. Please."

He stops kissing my mouth and his lips trail down my neck. Xan ends up on his knees right in front of me. And when I see him in this position, my erection jumps with excitement. He pulls down my pants, freeing my hard member from its confines. Xan doesn't waste any time and licks it from base to head before taking it completely into his mouth. I stifle a sound that's half moan and half grunt. This is likely to be a repeat of our first time. This is going to be fast; he's too damn good at this and I doubt I can hold back.

"Xan." I groan and gently tug at his blue hair.

I make the mistake of looking down at him. Our eyes meet as he sucks, licks, and takes the entire length deeper into his mouth.

"Xan . . . I'm going to . . . You have to . . ."

But Xan has no plans to stop. Instead, he increases the speed, and his mouth becomes more aggressive. And that's all that's needed to make me explode. I close my eyes and throw my head back. I moan and pump my hips forward, pushing inside his warm, wet mouth.

The tension that had built up in my lower abdomen rushes down to my shaft, making it jerk as I come. My shoulders rise and fall with each breath I take. When I open my eyes, Xan is licking his lips as he stands in front of me.

"I wanted to do that so badly," he admits with a playful smile. "Since the first day I saw you."

I arch an eyebrow. "You're not as innocent as you look, Xan."

"Says the boy who just came in my mouth."

I smile at him sheepishly. He takes a step back when I inch closer. I want to touch him and return the favor.

"No, that's enough for today," he says.

"Are you serious?"

"Yes, very serious." He puts his arms around my neck with an ease and familiarity that I enjoy very much. "Now, what was it that you wanted to talk about, Apolo?"

I look into his eyes and brush a strand of hair from his face. His eyes are beautiful and the perfect shade.

"Can I have a minute? I'm waiting for the blood to flow back to my brain."

Xan explodes in laughter and plants a kiss on my mouth. I don't mind the taste of myself on his lips. When we part, I give him a peck on the nose and stroke his cheek.

"What are we doing, Xan?" I ask in a hushed tone.

Everything about this moment is perfection. The soft light in the kitchen, the food on the kitchen island, and this boy in my arms who looks secure, happy, and at peace. I have never seen Xan this way. He never glowed or looked this relaxed when he was with Vance.

"I don't know, Apolo," he says frankly. "But it feels good."

"Are you attracted to me?" I have to ask.

Xan snorts. "Do you think I would give someone I didn't like a blow job?"

"Xan."

"Okay. Yes, I like you very much, Apolo." He gives me a quick kiss. "I thought it would be crystal clear by now."

"Xan, I don't just fuck—"

"For the sake of fucking. I know." He sighs. "I understand it may be too much to ask for you go with the flow. To share something without labels or expectations. But I just got out of a relationship, Apolo. I would be lying if I said I'm ready to jump into something serious. I still have a lot to work out and need time to heal."

"I'm not good at going with the flow, Xan."

"I know. And I don't expect you to change for me. Maybe it's best if we use this moment as a good-bye of sorts." I narrow my eyes and he pulls away. "We can still be friends, Apolo. If that's what you want."

"And that's it?" I look at him with disbelief. "We could be together as long as we're not serious. But if that doesn't work for me, then I have the option of just being friends. Is that right?"

"I'm sorry. I can't promise the impossible at the moment. I'm not ready for another serious relationship."

"But you're okay with kissing me and letting me come in your mouth?"

Xan is visibly hurt. He didn't expect to hear this from me. But I'm definitely pissed. When I came into the kitchen it was my intention to talk. I'm not interested in a hookup if all he wants is to have some fun. I don't know what else to say. I run my hand over my face, conflicted.

I play back in my head all the times I have been told to stop taking everything so seriously, to enjoy my life and revel in my youth. I try to picture what a friendship with Xan would be like. I couldn't stand not being able to kiss, touch, or feel him ever again. So I make a decision that goes against my core principles. The one thing I need most right now is to hold him in my arms.

"Fine," I reply, raising my hands in defeat.

Xan tilts his head to one side, looking slightly puzzled. "You're willing to go along with it?"

I walk up to him and cradle his face in my hands. "Let's go with the flow."

Xan smiles at me, then puts his lips on mine.

Thirty

XAN

This is a terrible idea.

I stand outside, facing the imposing Hidalgo mansion. When Apolo asked me to spend Thanksgiving at his house, it sounded like a great plan. But now that I'm here, I'm doubting my decision. Shortly after I suggested we should go with the flow, he brings me to his family home. I have a feeling that Apolo's version of taking things slow is very different from mine.

He at least promised that he would introduce me as a friend and that we would behave ourselves during this visit. I accepted his invitation mostly because I didn't want to stay in the apartment all alone. I've never been on my own during this holiday weekend, and used to spend it with Vance doing a bunch of silly things to pass the time.

Maybe I can use this visit as a distraction.

It's already dark. I feel bad about showing up at his family's place this late. I don't know why, but I have this image in my head of the Hidalgos as a serious and intimidating bunch. Probably because all I've learned from watching the news is that they're very wealthy and their company keeps expanding across the country.

"Come on in." Apolo leads the way into a spacious entry hall. It leads to a living room with a stairway on one side. The interior is illuminated beautifully and looks impeccable. It really is a gorgeous house. A very pretty woman comes out of one of the hallways. She has messy red hair that falls around her face. She wears leggings paired with a sweater in a dark color that is roomy and comes down to just below her thighs.

"Apolo." She greets us with a smile and I stare at her. "And you must be Xan. I'm Claudia."

She offers me her hand and I shake it gently.

"Nice to meet you."

From the same hallway enters a tall young man with a beard, dressed in a casual shirt and pants. There's a natural elegance about him. He stands next to Claudia and holds out his hand to greet me.

"Artemis Hidalgo."

"Xan." I don't know why, but I hesitate about whether I should add my last name. "Just Xan."

He nods and I swallow hard. There's something about this man. Despite his young age, he has a very intimidating presence.

"Welcome to our home," says Claudia.

"This is the first time Apolo has brought a friend to stay at the house," Artemis adds, looking at me as if he suspects something is going on. Or maybe it's just my nerves and I'm being paranoid.

Apolo and Artemis exchange intense looks. I don't know what it means. Sibling dynamics, I guess.

"Ah, lucky me," I reply, trying to sound nonchalant.

"I love your hair," Claudia adds.

"Thank you."

"Grandpa and my mom are already sitting at the table," Claudia explains to Apolo. "The others should be here any minute."

What does she mean by others?

"You must be hungry," Claudia continues. "Why don't you go upstairs and put your things away?" She speaks to Apolo. "I put you both in your bedroom since you told me you share a room in your apartment. I thought it wouldn't be a problem. If it is, I can fix up the guest room."

"No, we're fine sharing," I reassure her. "The last thing I want is to inconvenience you any further."

Artemis looks at me again and I swear something is clicking in his head.

"You two share a bedroom?" He sounds like he's fishing for information.

"Artemis." The serious tone in Apolo's voice is one I have not heard before. Artemis responds with a smile.

"Go get settled, we'll see you in a little while."

They step aside so we can climb the stairs.

Pictures of the Hidalgo family members hang on each wall along the hallway of the second floor. There are several portraits of people I assume must be Apolo's mother and father. There's one of the three children with their parents. They are all well dressed and look very elegant—they certainly were blessed with good genes. I stop in front of a portrait of Mrs. Hidalgo. She has gorgeous blue eyes that remind me of my mother's. As far as I can tell, only the middle son has inherited this trait. Apolo has told me a lot about him.

"Your mother is very beautiful," I say with sincerity.

Apolo purses his lips and doesn't reply. Did I say something wrong? It was just a compliment.

Apolo's bedroom is as organized as the one in the apartment. I'm a little surprised. As much as Vance would sometimes obsess about cleanliness, his room was never this tidy. I'd like to say I don't think about him or the life I had with him, because he surely doesn't deserve my consideration, but it would be a lie. We were together for years and there are nights when I still miss him. And moments when I entertain the thought that perhaps this time he will change for good and that my absence is the push he needs to make an honest effort. Even so, thanks to Apolo, I'm getting stronger and more confident. He may not realize how much his support means to me. Every time I look into his brown eyes, I'm reassured by the affection I see in them, which reminds me that I deserve more in this world; so much more than Vance.

During my time with Apolo I've experienced new and unfamiliar feelings. In his arms I feel safe, cherished, and protected. Maybe jumping into someone else's arms while I'm still processing what happened with Vance is the opposite of healthy, however, honestly speaking, I couldn't have stayed away from Vance if it wasn't for Apolo. He's my rock. I know he deserves much more from me, but this is all I can offer right now.

I'm browsing through the contents of a small bookshelf when I feel him standing behind me. He wraps me in his arms and places a kiss on the nape of my neck.

"Hey," I scold him in a playful tone. "You promised you would behave."

"Not when we're alone."

I turn around in his arms and grab that face that I like so much. "They're expecting us downstairs."

Apolo pulls me closer and kisses me. The contact is brief and gentle. Still, it makes my nerves tingle and awakens my senses. Sometimes I have a hard time believing that this is really happening; that I'm kissing this guy, whom I've found attractive since day one. I push away from him and take his hand, leading the way.

"Let's go."

Thirty-one

APOLO

I'm glad to see Xan relax as the evening progresses.

I wasn't completely sure this was a good idea. After all, bringing him to stay at my family's house isn't very "go with the flow." So it's reassuring to see him fit in. He's sitting next to me and Grandpa is asking him a million questions.

The doorbell rings, and Artemis goes to answer it. A few seconds later, we hear a cacophony of female voices growing closer.

I stand and step away from the table, flushed with excitement.

I see her coming out of the hallway, her face beaming the second her eyes land on me.

"Lollo!"

Dani sprints and jumps on me, wrapping her arms and legs around my neck and waist. We spin around for a few seconds. She buries her face in my neck and murmurs how much she's missed me. When I place her on her feet, I notice her haircut.

"Did you have an existential crisis?" I touch a lock of hair, the tips now reaching just to her chin.

Dani gives me one of her signature wide and playful smiles. "Always," she replies, before planting a kiss on my mouth.

The kiss is friendly and platonic. She and I are very close, and my family is used to seeing us show affection for each other this way. But this is completely new to Xan, and I have a feeling that this innocent gesture will bite me in the ass later.

Raquel makes her entrance with Artemis following closely behind. The moment she sees me, she hurries to my side and pushes Dani out of the way.

"My turn." Raquel hugs me. "It's good to see you, Lollo!"

"Likewise." I look at everyone, "I never expected I would miss these two crazy girls so much."

Grandpa, Claudia, and Artemis are all smiles when they greet the girls. I return to my seat. Xan doesn't look at me. Instead, he concentrates on the tea he's drinking.

"Raquel, do you know what's going on with Ares?" Artemis asks with concern.

"Yes." She waves with her phone in hand. "His flight was delayed an hour, but he should be landing very soon."

"I told him that it was best to fly out yesterday." Artemis shakes his head. "Traveling the day before Thanksgiving is always a mess."

"I told him the same thing." Raquel shrugs. "But you know how he is."

Dani and Raquel turn to stare at Xan. They have a look of expectation, and I realize my carelessness.

"Oh, this is Xan. He's a friend from university." I extend my hand, gesturing a formal introduction. "Xan, this is Raquel. She's Ares's girlfriend. And this is Dani, a friend."

"Nice to meet you."

The girls sit down. Dani takes the chair next to me, and her eyes land on Xan on my other side. Her plump, wet lips curl into a mischievous grin.

"Dani . . ." I mutter under my breath, warning her.

"What?" she replies, playing dumb.

"It's not what you think."

"I didn't say anything," she whispers. But I know her as well as she knows me.

After our meal is over, Claudia and Artemis say their good-nights and take a sleeping Hera to bed. The little girl fell asleep a while ago in the arms of Claudia's mom. Grandpa also takes his leave, leaving Dani, Raquel, Xan, and me on our own. We decide to hang out by the pool, and light the firepit to keep us warm. Xan excuses himself to go to the washroom, and I prepare myself for the onslaught of questions these two are surely about to lay on me.

"Don't even—"

"He's really cute!" Dani blurts out straightaway.

"Is this the guy you were waiting for that evening?" Raquel asks, her eyes sparkling with curiosity.

I let out a sigh.

"Stop it, both of you. Please don't make this awkward for him."

Dani observes me closely and gasps. She acts as if she's been hit with the sudden realization of a mind-blowing fact.

"You've done the deed."

I immediately turn red and say nothing. Raquel's jaw drops; she looks surprised.

"Really? Wow, the last time we talked it didn't sound like anything would ever happen between you two."

"And nothing happened."

"Apolo . . . lying to us—really?" Dani shakes her head.

I let out another sigh.

"Fine, but not a word from either of you."

Raquel zips her lips with her fingers.

"I promise."

They eagerly wait for me to elaborate.

"Yes." I come clean. "Something did happen. And we agreed to go with the flow."

They look at me with their eyes narrowed.

"Apolo Hidalgo going with flow?" Dani seems surprised. "I didn't expect that, but good for you. You've finally stopped living the life of an eighty-year-old."

"Dani," Raquel scolds her, then turns her gaze on me. "How was it? Amazing? Do you like him a lot?"

"It was—" I remember the night he went down on me. "It was great."

"And you're head over heels, aren't you?" says Dani, teasing me.

"No, we're keeping things casual."

Dani rubs her hands together. "Let me guess, the casual approach was his idea, not yours. Correct?"

"It doesn't matter."

"Apolo," she presses.

"Really. I'm fine with this arrangement."

They both exchange a knowing look, and it's Raquel who breaks the silence.

"Are you sure, Apolo?"

"Yes."

"Well," says Dani, "if it's going to be casual, you need to

protect your heart, Apolo. We don't want to see you get hurt."

I give them a weary look. "I'm not a kid who needs to be sheltered anymore, okay? I can have sex without complications."

Raquel makes a grimace.

"Sure. That's exactly what your brother used to say. And now look at him."

"It's not the same thing."

Xan returns and we stop talking, which is a big mistake. Our abrupt silence makes it obvious we were talking about him.

"So, Xan," Dani starts, and I watch her intently. "Apolo told us that you operate a café close to campus."

"That's right. You're both welcome to drop by anytime."

"Oh, thank you. When we visit him, we will make sure to pop in," Raquel answers. "Anyway, since Apolo isn't very good at sharing, we would like to use this opportunity to get some information from you. How is Lollo doing at school? Does he have any friends?"

"Raquel," I protest, feeling embarrassed. "You sound just like my mother."

She gives me a big smile as Xan jumps on the let's-tease-Apolo bandwagon. "Other than Gregory, I haven't seen him hanging out with anyone—well, except for . . ." His eyes search mine and he hesitates for a second. "Except for Rain."

"Oh yeah. Rain." Raquel recognizes the name. I stare at her with great intensity, hoping to convey without words that I need her to keep what she knows to herself.

"Do you know who she is?" Xan asks. "I guess Apolo told you about her."

Raquel chokes on her drink and coughs.

She's never been a very good liar. I don't know what made me think she could give a simple answer. It doesn't matter, though, because Xan drops the subject and moves on.

We pass the time talking about our experiences at school. Raquel compares the courses she took in her first year of psychology with the ones I'm taking and gives me some advice. Dani and Xan talk about the festivals held all over downtown Raleigh during the month of December.

The girls decide to turn in at midnight. They want to get a good amount of sleep to be in top form for tomorrow's festivities.

Xan is quieter than usual when we make it back to my bedroom. We lie down and he turns his back to me, pulling the covers up all the way to his neck.

"Are you all right?" I ask, sensing that something is wrong.

"All good."

"Xan."

He sighs and turns over, lying on his back with his eyes fixed on the ceiling. "I don't think this was a good idea."

"This what?"

"Me, coming here with you."

Although his words hurt, I do my best to remain calm. "Why?"

"I don't know. It's a lot . . . all of it. It's too much."

"I don't understand."

"I know, and I'm sorry, Apolo. You meant well. You didn't want me to be alone, but I feel out of place."

"Do you feel uncomfortable around my family?"

"No, of course not. They're all great. It's me. I'm the problem."
He sighs. "I'm sorry, but I'm a mess."

"But you're not."

Xan turns and faces me. Slowly, he inches closer until his forehead rests against mine.

"I know we promised we wouldn't do anything under your family's roof," he whispers against my lips. "But I need to—"

I kiss him before he can finish that sentence. The comfort we find in each other's bodies always helps drive away concerns. Yes, it's a Band-Aid solution, but it's fulfilling and soothing. I hold him tightly as our kisses turn fevered and more demanding.

"Xan," I say breathlessly.

He gives me a quick kiss. "I'll be quiet, I promise."

One look at the mischievous smile and I come undone. He gets on top of me while we continue to kiss. And we're swept up by a tsunami of lustful moans and heady sensations, drowning everything around us.

The next morning, I wake up in an empty bed. My chest tightens when I notice a note on the bedside table. With my heart pounding, I pick up the paper.

I am very sorry, Apolo.
I'm not up to being around people. I'm not in the mood to socialize and put on a fake smile while I'm still processing what I've been through.
Thank you for everything.

Xan

Thirty-two

APOLO

Xan. Xan. Xan.

I can't get him out of my head.

I'm enjoying the time spent in the company of my family and friends, and there are times when I completely forget about the boy with the blue hair. But there are other moments when all I do is think about him, and it saddens me that he's not here. For the past few weeks Xan and I have spent part of every day together, so I've gotten used to our little morning routine, the banter over breakfast, the affection he shows me.

Dusk stretches around the lake as the sun disappears behind the mountains that surround the town of Chimney Rock. I'm going back to the apartment tomorrow, and I can't wait to see Xan. I want to make sure he's okay. We've been texting, but the messages are few and brief.

I sigh and lean on the side of the boat. We stop in the

middle of the lake to enjoy the view. Everyone is bundled up as the water is too cold for a dip. But it's tradition to take the boat out for a ride and drink hot chocolate on board. Grandpa, Dad, Claudia, and Artemis stayed behind at the cottage. They weren't in the mood for the ride and didn't want to bring Hera out in this weather. My niece is hypersensitive to colds and she catches them easily. So Ares, Raquel, Dani, and I are the only ones along for the ride.

In a way, this reminds me of the old days—when the four of us used to hang out and have fun as a group. Back in the days when I believed that Dani and I made a perfect couple and could go the distance, just like Ares and Raquel. I look at Dani on the other side of the boat, sitting next to Raquel. Their feet dangle over the icy water, their toes skimming the surface.

Ares comes to sit next to me. He wears a coat and a cap, the tips of his hair peeking from underneath it. His hair is longer than usual. I wonder if the colder weather up north where he's completing his studies has something to do with this new look.

"So you finally decided to see a psychologist," he says, a cloud of icy vapor exiting his lips.

"Grandpa is not very good at keeping secrets." I sigh.

Ares puts his hand on my shoulder. "That makes me very happy."

I say nothing and he arches an eyebrow, waiting for my response.

"What?" I ask.

He shrugs. "So, you're sharing your bedroom with a guy?"

I give him an eye roll. "And Artemis can't mind his business either. Seems like the Hidalgos struggle with keeping their mouths shut."

Ares watches me with an amused expression. And his lips curve into a smile that screams *A-ha! I knew it!*

"Why are you being defensive? It was just a question."

"I'm not . . . it's fine. Xan needed a place to stay and I offered, period."

"I didn't ask for an explanation, Apolo." His voice changes as he grows more certain that I'm hiding something.

"What about you? How is everything going?" I change the subject.

Ares exhales; his gaze turns to the sunset.

"Medicine is as demanding as ever. Just when I think I'm about to get a breather, the pressure and stress intensify. I'm completely drained." His gaze turns to Raquel, who is sharing a laugh with Dani. "And it's getting harder and harder being away from her."

"I can imagine." It's my turn to put my hand on his shoulder. "But you'll get through this, Ares. I have so much faith in both of you."

He smiles at me and nods. "What about you?"

"What about me?"

"I missed meeting the boy, and Raquel wouldn't tell me anything. The way she reacted was quite suspicious, which leads me to believe there's something going on between you and this roommate."

"There's nothing, I swear. We're just going with the flow and taking things as they come." Ares raises both eyebrows. "I know, don't say it. Yes, it was his idea. No, it's not something I usually do. It's just that it hasn't been long since he left a very . . . complicated relationship."

"Fine."

"Fine?"

"You're old enough to make your own decisions, Apolo."

"Thank you."

I'm grateful to him for not judging my choices. Ares gives me a quick hug from the side. "I miss you."

"And I miss you, too, idiot."

I get back to the apartment Sunday afternoon, walking past Gregory straight to my room.

"I missed you too, ingrate!" Greg shouts from the hallway.

The first thing I notice when I enter the room is the bed. It looks exactly the same as the day Xan and I left. Except the clothes I lent him are washed and neatly folded, lying on top.

No.

When he stopped answering my texts, I was afraid something had happened.

Greg comes down the hall and leans against the doorframe. "Where's Xan? I thought he left with you." He shows me a set of keys. "He left the spare set with the concierge."

I feel a void in my stomach.

"Apolo?" Greg persists, looking at me. "What happened?"

"I don't know." I sit on the bed and run my fingers through my hair, feeling frustrated. "I don't know what the hell happened."

"He should be at the café—though it's almost closing time," Greg says. "You said it closes early on Sundays, correct?"

"You're right." I grab a jacket from the closet.

"Apolo."

I stop and look at him. Gregory very rarely uses a serious tone. He reaches out with one hand, placing it on my shoulder. "You can't save someone who doesn't want to be saved."

"He came to me, Greg. He does want to be saved, he just doesn't know how to ask for help."

Gregory gives my shoulder a gentle squeeze. "There are some things he needs to face alone, Apolo. Don't let your feelings cloud your judgment."

"And what am I supposed to do? Nothing? Just let him walk away?"

Greg lowers his hand and looks at me with a tight-lipped smile.

"I just want to make sure he's okay," I tell him before I head out.

I need to make sure that he's okay. The urgency and uncertainty make the walk to the café seem longer than it really is. I keep telling myself that it can't be what I think. He's not back with Vance. It's possible that he's staying at the café. It's not my preference, but it's certainly better than being back in the clutches of that monster.

My heart skips a beat with every step I take. I notice the dim lights inside Café Nora from a distance. But its neon OPEN sign has been turned off. When I step up to the glass doors, I can make out someone moving around inside. Then Xan comes into view, and I feel like I can breathe again. He's clearing a table. His blue hair is held away from his face by a headband. I place a hand over my chest, feeling relieved. It's like a weight has been lifted off my shoulders.

I tap on the glass to draw his attention.

Xan looks surprised to see me. He runs to the door but doesn't let me in. Instead, he joins me outside, pushing me a few steps back.

"Xan?"

"What are you doing here, Apolo?"

"I wanted to make sure you were okay. Why did you leave the apartment? Why aren't you answering your phone?"

Xan looks away. "Apolo, I'm sorry."

Then everything begins to move in slow motion. I catch a glimpse of someone else inside the café, and notice Vance through the glass. He comes out of the storage room wearing an apron. He lifts his head and I look into those eyes that have always given me the creeps. He starts to walk toward the front door but Xan turns around, gesturing with his hand for him to stay inside. Vance obeys him and Xan shifts his gaze to me.

"Are you back with him?" The words hurt as they slip out of my mouth.

Tell me that you're not, Xan. Tell me you're just trying to work out a business arrangement for the sake of the coffee shop. Please.

"Apolo . . ."

Disappointment and anger sweep through me. My heart sinks, my muscles become stiff, and my eyes burn with unshed tears. I take a step backward in total disbelief.

"Shit, Xan!" I raise my voice, losing my cool. "He almost killed you last time. I thought you were never going back to that fucking abusive relationship."

Xan looks pained, seemingly burned by my words. I really don't care. Beating around the bush with him doesn't work.

"It's different this time, Apolo," he explains, and I snort, shaking my head.

"Do you really believe that?" I inch closer. "Look me in the eye and tell me you truly believe that's possible."

"He's really trying," he says. "I didn't believe it at first. But he asked Rain to talk to me, and she corroborated everything he swears he's doing to change."

"Rain?"

My fury erupts. I already knew Rain wouldn't send her brother to jail, but persuading Xan to give him another chance is taking it too far. She's behaving shittier than I could have ever imagined. It's one thing for her to fall for Vance's bull; it's quite another for her to push Xan back into his clutches. I don't care if Vance is on his way to becoming a saint. He inflicted a great deal of pain on Xan. The abuse Xan suffered at his hands may be over, but the damage is done.

I do believe that people can change. But there are instances when the only and much healthier option for survivors is to move forward and away from those who caused them harm.

"Rain is his sister, Xan. She'll always take his side."

Xan shakes his head. "You're wrong. In the past, she insisted that I should leave him. You know that. I don't think she's lying this time."

My face twists in a grimace. This whole situation makes me sick. Maybe Rain and Vance aren't that different.

"I think you should leave, Apolo," Xan whispers, without looking at me.

"And what were we? A rebound from your toxic relationship? A screw out of pure convenience? Oh yeah—I was the nice, dumb guy you used while you were on a break from your abusive boyfriend."

"Apolo . . ."

I purse my lips. I'm fuming. At that very moment, Xan trains his gaze on something behind me.

When I turn around, I find Rain. She steps closer, watching us cautiously.

Great, the gang is all here.

"Did you tell him to get back with Vance? Really?" I ask her in a tone that oozes contempt.

Rain is quiet for a few seconds. "I only told him the truth," she finally responds.

"The truth?" I let out a laugh dripping with sarcasm. "Oh, that's rich coming from you."

Rain tightens her lips, walks over to Xan, and grabs him by the arm. "Let's go inside, Xan."

"Why? Are you afraid I'll tell him the truth?"

Xan stops and his gaze jumps from me to Rain. "What truth?" he asks.

"It's nothing, Xan." Rain is quick to respond. "Let's go."

Xan pulls away from her grip and looks at me. "Apolo?"

"When she told you to get back with Vance and swore he had changed, did she tell you that he was the one who attacked me during my first week of school?" Rain lowers her gaze and Xan looks horrified. "Did she tell you that I would have died in that alley if it wasn't for a sliver of moral sense that persuaded her to go looking for me?"

Xan puts his hand to his mouth and looks at Rain in shock. "Rain?"

She says nothing, just nods.

"I bet she failed to tell you that she refuses to testify in my case. And that Vance will never pay for what he did to me because he's her brother."

Xan is speechless. Rain doesn't dare look up, clearly avoiding my gaze. The pain I feel takes its toll and I shut down. My empathy for others disappears; all I can feel is rage and sadness.

"You know what? Fuck the three of you," I declare as I take a step back.

Xan takes a step forward but I raise my hand.

"No. You've made your choice." I turn around and walk away. "Good-bye, Xan."

Thirty-three

XAN
Three days earlier

I leave a note on Apolo's bedside table and sneak out of the Hidalgo mansion.

I feel terrible. I know Apolo wanted to spend this time with me, but I'm not ready. I'm not in the mood to be around people I don't know while I'm sorting myself out. I don't even have the exact words to explain what I feel. Is it anguish? Or heartache? The realization of what I truly shared with Vance hits me like a ton of bricks and I feel a heavy weight on my shoulders and a constant tightness in my chest.

Apolo's family doesn't deserve my forced smiles or pretend enthusiasm. They've been nothing but nice, welcoming me with open arms. They have a right to a pleasant Thanksgiving celebration.

I haven't formed a plan, so shortly after my arrival at the apartment, I distract myself by cleaning and organizing the place. Café Nora is closed today and tomorrow. There's no point in opening since there's only a handful of customers left on campus. Most folks use this time to visit family or to go shopping. I sit on the bedroom floor and fold laundry while listening to music. It's not my ideal way of spending the holiday. Nevertheless, I find it peaceful. Maybe later I'll watch a movie or a show. I needed this solitude and time away from others. No need for polite pleasantries and forced smiles. I hope Apolo understands.

The song playing on my phone ends and "& Cry!" by Middle Part starts. It's one of my favorites. I immediately fell in love with it the moment I heard it at the coffee shop the day I was sampling different Spotify playlists. I sing along and stare at the bed. I can almost picture us on it, tangled under the covers, kissing until our lips are swollen.

Apolo.

I'm still amazed at what we have together. Every day my attraction for him grows stronger, and my feelings for him intensify with every look, touch, and kiss. Even the simplest things, like a smile, gets my heart racing. I wonder if I'm making a big mistake by letting myself get carried away with him.

No, Xan. You've been clear with Apolo from the start. He knows where you stand relationshipwise.

I place the folded clothes on the shelves of the walk-in closet. When I come out, I listen to the sound of the rain hitting the window. Of course it had to rain. The weather had to match my melancholic mood. The noise is louder than usual so I walk over to the window. When I get closer, I realize the rain is mixed with tiny pellets of hail. The temperature was ridiculously low today, so it makes sense. I'm both surprised and relieved it's not snow. Apolo and I promised we would spend the first snowfall together. It's something silly we picked up from a Korean romance movie we watched last Thursday with Gregory. According to the storyline, if you're with your partner during the first snowfall, then you will share true and everlasting love.

I don't know why we latched on to that idea when we had already promised each other to keep our relation casual. Truth be told, I'm not exactly sure where we stand anymore.

I spend the rest of the afternoon tidying up. The apartment feels empty without him. I can't help but picture him hanging around in the kitchen or lounging on the couch. I miss him a lot, which is ridiculous since we've only been apart for one day.

In the evening, I warm up some turkey slices and eat a salad that Gregory left in the fridge. Once I'm done eating, I sit on the couch wrapped in a blanket and ready to watch *Pirates of the Caribbean*. These were my mother's favorite movies. I suspect that she would have preferred to live somewhere along the coast, close to the sea. Her fascination with movies where the ocean played a big part was never-ending.

This may not be the best Thanksgiving, but, surprisingly, I'm enjoying the solitude. I'm glad I get to be in my own company and no one else's. It's the first time I've spent this holiday on my own. Here, in this moment, I'm not Vance's boyfriend or Apolo's whatever we may be. It's just me, wrapped in a blanket and snacking as the hail falls.

At night, I fall asleep feeling calm and at peace. The following day, I psych myself for what I need to do next. I have to gather my things from Vance's apartment.

I decided today was the day. It's likely that he's with his family, so the chances of running into him when I drop by to collect my things are very low. I won't lie and say that I'm not scared. And this may sound strange, but I'm also curious. What will I feel if I see him? Will it be resentment? Perhaps love? I know that it's impossible to erase him from my memory in a matter of weeks. However, I don't love him like I used to, and I'm no longer blind to his deception.

Outside his door, I gather my courage. I use my key to enter—the same key I will leave at the front desk once I'm done gathering my stuff. The apartment is quiet and partially engulfed in darkness. It's overcast outside and the clouds are preventing the usual flood of natural light.

Everything looks the same. The place is clean and the sweet smell of Vance's favorite scented candle permeates the air. I step out of the hallway and freeze when I see him sitting on a cabinet, his legs spread apart and with his phone in hand. He looks up, and I swallow hard when our eyes meet. He watches me carefully, as if he's dissecting my appearance.

What is he doing here? Why isn't he with his family?

I break the silence.

"I've come to collect my things."

"All right," he replies matter-of-factly, and returns his gaze to his phone.

It looks like he's texting.

I walk past him to the bedroom. I proceed to fill the backpack I brought. It's not big and won't fit much so I'll only take the essentials with me. Underwear, socks, jeans, and a shirt or two. Maybe I'll go shopping later. I worry that most of my clothes will be reminders of Vance.

"You thought I'd be with my family, didn't you?" I'm startled by his voice. I didn't realize he'd followed me. He leans against the doorframe and folds his arms over his chest.

"Yes. I thought it'd be better if we didn't run into each other."

"Why?"

I keep my eyes fixed on the clothes I'm shoving into my bag.

"Because it's over and there's no need for us to see each other."

"Just like that, Xan? Years poured into a relationship, and we can't even have one conversation?"

I zip up the backpack and turn to face him. "We have nothing to discuss, Vance."

"You know"—he steps into the room—"I've been wondering where this sudden courage of yours stems from. I think I know who's behind it. It's Apolo, isn't it?"

I slump. I'm tired of his accusations and paranoia. "He has nothing to do with it."

"Really? This has nothing to do with the fact that you're staying with him?"

"Vance."

"Are you fucking him?"

I hoist the backpack to my shoulder. "I have to go." I head for the door but Vance stretches his arm across the frame, blocking my way. "Vance."

"A conversation is the least I deserve."

"What you deserve?" I snort. I can't believe he has the gall to say this to me.

The doorbell rings and I frown, wondering who it could be.

"Are you expecting someone?"

"It's Rain." Vance steps aside and we walk out of the room together. "I'm trying hard, Xan. I know you don't believe a word that comes out of my mouth. She was visiting a friend who lives nearby so I asked her to come and talk to you."

Rain sits with us in the living room. She's earnest as she speaks.

"Xan, you have every right to leave him, and you're free to do so after our talk. Not so long ago, I encouraged you to break up with him. I'm just here today to verify that what Vance has told you is the truth. He's really making an effort and wants to change."

I nod and she keeps talking. Rain goes over everything her brother has done these past few weeks. She tells me he's seeing a psychologist and has enrolled in an anger management program. Apparently, he stopped drinking and no longer smokes because those substances fuel his violent behavior. In addition, he's staying with his parents. If I decide to get back together with him, I can have the apartment all to myself while Vance gets the support he needs at home. I listen to every word she has to say. She stands up as soon as she's done with her detailed account.

"Well, you have a lot to discuss. Whatever you choose to do, please know that I'm here for you, Xan."

And then she leaves.

I remain seated, contemplating everything I've heard. I wish I could say that this information has little impact on where I stand, but I would be lying. Vance is on the other side of the room. His anxious gaze is pointed at me, eagerly waiting for my reaction. I won't deny that I used to love him, and perhaps a part of me still does. But the sound of his fist crashing into my face and the feel of his tight grip around my neck are forever seared in my memory. Then there's the incident at the café the morning when he prodded me with his finger, checking for someone else's semen.

That moment was the turning point for me. Deep down I know that if I give him another chance, the next time he has a meltdown I may not be lucky enough to survive.

"Vance, I'm glad you're getting the help you need." He smiles at me. "But it's over between us." His smile fades.

"What?"

"I don't want to get back together. I hope we can get along for the benefit of Café Nora, but you and me—there's no turning back now." Although it hurts to admit this, it's liberating to say it out loud. In a way, this is a bittersweet moment.

"Xan, I'm trying everything. Can't you see?" The desperation is clear on his face. "Please. We've been together for so long, and our relationship deserves one more chance."

"No." I shake my head. "Maybe you'll stick with this plan and manage to change for the better, which I sincerely hope you do. But what if you don't? What if I give you another chance and it lands me in the hospital? Or even worse, what if you kill me the next time?"

"You're exaggerating. I've never hit you that hard, and there won't be a repeat, okay? I'm doing everything in my power so it doesn't happen again."

"So I should light a candle and pray that this is your turning point? Why should I risk my life to help you prove that you have really changed? It's not worth it. Not anymore. If you had done this in the beginning, right after you first screamed at me in a fit of rage, maybe we could have had a future together. Not anymore, Vance. It's too late."

I stand and Vance does the same. He comes closer and takes my face in his hands.

"Xan, please. I'll do anything you want," he begs. "I'll come out and tell everyone, including my followers, that you're my boyfriend. I'll take you home and introduce you to my family. Things will be however you want. I won't come back to the apartment until you decide it's time. And you can have your friends over."

I take his hands off my face.

"We're done, Vance."

My voice breaks. This is hard. We were a couple for a long time. I wish I could trust him and believe in his promises. But the memory of last night's solitude is fresh in my mind. It felt good to be on my own. And my time away from him has been healthy and healing.

I take three steps, moving in the direction of the hallway. When he speaks again, a coldness has replaced the agony.

"I wanted to give you the chance to make this decision on your own, Xan."

I turn around, fearing an attack. But Vance stands in the same spot. Then he takes out his phone and shows me a video playing on the screen. I have a hard time figuring out what it's about at first, but I soon realize it's a clip that shows Apolo punching him at the fall festival. The scene plays out differently from what I remember. On camera, everything looks more violent and barbaric. It also paints Vance as the victim.

"What the . . . ?"

"Xan, If you leave me I will release this video. Given my platform's reach, I can make this go viral in a matter of minutes. I'll post it with a juicy description retelling how I was attacked by a hater who happens to be none other than Apolo Hidalgo, the son of one of the richest families in the state. It will come across as the story of a privileged rich kid assaulting a poor freelance streamer."

I'm shocked. I know he would follow through. Everything he just told me will unfold exactly as he's planned. His followers are a passionate and dedicated bunch. It wouldn't be the first time they've helped him go viral. I immediately think about Apolo's family. They're good people who have done nothing wrong and don't deserve a scandal soiling their reputation.

"Apolo would be in so much trouble, there's no doubt about that," Vance continues. "His life would be turned upside down because of you. Can you live with that?"

I clutch my stomach, feeling like I'm about to throw up.

"It was all bullshit, wasn't it?" I ask with disgust. "Everything you said about having changed. It was all a farce."

"No, it's not. But you leave me no choice, Xan. I can't let you go like this. I won't be able to win you back. So get your things from that brat's apartment and come back here where you belong. Come back to me. As promised, I won't stay here. You can have the place all to yourself."

I want to yell and punch him, then run away. But I restrain myself. I can't look at his face.

I sob as I make my way back to Apolo's place and shed more tears the second I walk in. I'm assailed by the memories of our time spent together, the safety I felt here, and the hopes of what could have been.

I gather my belongings and take one last look. I feel a sudden rush of sadness when I notice the blanket on the couch. I enjoyed my time last night. Now I have to leave everything behind and return to a cold place tainted with Vance's energy. I clean up and drop off the spare key at the front desk. I stand on the sidewalk and stare at the building as tears blur my vision.

I'm so sorry, Apolo. It seems like I will never be able to get Vance out of my life.

Thirty-four

APOLO

You must learn to let go, Apolo. Let it all go. You can't save everyone.
You can't force someone to choose when they're not ready to do so.
You were there to help him and provided him with a safe place. You
did what you could, and it's more than enough. It's time to let go.

The advice of my psychologist replays in my head while I
stare at my bed. It has felt empty these past few days. A week has
gone by since I confronted Xan and Rain outside Café Nora. I
haven't stopped by or texted him.

I'm letting go.

I'm focusing on myself and school instead.

The odd time I've been tempted to drop by Café Nora, I
remind myself that it's not worth it. They both made their choices
and are no longer my concern. It's not healthy.

"Ah, but I miss him," Greg complains next to me.

"He made his decision, Greg. We weren't good enough for
him," I joke.

Greg laughs and then lets out an long, exaggerated exhale. "You know what, Apolo? It's all so weird."

I cross my arms over my chest. "What exactly?"

"Xan was so determined—" He strokes his chin, appearing thoughtful. Greg knows Xan's full story. "He was looking into all the legalities behind taking over sole ownership of Café Nora and severing all ties with Vance. Then all of a sudden, he's back with him like nothing ever happened."

"I don't know what to tell you. Apparently, Rain convinced him to give it another go."

"That's also very odd. Rain talking someone into giving an abusive relationship another chance? I don't know. Something doesn't add up."

"Trust me. Rain has really surprised me lately."

"If you say so." Gregory sighs. "Well, how about a vegetable-and-shrimp stir-fry?"

"You read my mind."

"Come on, I could use some company after the day I've had."

"Erica?" I ask, and he nods.

"She's made it crystal clear that we can only be friends. And I get it. But I'll admit, I was hopeful."

"Poor thing," I mutter, earning a slap on the arm.

"I'm in the same boat as you. I need to let go," he says sadly.

I smile at him. "Welcome to the club."

I grab him by the shoulder as we make our way to the kitchen, and talk about the Christmas break, which is only two weeks away.

The persistent and constant vibration of my phone wakes me.

I reach for it with one eye half-open and the other fully shut. I'm half asleep and clumsy so the phone slips from my hands, slamming against my face. I touch my nose and groan in pain. I'm fully awake now. I freeze when I look at the screen. It's four in the morning and Rain is calling.

I feel a sense of déjà vu and flash back to the night Xan showed up at my apartment in the dead of night. I answer her call, feeling a lump in my throat.

"Rain?"

"Apolo! I'm so sorry, he—" Her voice breaks between sobs.

"Rain, what happened?"

"We're at the hospital."

I jump out of bed.

"We? Rain, for god's sake, what happened?"

"It's Xan."

No. No. No.

"You have to come," she says, sobbing. "I'm so sorry . . ."

I ask for the address and hang up. I put on a shirt and jeans. In my haste, I nearly forget my coat. In the taxi all I can hear is the sound of my agitated heart, beating loudly in my ears and the back of my throat. The ride feels like forever. I just pray that Xan is okay. Rain struggled to piece together a coherent sentence, so I couldn't get much out of her.

The second I arrive, I bolt down the corridor that leads to the emergency room. A tall nurse with a friendly smile stops me when I reach the nurses' station.

"Can I help you?"

"Xan—" I reply, out of breath. "A guy—"

"Apolo!"

Rain's voice spills from the corridor. She runs toward me. Her eyes are red and her hands are covered in blood, as is the front of her shirt.

There's a tight feeling in my stomach, and I'm having a hard time breathing.

"Rain." It's all I can say in a choked whisper. I'm riddled with panic, expecting to hear the worst.

"He—"

I grab her by the shoulders. "What happened?! Tell me, damn it!"

"It was Vance," she tells me between sobs. "Vance beat him. It was so brutal that—"

"So brutal that what?"

"Xan called me. When I got to the apartment—" Her expression is pained as she relives the horrific and haunting memory. "There was so much blood and the ambulance took a long time and when it arrived here they had to resuscitate him twice and they're—Apolo, I'm so sorry." She clutches my shirt and cries inconsolably. "This is my fault, I'm sorry, I'm sorry . . ."

I want to scream at her and make her feel worse but I lack the strength or the willpower to do so. I'm frozen with fear at the possibility that Xan might not make it. Rain is a wreck and can't stop crying. I should rake her over the coals for her role in this tragedy, but she feels bad enough as it is. Anyway, it won't do any good or turn back the clock. I help her to a seat in the waiting room and bring her a glass of water.

"Thank you," she murmurs, and hiccups. After her long bout of sobs, her whole chest is heaving.

Memories of Xan replay in my head. I think about his hair, his smile, the passion in his eyes when he talks about Café

Nora, how full of life he is. He can't die. This can't be the end for him.

A tall doctor comes out of Urgent Care.

"Are you Xan Streva's relatives?" he asks.

Rain and I stand up. Instinctively, we hold hands.

"We're his friends. Xan has no one else," Rain explains.

The doctor watches us carefully for a brief moment. He appears to be assessing whether we're telling the truth. As soon as he notices the bloodstains on Rain's clothes, it registers that she's likely the person who was with Xan when he was admitted.

"Xan has suffered an internal hemorrhage. We managed to get it under control, but he needs surgery right away. The X-rays show several broken ribs and fingers." My chest tightens. "We also found various hematomas and external bruises from days ago. All his injuries are consistent with—"

"Abuse," Rain concludes.

The doctor nods.

"I had to report it. The police are already on their way. What happened to him?"

Rain's lips tremble and she squeezes my hand before giving an answer.

"It was his partner, Vance Adams."

"The police will want to talk to you when they arrive. Your friend is being prepared for surgery as we speak. I'll be back as soon as he's out."

The doctor turns around.

"Wait," I ask, my voice slightly breaking. "Please save him. He doesn't deserve to die this way."

The doctor smiles briefly, conveying without words his understanding. Then he leaves.

While we sit in the waiting room, Rain keeps sniffling and wiping away the tears that roll down her cheeks.

"You were right, Apolo. So right," she whispers. "I'm an idiot and a horrible person. This is my fault. How could I believe that Vance would change? How could I fall for his lies? Xan is in there fighting for his life and it's my fucking fault. I used to believe I was a decent human being with good morals and principles. But I pushed all that aside and turned a blind eye simply because Vance is my brother. I wanted to believe he was different. I didn't want to face the truth that he's a monster—and look at me now."

She points at her blood-splattered clothes.

"Rain, this isn't about you." I speak in a cold tone, and she stares at me. "Xan is in there barely holding on. The last thing I need is for you to sink into the guilt and sadness you feel. This moment belongs to Xan. The focus needs to be on him getting through surgery and whatever may come of it. There's plenty of time ahead for you to face up to the mistakes you've made."

She looks away. "You're right."

We wait in silence. When the police arrive, Rain accompanies them to a more secluded place where they take her statement, and I'm left on my own for a while.

Rain returns just as the doctor comes down the corridor. We rush to meet him, anxiously awaiting his update.

"The surgery went well," he says. I let out a breath I didn't realize I'd been holding. "We're keeping Xan in the intensive care unit tonight. These first hours are crucial. He has to remain lightly sedated while he heals internally. Do you want to go up to see him?"

I nod and start to follow him, but Rain lags behind. She shakes her head.

"I can't, I'll wait down here."

I don't say anything and let the doctor lead the way.

Nothing could have prepared me for what I experience the moment I enter the ICU. Xan is bandaged and hooked up to a bunch of tubes and machines. I'm petrified, taking it all in.

I feel a deep sadness as fat tears roll down my cheeks. I'm hurting badly. I did everything I could. Still, I feel like maybe I could have done more. This shouldn't have happened. His hands are covered in bandages so it's impossible to hold them, so I wrap my hand around his wrist.

"Hi, Xan," I whisper, wiping my nose with my free hand as tears keep rolling down my cheeks. "You're going to be okay. I'm here now. I'm so sorry it's come to this, Xan. You don't deserve it, no one does. I will stay by your side, I promise."

And I make good on that promise.

"I'm back," I tell him. I carry a thermos filled with freshly brewed coffee from the hospital cafeteria and place it under his nose. "Do you smell that? I do. It's not the best coffee in the world, but I thought the familiar smell would help. To be honest, I miss going to Café Nora and watching you in your element, preparing the lattes you love so much."

The swelling on his face has become worse as the bruises run their natural course. There is a huge contusion under his left eye. His long eyelashes brush against his cheekbones and I miss being able to look into his eyes, watch his expressions, and notice every little quirk.

I miss him terribly.

"Xandwich!" Gregory exclaims as he approaches Xan, who remains unconscious. "You have to get better soon. I miss my cooking partner. You know how useless Apolo is." I roll my eyes at the remark. "So I need you."

"You had no issues with my muffins yesterday, and gladly ate them."

"I'll admit that it's the only half-decent thing you have going for you, Apolo. But please, don't push it."

I sigh. Despite Greg's cheerful energy, it's difficult to keep my spirits up when I'm in this room. Greg points to Xan.

"When do they think he'll wake up?"

I respond with a shrug. "I don't know. They started to reduce the dosage of his sedatives. According to the doctor, he should be waking up soon."

"Maybe he doesn't want to wake up," Greg murmurs, sounding a little sad as he leans over Xan. "Hey, Xandwich. I get that you went through something terrible, and that you may not want to come back to us and face reality, but we need you. You won't be alone. We're here for you. Please remember that."

I smile. I hope that Xan is listening.

"They found Vance," Rain informs me as she enters the room. Xan was transferred out of the intensive care unit into a room in the recovery ward. Still, he remains unconscious. "He's being held at the Raleigh police station."

I don't know what to say. That I'm glad? Or that there's nothing Vance can do in this world to make up for what he did to Xan? I remain silent and Rain hands me a piece of paper.

"It's a copy of the written statement I gave at the police station this morning." I look at it in confusion. I attempt to give it back. "Maybe you should give it to Xan when he wakes up."

"No. This is the statement I gave about your case."

I freeze.

"It's not enough to say I'm sorry for what I did or didn't do. However, this is something that can give you and Xan some of the justice you both deserve. Vance will finally face the consequences of his actions." She hesitates for a few seconds then proceeds. "I'm aware this isn't about me, but I need you to know that I made a mistake out of pure stupidity. I didn't want to put my family through a difficult time. As it is, my mother is devastated and my father is at a loss, which is exactly what I wanted to avoid. I know it was very selfish of me, and I have to live with the guilt for all the pain caused by my lapse in judgment." She points to Xan, looking sad. "I'm partly responsible for this. So I'm deeply sorry, Apolo."

I'm at a loss for words so I just nod. I would like to tell her that I understand where she's coming from, but I can't lie to her. Not when I'm standing next to a still unresponsive Xan. Suddenly I recall the words spoken by my psychologist and my grandfather. They both said that when we're unable to forgive, we can harbor resentments that may end up causing us more harm.

I get up from my chair and give her a hug. The smell of citrus assails my nostrils. Although it's not unpleasant, it's doesn't offer the comfort it once did.

"You did the right thing and I accept your apology," I say with utmost sincerity.

It's up to Xan to decide whether to forgive her or not. As far as I'm concerned, I'm letting go of the hatred and anger. And in doing so, I let go of the girl who saved me. A girl I placed on a pedestal only to see her fall from it in a most devastating way. Rain wipes her teary eyes when we pull away from each other.

"Thanks."

She turns around and I watch her walk down the hallway, her blond hair bouncing with each step she takes. And I feel at peace.

I've slept on this chair a few times. During the week I come to the hospital right after I'm done with my classes, and I hardly go anywhere else. I'm happy that tomorrow is Saturday so I can spend my whole day here. The doctor said that Xan should have regained consciousness by now, and that worries me. Why doesn't he open his eyes? I don't think I'll be able to breathe properly until I see him fully awake.

I'm checking my phone when I hear his voice.

"Apolo?"

I jump out of the chair and move next to the bed. Although his eyes are still half shut, I manage to catch specks of brown behind his semiclosed lids.

"Xan?" I speak to him in a soft tone and he looks at me. I let out a long exhale and smile, feeling relieved. "Hey . . . welcome back."

Xan blinks and attempts to reciprocate the smile. He has a cut on his lip and the effort makes him wince. Then he tries to move his hands but I shake my head.

"You're healing and need to be still."

Xan's eyes well up with tears.

"I thought I was going to die, Apolo." His voice breaks and I make an effort not to cry along with him. "I thought . . . that . . . he . . . Everything hurt so much."

"Xan." I caress his face, and brush his hair back. "You're safe, it's over. He was arrested. He can't hurt you or anyone else, okay?"

He nods and I wipe the tears from his cheeks. I try to distract him by telling him about Gregory's visits. The doctor suggests he try to eat something light. I help him sit up in the bed. While I feed him, Xan comes clean about why he gave Vance another chance.

"I didn't want to be with him, Apolo. Rain had a talk with me but only to corroborate his story. She wasn't there to convince me to get back with him. She laid out the facts and left the decision in my hands. In the end, I decided to leave him."

I lower the spoon and watch him intently.

"Then how . . . ?"

"He threatened to post a video of the fight at the fall festival. He was going to paint you as the villain and I didn't want you to get hurt."

My brows knit in a frown. "Xan."

"I know. Please don't say it. I just couldn't allow that to happen. But as the days went by, I realized that I couldn't live with him anymore so I left him, which led to this."

"I'm so sorry, Xan."

I comfort him with a hug. He looks so sad and hurt sitting in this hospital bed. I lose track of time as we hold each other tightly.

Two weeks later, Xan is finally discharged. I convince the doctor to release him after four o'clock in the afternoon. Though it's a strange request, there's a reason for it.

"I don't understand why I was discharged so late," Xan complains.

He takes small steps as he walks. He needs to be careful with the bandages around his rib cage. Also, there are a few fingers on his hands that are splinted to protect them while they heal. We walk through the main entrance of the hospital. It's almost evening. Since it's winter, the sun sets earlier and the sky is near dark. Xan stops dead in his tracks and stands under the overhanging roof of the hospital. He turns to look at me.

"Apolo."

I smile and we both admire the snowflakes that started falling not so long ago. The sidewalks are blanketed with a thin, powdery layer of snow.

"The first snowfall," I say proudly.

Xan stretches out the hand that is the least bandaged and lets the snow collect on his palm. He looks at me, and we seem to be thinking about the same thing. We pause to reflect on what we've shared these past two weeks and what led us to this moment—the time I spent caring for him, the laughs we've had together while he was recuperating, the first time we saw each other, and the friendship that blossomed between us. A friendship that turned into something entirely unexpected and special.

Xan moves away from the overhang and the snow falls on his blue hair. I do the same and he turns to look at me with a smile.

"I have a lot of healing to do."

"I know."

"I can't make any promises. Even after sharing our first snowfall together."

"I understand that too."

Xan comes closer and I cup his face with my hands to give him a kiss on the forehead.

"No rush, and no pressure," I say.

I pull away and lock eyes with him. In my head I replay the memory of my afternoon at the beach with Dani.

True love doesn't bind, suffocate, or constrain.

The road to recovery is long for the young man standing in front of me, both physically and emotionally. One thing I've learned from this ordeal is to let go and to stop obsessing over every little thing.

And I, too, have a few things to work through.

I caress Xan's cheeks and lean in to kiss him under the snow. My lips touch his in a warm and loving manner. The fear of losing him has faded. It has been replaced with a sense of peace and a feeling of relief.

Snowflakes land on my jacket, my hair, and my hands, which cradle Xan's face while we share a kiss. I flash back to the beginning of this story. The rainy night that put me in Rain's path, which led me to Xan.

Snow is also a form of precipitation. Unlike the rain, it's much gentler and calmer. And just like my feelings, it changes over time.

I will never forget the girl I met through the rain. It's because of her that I found my way to him. The boy with the blue hair I'm holding in my arms, who softly whispers a promise in my ear.

"Together we will find our very own flow, Apolo Hidalgo."

Epilogue

APOLO
Four years later

CONGRATULATIONS, APOLO!

A huge sign hangs between two very tall pine trees that are decorated with beautiful yellow lights placed in a diagonal criss-cross pattern. They give the patio a soft, warm glow. The placid lake stands on one side, and the wooden dock that leads to the water is also decorated with fairy lights and ornaments. The curtains are open and the glass windows allow a clear view of the illuminated interior. It's past dusk and already dark outside.

This is my graduation party.

The last semester was not easy. Truth be told, I had serious doubts I would make it through. I was completely burned out after my finals. I didn't let anyone plan a celebration until I was sure that I had passed every subject and my practicum.

There are more people in attendance than I expected. Some are friends of my mother's. It was my idea to hold the party here, at her lake house. My mother and I had a heart-to-heart talk about what happened years ago with Rain's family. She told me that at the beginning she wasn't aware the father was married. In fact, she was breaking up with him the night Vance found out about the affair. She realized he had a wife the night of the party, when he brought his family along. After that, she ceased all contact with him. To be honest, my mother has changed a lot and for the better. I was the first to notice and the one who convinced my brothers to give her another chance, serving as a bridge between them. It wasn't easy at the beginning. Ares and Artemis refused to see her. I invited them to dinners and gatherings but they never showed up. As I advanced in my studies, I picked up a handful of mediation skills that came in handy. In the end I was successful in getting them to agree to get family therapy.

We needed this. As a family, we could no longer run away from our problems. My mother has made her fair share of mistakes, and some will have a long-lasting impact on my siblings. However, they all needed to heal. Deep down, they never stopped loving her. After all, she is still our mother. And she was truly sorry for everything she had done in the past. Maybe it was age. Perhaps it was time. Whatever it was, she made positive changes in her life. I'm still amazed at what came out during our sessions with the psychologist. There were tears and apologies. It was a painful but necessary process.

Nowadays, our mom plays a part in our lives. Ares spends time with her in this house on the occasional weekend. My niece and nephew adore her and love to spend time at the lake, so Artemis and Claudia visit frequently. And I try to visit as much as I can.

I believe we Hidalgos have finally learned to let go. And it was about damn time.

"I still think it should read *Congratulations, Lollo*. Or better yet, *crazy fingers*?" an enthusiastic Daniela says as she takes a place next to me.

In keeping with the theme for this all-white party, she wears a knee-length white dress. This was my mom's idea. Now that I look around and see us all dressed in white and gathered under the glow of these lights with the lake and the dock in the background, her concept makes sense and comes together nicely. And the pictures will turn out great.

"Are you ever going to get over it?"

"Never." Dani places one of her cheeks on my shoulder. "It feels nice to be here all together again."

I smile and give her a hug. We watch the rest of the guests. Claudia is laughing at something Artemis is telling her. Meanwhile, Hades is fast asleep in my brother's arms. My newborn nephew is the precious youngest member of the Hidalgo family. Though he's just a baby, he's managed to steal all of our hearts. Hera is running all over the place while Martha, her other grandmother, chases after her. My father and mother are sharing a glass of whiskey and having a pleasant conversation.

Gregory, Marco, and Samy are sitting at one of the tables. They're having a laugh and catching up on new gossip. At least that's what they told me when I sat with them a while ago.

Ares and Raquel are sitting on the dock. Their feet are dangling and their toes are skimming the water. Raquel's dress is bunched up to her knees so it doesn't get wet. They are staring into each other's eyes and giggling like fools in love.

"From this angle," I mutter, "those two look like the cover of a Nicholas Sparks novel."

Dani bursts out laughing.

"Nah." We hear a voice behind us. Xan comes to stand next to us. "More like a Nora Roberts novel."

I smile at him. He still has blue hair. Some things never change. Xan and I are now very good friends. After his experience, he had a long journey to fully heal and recover. We went with the flow and kept things casual for a few months, but decided that it wasn't the best arrangement for either of us. I also needed to heal, and had a lot to learn about myself. As time went by, and with the help of my courses, I discovered more about the human mind, and I realized that we'd made the right choice.

We didn't force a relationship out of fear of being alone. We ended things before we could hurt each other. The experience I had with Xan was similar to the one I had with Daniela.

The right person, but the wrong time.

I'm very happy that I met them and that they're in my life. A part of me will always feel love for them. And this is a beautiful feeling that doesn't bind or constrain me. I can always count on them. Perhaps I'm not the type of person who needs to be locked in a serious relationship. And I'm okay with that. Maybe, in my case, what I treasure most is the individuals I let into my life and the bonds we form over time.

"Attention, please!" Ares's voice echoes across the patio. He stands in the middle while Raquel joins Gregory and the others sitting at their table. "I can't believe Apolo asked me to give a speech at his graduation party. But his other choice was Artemis, so I get it."

We all laugh, and he continues.

"Apolo and I used to argue a lot. I've always been stubborn. Meanwhile, he's always been too nice. Growing up, we were very different and didn't agree all the time. However, every argument

I've ever had with him has always left me contemplating. My brother has the ability to talk sense into anyone. He is empathetic and can put himself in other people's shoes. He has the ability to understand and is a great advocate. I believe all these qualities will make an excellent psychologist out of him." He raises his champagne glass to me. I do the same and smile. "To be honest, I think I was his first patient."

There is laughter and murmuring. Ares watches me, looking nervous. I give him a nod because I know what he's about to say.

"In fact—" He gives his glass to Artemis. "My brother is so nice that he let me do this on his special night. He said this will make this celebration even more special since he loves to play a part in other people's happy moments. So here it goes. Raquel—"

When he says her name, Raquel stands up and gives him a confused look.

"We have been in a long-distance relationship for many years. We fought, struggled, and gave it our all. Last year when you graduated you did the impossible to find a job close to where I was. You succeeded and didn't hesitate when I suggested that we live together. This past year, you've been my rock and my support while I finish my degree. The journey to becoming a doctor is long. You know this better than anyone, and haven't thrown in the towel. I know without a doubt that you are the one for me. Even though I'm not standing by a window at this moment"—she laughs and looks at him with red eyes as he kneels down—"will you marry me?"

We are all very emotional. Suddenly Raquel bursts out laughing as her tears flow.

"You are crazy, my Greek god," she teases him.

Ares raises an eyebrow. "Is that a yes? Because I'm getting a cramp on my knee that's—"

"Yes! Yes!" She leans in and kisses him.

We all applaud. Dani, Xan, and I discreetly wipe our wet cheeks and walk over to congratulate them.

Once the commotion dies down, I sit on a chair and watch the newly engaged couple. Ares and Raquel are out on the dock, dancing in each other's arms to a soft melody coming out of the speakers, with the lake and the moon in the background.

Xan appears at my side. "They would look great on the cover of an erotic novel."

I smile and take him in. Xan now plays sports. His arms are no longer slim, but toned and muscled. And his blue hair is long.

"Do you think you'll ever have something like that?" Xan asks, pulling up the chair next to me.

"I'm not sure if I want something like that."

"This is the part where you give me the speech that you don't need someone to feel better and that you're a self-sufficient human being."

"You already know it by heart," I mutter.

"I always thought of you as a romantic."

"And I think of you as the boy who likes to go with the flow."

Xan laughs. "Okay, I deserve that." He sighs. "Actually, I'm proud of you, Apolo."

I turn to him, resting my elbow on the back of the chair. "Really?"

"Yes, you've matured a lot. You're not the anxious and inse-cure boy who first walked into Café Nora. You're also not the boy who couldn't let go and kept clinging to me, even when I kept pushing you away."

"Now you're exaggerating. I wasn't that intense and obsessive." He arches an eyebrow. "Okay, maybe a little."

He exhales. "You taught me a lot too. This friendship we've nurtured over these past years has been one of the best things that ever happened to me. You brought me into your family and allowed me to play a meaningful part in your life. Your brother is wrong. I was your first patient."

"Now everyone is competing for that title."

"No! No! Marco! I swear, if you throw me . . . !" I hear Samy's screams coming from the shore. Then I see Gregory coming right behind him with Daniela in his arms.

"Nooo! We're wearing white! You can't do this!"

Xan looks at me and I freeze.

"Xan . . ."

"I knew that all this exercise would come in handy one day."

Xan is too quick, giving me no time to escape. I manage to grab my phone and toss it on the ground. The next thing I know, he's throwing me into the lake.

And wham! I hit the warm water. When I swim back up to the surface, I find Raquel. Her hair sticks to her face, and I'm spooked at first glance. Dani is coughing and Samy is hitting Marco. The hems of their white dresses float around them and their nipples are visible through the white fabric of their wet clothes. But no one feels awkward or uncomfortable. We've been close friends for a very long time. We've all suffered through Raquel's loud moans, so this is nothing.

We have a great time. We make jokes, laugh, and play-fight in the water.

I pause for a moment to watch them. This sweet moment is perfection.

Just like that afternoon spent on the beach years ago. Or the Fourth of July holiday we spend as a family. And the rainy days that no longer frighten me.

About the Author

Ariana Godoy is the author of the bestselling novel *A Través De Mi Ventana*, which was adapted into a film by Netflix Spain. A Wattpad star, Ariana has over two million followers on the platform and her stories have accumulated over eight hundred million reads. She is also very active on social media and is a successful YouTuber. Ariana enjoys K-dramas, coffee, writing, and spending time with her dogs in her house in North Carolina.

CHECK OUT THE FIRST
TWO BOOKS IN ARIANA GODOY'S
The Hidalgo Brothers series!

Available now, wherever books are sold.